GODS & THIEVES

GODS & GHOSTS BOOK 2

CYNTHIA D. WITHERSPOON

T.H. MORRIS

PROLOGUE

EVA MCRAYNE

JANUARY 16TH

TODAY IS MY TWENTY-SIXTH BIRTHDAY. I didn't think I was going to make it this far. Five years ago, I was falling deeper into the despair that would find me taking a blade to my wrists. Elliott Lancaster was the one who saved my life then.

He's dead now. Physically dead, since there is no such thing as death forever. The spirit changes. It shifts and transforms as we all do, I suppose.

I have changed, too. I have spent the past five years searching for myself. Am I Evangelina, the girl who wanted nothing more than her grave? Or Eva, the badass who has no problem running her mouth?

I'm still trying to figure it out. There are days – moments – when Evangelina slips through, but those times are becoming less and less since Cyrus is no longer around. I shouldn't be surprised by that. Time and distance have shown me just how negative my Keeper's influence has been. He's still tied to me through the Olympian bond, but I hope that Apollo can see that I don't need a Keeper. I don't need a babysitter.

Maybe I can ask my father to take back the gold necklace he sent me this morning and ask for freedom instead. Not

1

freedom from my Olympian duties, but from a Keeper who can track me whenever he damn well pleases. Then again, Cyrus never cared for me. Perhaps my worry is misplaced.

Either way, I am getting older though I don't look like it. The eternal twenty-two-year-old who rejected Joey's attempts to get me to go out on the town tonight despite the fact we've been on the road for months. How much fun could we have possibly had if he's exhausted?

Joey doesn't know I have other plans. Plans that involve hanging out with Jonah Rowe on the ancient streets of London.

What could I possibly write about Jonah that would do him justice? That he is kind? He is handsome? He makes my heart flip every time he smiles? Or that he is a hero in every sense of the word? He is all of these things and more.

I haven't been able to see him since we returned from Romania. Not really. The virtual research meetings I crashed at Theia don't count, but David is pleased with his work. I'm pleased, too. Jonah's research packets are filled with all sorts of tidbits and maps. Legends and news articles. Joey says Jonah produces high-quality work so he doesn't have to come in to save my ass. I say it's because that's just Jonah.

I've rambled on for too long. Jonah could be here any minute. I am nervous. Excited. You'd think he was taking me on a date instead of simply hanging out with me. Maybe someday. Maybe not.

Only time will tell.

———

I shouldn't have been this excited. I was fidgety enough to rearrange the salt and pepper shakers. I straightened the napkins. Hell, I kept glancing out the window just in case I saw him. I knew I had to sit still, so I forced myself not to move. That lasted for all of two minutes before I checked the clock on my phone for the tenth time since I sat down at the back booth of London's Hound and Bone pub.

Maybe it was because my European filming spree had gone off without a hitch after Romania. We'd hit a castle in Scotland. A haunted monastery in France. More historically haunted sites than I could have imagined. And just last night, we'd wrapped up a London investigation on an old brownstone.

Or maybe, it was because Jonah Rowe had agreed to meet me this morning. I hadn't seen him since the Hoia-Baciu episode. But we texted constantly. Facetimed whenever we could. It was crazy how easy it was to talk to him. Or how happy I was that he agreed to meet with me a whole world away from Rome, North Carolina.

"Anyone ever tell you that you look just like Eva McRayne?"

I tossed my phone down and grinned up at Jonah as he stopped next to the table.

"Every damn day. But enough about me. Anyone tell you that you look just like a badass Blue Aura?"

Jonah laughed when I stood up then threw my arms around him. I had to stomp down the butterflies in my stomach as I took in his scent. See, I'd been captivated by this man since the moment I met him. Neither time nor distance seemed to lessen that.

I released him with more than a little reluctance to sit back down. Jonah lowered himself down into the booth across from me.

"You look good, Superstar." He waved the waiter over then ordered coffee. When we were alone again, he continued. "I can't believe it's been so long since that Hoia-Baciu episode."

"Me neither." I sat back as the waiter returned seconds later with a refill for me and a steaming mug for Jonah. "Last night was our final European episode."

"I know. David already has my ass working on Japan."

I grinned, then sipped from my mug. Jonah had accepted a position as a researcher with Theia Productions, but since we were friends, his assignments centered around my show. And he was all for the international locations. Researching haunted locations in Japan must be fascinating to him.

"Where's Joey? Cyrus?" Jonah sipped on his black coffee. "I was surprised to see you sitting here alone, to be honest."

"Joey's sacked out back at the hotel." I doctored my coffee with sugar and creamer. "As for Cyrus? No clue. Haven't seen him since he showed up at Hoia-Baciu."

"That's a good thing. The less you have to see him, the better."

"It seems to be working out. Things are a lot more peaceful for me. The truth is I just don't know where to go from here."

"What do you mean by that, exactly?"

I stared at my coffee for a minute before I looked up at him. "Jonah, do you think it's possible for someone not to have a soulmate?"

"I think that depends on if you believe in soulmates. And if you do, maybe you just haven't met them yet."

I stirred my drink as we sat in silence. Finally. I spoke.

"That's just it. I thought that I had. I thought that Cyrus was bound to me for a reason other than the whole keeper thing. You know? Like fate or something? But if Cyrus had been my soulmate, I wouldn't feel the way I do now."

4

Jonah reached over and caught my hand. He smiled as he pulled the spoon I was holding out of my hand.

"You keep going like that, you're gonna break that mug, Evie." He kept his hand over mine, and I tried like hell to calm the beating of my heart. It was just like when he held me in the gazebo. "Being soulmates isn't bullshit. But the person you might be with could be bullshit. The way you feel now confirms that you aren't soulmates. The way he treated you confirmed it for me. Your soulmate lay elsewhere."

I sighed then flipped my hand, more than a little surprised when he took the opportunity to lock our fingers together.

"Jonah, I thought it would get better. That if I was just good enough, then he wouldn't be so hard on me," I confessed. "You know how he talked to me. I would make excuses. I built up a wall and believed everything he told me about myself. I just didn't care. And that's not normal. How can that be normal?"

"It's normal if that's all you've known for four years," Jonah said. "O.k., look. I'm far from the expert, but Nana used to say that when you love someone, they make your heart flip. Make your flesh warm up without heat. Your life doesn't make sense when they aren't there. Your dreams get all crazy and dizzy. She said that all the time. Did Cyrus do that to you?"

I released a slow breath at his words because the answer was so simple. Cyrus never made me feel that way. But Jonah had from the moment I first laid eyes on him. Like now, when I felt giddy that he was holding my hand.

"No," I managed over my nerves. "If anything, I feel relieved that he's gone all the time now."

Jonah squeezed my fingers before he released my hand. I grabbed at my mug again as he poured himself another cup of coffee from the pot the waiter left behind.

"Then you need to move on, Superstar. Tell Daddy Gold it ain't clicking, and you require a new Keeper. He's useless."

I knew he was right. But I was not looking forward to that conversation with either Apollo or Cyrus. Jonah cut his eyes over at me before he spoke.

"Do you think he believes you two are still in a relationship?"

"It doesn't matter if he does or not. Any relationship we had outside of the Sibyl-Keeper agreement is over," I said with a sigh. "You said it yourself. We weren't even in a real relationship. It's more like we were just together."

"You weren't even together." Jonah gave a snort that had no mirth. "He was playing Daddy. It's time you dropped dime on him to Apollo. I'm glad you're immortal because Cyrus could very well be exposing you to STDs."

"No, he wouldn't have." I shook my head as another confession came out of me. "I haven't gotten past first base with anyone, much less Cyrus. Remember that story? I tried once. But he told me that he didn't want me."

"He is a fucking fool not to want you." Jonah took my hand up again then squeezed my fingers. "You're one of the most desirable women I know, Superstar. Believe that."

It took a minute for me to remember how to breathe. How to form words. Jonah thought I was desirable? I felt a thrill before I realized something I should have known the moment he said those words. He was just trying to make me feel better. That was all.

"Thank you, Blueberry," I said in a level voice.

"That means more than you could imagine. In any case, I won't be able to talk to Apollo until after we get back to L.A. We're supposed to leave out tonight."

I took a sip of coffee to moisten the back of my throat. I needed to change this conversation before I said something out of line. Like how much I wanted him to be telling me he really did desire me.

"What about you and Vera?" I ventured. "Have you talked to her since the Facetime disaster?"

Jonah rolled his eyes, and I frowned at the sudden pain in his expression. He smoothed it out before he answered me. "She came to the estate to visit, then went back to Seattle. I didn't tell you that?"

"No." I leaned forward as I watched him. He was tense all of a sudden. I could feel it. "Did something happen between you two?"

That dark expression passed Jonah's face again. "No." He ran his hand through his hair. "She ignored me the entire week she was there. I guess all that talk about 'seeing where we stood' was just bullshit."

I felt myself grow cold at his words. Not with jealousy, but anger. Everyone knew how Jonah had fallen for Vera Haliday, but one Facetime session where I sat on Jonah's lap pissed Vera off to the point that she became insistent that she and Jonah could work something out when she was done 'finding herself.' Jonah had told her that he was worth more than the backburner, and she punished him for it?

I narrowed my eyes when I responded. "Excuse me? She ignored you the entire week?"

"Apparently, she was trying to punish me for that Facetime call before Romania," Jonah spoke my very thoughts out loud. "Haven't seen her since."

"Wait." I took a deep breath, then another to calm down. It wasn't working. I wanted to go to Seattle, find that bitch, and snatch her up by the neck. "She punished you for not wanting to be put on the back burner while she screwed anyone she could find? Surely to the gods, she realizes what she has thrown away. Any woman would be lucky to have you, Jonah."

Jonah seemed to blush at my words. I tilted my head at him before he cleared his throat.

"Yeah, well, Vera, like Priscilla before her, wants me to realize that dropping the ball was *my* fault. I know the fact that Inimicus was her sister, but I could have gotten past that."

"Inimicus?"

"Yeah. The pseudonym for the bitch who murdered a friend of mine. Jessica Hale. She's Vera's sister."

I couldn't contain my anger any longer. I knew my eyes were practically on fire when I responded.

"Good. I'm glad you didn't fold when you saw her again." I squeezed his hand. "You deserve so much more than someone who wants you to wait on them, Jonah. I mean, by the very gods. You must know how special you are. If she didn't see that, it's her loss. Not yours."

Jonah looked genuinely touched by my words. With a warm smile, he shrugged.

"Look, let's not talk about depressing shit." He shifted against his seat. "Let's get away. Use ethereal travel, and just get away. We can find a spot and just explore. Interested?"

Gods, that sounded amazing. Time away from my life? Time with Jonah? I'd give anything for that. It took me two seconds to make my decision. I grinned at him over the table so big, it hurt my face.

"You have no idea how interested I am, Blueberry." I clutched the edge of my seat. "Where are we going?"

"I've always wanted to visit Santa Fe. Pretend to be a different person even. You down?"

A different person, huh? I could understand that completely. There were times where I felt the same way. I willed a twenty in my hand to cover the coffee, then placed it on the table.

"Oh, I'm down," I told him, suddenly feeling devilish. "Tell me who you want to be, and I'll pair up with you."

Jonah thought for a second before he pulled out his phone. A few minutes later, he glanced up at me. "Santa Fe Suites? We can meet up like college friends or something."

"You get us to Santa Fe, and I may just be able to do you one better." I slipped out of the seat then reached for his hand. "Wanna go play, Blueberry?"

Jonah grinned when he realized I was serious. He pocketed his phone, then stood. "All you had to do was ask, Superstar."

I shivered when he wrapped his hand around mine to lead us out of the pub. I kept my head down as we melted into the crowds until we found an alley to duck into.

Jonah initiated the Astralimes, and within moments, the chilled London streets became warm. I looked around the park we appeared in as I was hit with a stroke of genius.

"Meet me back here in one hour." I released his hand. "And don't worry about changing anything. You look perfect for what I have in mind."

"Which is...?"

"Nope. It's a surprise." I leaned up to kiss him on the cheek. "See you soon, Blueberry."

I was gone for exactly one hour. Just long enough to make myself almost unrecognizable. I'd let my curls go wild. Changed into a tank top and short shorts. Doc Martens completed the look. If Jonah wanted us to pretend to be other people, then I was going to be the exact opposite of what he expected.

I found him on a bench by a small fountain. Watching the people who passed by with kids and dogs. I strolled up behind him then leaned in to whisper in his ear. I even altered my voice. Thousands of dollars' worth of voice lessons made it easy as hell to do.

"You look like you're a man who can show a girl a hell of a good time. Interested?"

Jonah jerked then turned around. He blinked as he took me in. "And who might you be?"

"Just call me Sibyl." I trailed my fingers over his shoulders as I came around to face him. "Or lost. Cause I don't know my way around this damn place. You a local?"

"No, but I know my way around quite well. I try to get out here a few times a year." He tilted his head back as he looked up at me. "You're lost? You a drifter, or something?"

"I go where the world takes me." I pulled him up to his feet then leaned in. Close enough that I could have kissed him if I wanted. "And the world has brought me right here. To you. What's your name, stranger?"

Jonah studied me as his eyes gleamed. He seemed to be having as good a time as I was with our little game. "James. You got a last name, Sybil?"

"No," I replied. "Don't need one. I ain't applying for a damn job, James. I'm too busy livin'." I had no idea how I could be so bold. Maybe because it was Jonah. Maybe it was because of the feelings he brought out in me. Feelings I didn't even realize I had. I ran my finger down the buttons on his shirt before I continued. "So, what do you got to show me?"

"Not so fast, oh, wild one." Jonah reached out to run his thumb down from the top of my shirt down to the zipper of my shorts. I shivered when he did that, then tried to hide that fact when he spoke. "I'm a gentleman. Ladies first. What do you have to show me?"

I had to slow this down because the way he was looking at me made me want to say forget the Keeper. Forget his stupid actress. Find a place where we could get lost for a while. "A hell of a lot more than a park if you keep that up."

"You are a most refreshingly direct woman, Sibyl." Jonah gave me a crooked smile as he tucked his hands in his pockets. "What could be better than this park? Do tell."

"Oh, no, you don't. You ain't getting those words from me. Not yet." I turned on my heel to see the Georgia O'Keefe museum across the way. "Let's go cool off in there."

"If you lead the way," Jonah invited, his voice far more direct than I'd ever heard it. "I have a feeling I'll enjoy watching the way you walk. Is that for me?"

Was Jonah flirting with me? I felt the blood rush to my cheeks before I realized this was all part of his character. Obviously, he'd gone for the charmer route. I threw a coy smile at him over my shoulder. "You'll never know, Jamie-boy. But since you're the one watchin', that means it must be for you."

I started across the lawn, but after a minute, I realized I was alone in my trek. I turned back around to see him still standing in place. His expression was completely unreadable. So I beckoned to him with a crooked finger.

"You gonna come like a good boy? Or are you gonna make me work for it?"

Jonah's face was priceless at my words. He looked shocked. For a second, I wondered if I went too far. But his expression was too funny. I cracked up when he grumbled something under his breath then crossed the lawn to get to my side. I wrapped my hand around his arm then hugged him.

"Good boy," I teased. "I knew you were the type. Now come on. This sun is blazing, and I ain't trying to get burned."

"Yes, ma'am." Jonah took the lead as we walked. "Yes, ma'am."

———

We spent the rest of the day pounding around Santa Fe, alternating between ourselves and the characters we were playing for each other. By the time night fell, we rented a truck and headed into the desert.

It had been an amazing day. Neither of us mentioned the reasons that made us flee London in the first place. Though I did call Joey to tell him I was with Jonah and to take the flight without me. He complained for a good thirty minutes before he agreed to get my luggage and bring it home too.

"I can't believe the skies are so clear out here."

I turned my attention back to Jonah, who offered me his hand from his position in the truck bed. I let him lift me onto the pile of blankets and pillows we had laid out. When Jonah got situated beside me, I passed him bottled water then tapped mine against his.

"Here's to roughing it."

"Superstar," Jonah chuckled. "This is not

roughing it. This is a damn luxury hotel compared to actual camping."

"Sure, it is," I teased. "There's no shower, nowhere to plug in a hairdryer." I leaned back against the pillow behind me. "I think you're just not used to being spoiled."

"That's very true." Jonah bumped his shoulder against mine as he opened the pizza box he'd sat between us. "I'd never get away with eating this much crap back at the estate."

"It's not going to hurt you one bit tonight." I snagged a piece and took a bite. Once I swallowed, I continued. "We walked a lot today. That counts as a workout."

"You, my dear, have a very loose definition of working out."

"So, do you do this often?" I asked him. "Camping, I mean?"

"Often enough," Jonah answered. "I have a tent set up in the Glade where I go to clear my head. Spent four hundred bucks on that thing, but I love it."

"Tell me about what it's like to live with so many people." I passed my half-eaten slice to him. "And finish this. I don't want it to go to waste."

"You only took like two bites."

"I'm good. Never been a big eater." I took another sip of water when Jonah took the food from me. "Now, on with it, mister. I want stories. Gossip. The good stuff."

"Are you always so chatty after dark?" Jonah smirked at me. "Because I distinctly remember trying to sleep on the floor at the end of your bed and you chitter-chattering my ear off."

"Uh-huh." I nodded in agreement. "It's the night owl in me. Can't help myself."

Jonah ate as he told me about the other Eleventh

Percenters who had been away when I was there. He had me cracking up over their lives. How they were a family forged through their trials. We spent the following hours swapping stories about our lives. Much more than what a simple phone call could do.

By the time we cleaned up dinner then stretched out to look at the stars, I was exhausted. I snuggled up against his side beneath the blanket to rest my head on his shoulder. Jonah didn't seem to hesitate when he wrapped his arm around mine.

"You're wiped out, Evie." He glanced down at me when I yawned. "God, I completely forgot you spent last night filming."

"Totally worth it, Blueberry," I muttered' as my eyes grew heavy. "I can't remember the last time I've been this happy. Thank you for such a wonderful birthday."

"Birthday? What the hell, Superstar? Why didn't you tell me?"

"It's just another day. But you made this one special. Thank you."

Jonah didn't respond, but he started playing with my hair. Running the strands between his fingers before he brushed his nose against the top of my head.

"Sweet dreams, Superstar." He whispered against my head. "Happy birthday."

"Honey, I'm home!"

I called out to Joey as I entered the condo. I dropped my keys on the table by the door and all but skipped into the kitchen. There were only two places Joey would be if he was home: the kitchen or his bedroom.

The kitchen was empty, so I turned to walk back

out when I crashed headlong into the chest of my Keeper. One Cyrus Alexius. A man I hadn't seen in months.

"Cyrus? What the hell are you doing here? I thought Apollo—"

"Where were you, Eva?"

"Excuse me?" I glared at him. "What do you mean, where was I? Don't you always know where—"

I didn't get to finish my sentence when Cyrus struck out. He smacked me so hard across the face, I tasted blood. I caught myself against the stove and stared at the red drops of blood that fell onto the flat surface.

I blinked away the pain. I had to talk to him. I had to explain myself. I turned and ducked when Cyrus took a swing at my head.

What the fuck was happening?

"Cyrus, stop it!"

I saw him pull a dagger from his boot. Now, I was terrified.

"Tell me the goddamn truth, Eva," he seethed. "Where were you?"

I didn't bother to respond as I took off towards the front door. I needed to get away from him. I was fast, but he was faster. Cyrus caught my arm as I reached the door. He jerked me around, and I gritted my teeth against my scream when I heard my wrist snap.

"Where were you?" He pressed the tip of the knife against the base of my throat. "Bitch, I will slice your goddamn head off—"

"Santa Fe," I managed as I fought against the fire racing up my arm. "We left London to get away from our lives for a little while. It was safe, Cyrus!"

"I warned you." He pressed the knife deeper. "I

warned you not to get close to them. And what do you do? You run off with the man who insisted on insulting my honor! I swear upon the grave of my father, I will see Rowe dead, do you hear me?"

"No!" I didn't dare move. I knew the power he held in that blade. One slip and my immortality would be stolen from me. One slip and nothing could save me. "Cyrus, stop. Listen to me! Nothing happened between us!"

"You are not to see the Elevenths again. Understand me?" He snarled as he removed the blade. "Move."

Cyrus jerked me up and shoved me forward. I found myself in the bathroom. Staring at myself in shock. The girl in my reflection was so different than the one I used to seeing. This one was hurt. Her eyes were wide with a fear I understood all too well.

Within seconds, my reflection shifted. No longer did I see the woman I had become, but the child I used to be. Fourteen years old. I recognized this horrific memory. The sadness in her green eyes was the only emotion on her emancipated face.

"This is your own doing, Eva." Cyrus shoved me harder against the sink. Closer to the mirror. "Look at what you have caused. If you had only followed orders, this wouldn't have happened."

I didn't dare break down. The girl in the mirror didn't either as Janet jerked her hair back with a brush. The strands were too thick. It had hurt like a bitch when she detangled it.

"This is your own doing," Janet's voice echoed through the pain in my heart at the memories and over what Cyrus was doing to me now. "Look at the trouble you cause! If you'd listen to me, I wouldn't have to hurt you!"

"Yes, m'am."

"You are not worthy to be the Sibyl,"Cyrus jerked my head back by my hair. "The sooner you relinquish the mirror and kill yourself, the better for everyone."

"You do not speak!" Janet jerked the girl's head back by the hair. "The sooner I am rid of you, the better!"

The girl in my reflection grabbed at the counter to keep herself upright. The result was a clatter of bottles and makeup that were knocked to the floor. My mother jumped back. Her face twisted as she picked up the hand mirror closest to her hand. Janet slammed it against the girl's head as she tried to stammer out her apologies. Blood ran down the side of the girl's face as she collapsed with Janet still striking her.

I choked back a sob as a lash of pain rushed through my heart. Violence and hatefulness had been all I had ever known. It was the only thing I would ever know. The happiness I had felt when I was with Jonah in Sante Fe wasn't meant for me. I had stolen those moments when I agreed to go with him in the first place.

"You are not to speak to Rowe again." Cyrus whispered. "Ever. Or his death will be on your consciousness."

Cyrus released me with a shove so hard, I cracked my hip against the bathroom counter. I folded over as he vanished back into the shadows.

He was right. He was always right. The sooner I left this world, the sooner I could be free from the pain of it. I was shaking as I grabbed a razor from the drawer. I could barely see through my unshed tears when I broke free the blade. I snagged it between my fingers then dropped down so that my back against the cabinets.

The sooner I am rid of you, the better.

I knew what to do. I followed the pale white scars that remained from my first attempt. I felt my emotion catch in my throat as I began to bleed.

"Eva? You in here?" Joey froze at the door, but I ignored him as his tone switched to one of horror. "What are you doing-Jesus! Stop!"

He grabbed at my hand and the blade clattered to the floor as I struggled against him.

"Let me go, Joey," I sobbed. "Let me go! I can't do this! Not anymore, please. Let me go!"

"You don't have to do this, Evie," He tightened me up in a bear hug so that I couldn't move. "You can't do this."

Maybe it was the kindness in his voice. Maybe it was his emotion, but I broke down against him. I sobbed into his chest until he was forced to sit next to me in the blood puddled on the white floor.

"It's ok, Evie," He whispered. "It's going to be ok."

I knew it wasn't. Nothing was ever ok for me. It never had been, and it never would be.

I didn't know what to say to Joey as he wrapped my sliced wrist. He didn't seem to know what to say either. My friend worked in silence as he wrapped the bandages with tape. There was no attempt at humor. No attempt to tease me.

"It's broken," Joey announced when he was done. "You might need to get this hand looked at. The bones could set wrong."

"No."

I couldn't, even if I wanted to. Any doctor who saw me would call the cops the second they saw my face. Then, they'd call the psych ward when they saw the damage to my wrist.

"You shouldn't have stopped me." I whispered. "You should have just shut the door, Joey."

"First off, there's no way in hell I could have done that." Joey's jovial face was serious. His mouth set in a hard line. "What happened?"

"Nothing worth talking about."

"Yeah, ok. So you busted your own face in? You broke your own wrist?"

He knew what happened. This wasn't the first time Joey had bandaged me up from one of Cyrus' fits.

"Eva, we have been friends for a long time," He sat back against the kitchen chair. "You've never re-acted to one of Cyrus' episodes like this. Why? Why did you try to hurt yourself?"

I remained silent for a while. I looked at the first aid kit without really seeing it. The balled up packaging discarded across the table surface.

"Eva?"

"I want out," I whispered. "I want out, Joey. I'm sick of this life."

"But suicide-"

"It's my only way out." I caught myself before the tears could begin again. "Violence. Pain. Disappointment. It's all I've ever known, Joey. I'm not strong enough to handle it anymore. I'm not."

"So that's it?" He tapped the back of my good hand. "You're just going to throw everything away for a little heartache?"

"It's more than just a little."

"I want you to do something for me, Evie," Joey grabbed a piece of packaging and tightened his fist around it. "I want you to realize that the second it's over for you? It's over. There's no going back. I want you to talk to someone. Promise me that you will take it one day, one minute at a time."

"There's no one to talk to."

"There's always someone to talk to, baby girl."

"Not for me." I held my bandaged wrist against my lap. "It wouldn't have worked anyway. What does it matter?"

"You matter, Evie. To me. To the Council. To Apollo." He locked our fingers together against the table. "Promise me that you won't do this. Not again. I don't give a shit what happens."

I closed my eyes as a single tear trailed down my cheek. I couldn't make that promise to Joey. He knew it as well as I did.

"Did something happen with Jonah?"

"No," My eyes flew open. "No. I was happy. Happier than I'd ever been. When I got home-"

"Cyrus was waiting for you?"

I nodded. Joey sighed.

"Evie, I'm not going to tell you who to be friends with. Not my place. But hanging out with Jonah seems like a bad idea."

"This has nothing to do with Jonah."

"So Cyrus didn't lose his mind when he found out who you were with?"

I swallowed at that.

"That doesn't make this Jonah's fault. It's mine. Besides, I'm not supposed to have anything to do with Jonah or any of the Elevenths from here on out."

"Is that an order?"

I nodded a second time.

"That's going to be an impossibility, you know." Joey spoke slowly. Carefully. "You know the Emmys are being announced tomorrow and rumor has it the Covington episode is on the top of the list. Theia is going to want them to be there."

I covered my eyes with my palm. There was no way I could get out of that. Cyrus would just have to understand. Maybe I could talk some sense into him. Maybe I could make him see how the Elevenths were now a part of our world.

And despite the threats, I knew that if I was physically alive, I couldn't go without seeing Jonah again. Even if my moments of happiness with him were stolen ones.

"Ok." I whispered as I dropped my hand. "I'll figure something out."

"I think you need to talk to Apollo. See if he can knock some sense into Cyrus' head."

"How am I going to explain my injuries, Joey?" I studied the table top again. "If I see Jonah sooner rather than later, he's going to ask questions."

"Will he?"

"What does that mean?"

"Now isn't the time for that conversation, Evie."

"Yes, it is." I frowned at him. "What do you mean?"

Joey stood up then gathered all the trash from the table. He tossed it in the trash can before he leaned against the counter.

"I told you before. Jonah doesn't seem all that invested in you."

"He's my friend, Joey."

"A friend, huh? What does he know about you that you haven't offered up after he's answered a question you asked him?"

"That's not true. Jonah asks me things."

"What sort of things? Things about work? About your locations? Or about you?" Joey ran his hand through his hair. "Did he even know it was your birthday yesterday?"

I opened my mouth to speak, then shut it.

"I knew it."

"Jonah doesn't have to know everything about me. It's not fair to put that on him."

"Not everything. But I sure as hell know when my friend's birthdays are so I can celebrate them."

"There's nothing to celebrate. It's just another day." I stood and my knees started to shake. "Don't talk about Jonah like that to me, Joey. I don't let anyone talk bad about my friends."

"Even me?"

"Even you."

Joey pushed away from the counter and crossed the kitchen to hug me again. I hugged him back as he whispered.

"Don't ever do that shit again, Evie. Ever. I mean it."

I didn't respond. There was nothing I could say that would ease his mind. Instead, I let him lead me upstairs. Joey walked me to my room.

"I'm going to stay with you tonight. I don't think you should be alone right now."

"You don't have to." I opened the door but he didn't follow me inside. "I can promise that you won't find me in the bathroom in the morning."

"Give me five minutes to change clothes. I gotta throw this shirt away."

Joey ran to his own room, so I stripped out of the clothes I was wearing and changed into pajamas. I couldn't get the image of myself in the mirror out of my mind. I couldn't ease the pain in my heart.

"Take it one minute at a time, Evie," I told myself as I slipped into bed. "One minute at a time."

ONE

EVA MCRAYNE

I KNEW JUST ENOUGH about the internet to be dangerous. Don't get me wrong. I posted on the standard social media sites when I had to. But I tended to leave that crap to the ad department. And Joey. Not to mention how I had a team of researchers to comb through the pages when I needed to get information. This time though, it was personal. I wanted to search out Jonah's enemies. The ones he only talked about when he had to. It was enough to distract me from my memories of the night before.

I decided to focus on the one he had mentioned when we were in London yesterday morning. Seemed as good a place as any to start.

One of whom he mentioned when we were in London yesterday morning.

I let the fingers of my good hand hover over the keyboard for a minute as I recalled our wonderful day together. It was my happiest memory to date. I'd known Jonah for less than a year, but I couldn't get him out of my mind. I wanted to protect him.

Flashes of my fight with Cyrus began to overtake my happier thoughts. The image of Janet in my bathroom mirror was enough to take the small smile off my face.

I had to focus on something else. I wouldn't last very long if I didn't.

Which is why I was doing this. I typed *Inimicus* into the search bar. Got the standard definitions. Even came across a book by that name. So, I switched my research to his enemy's sister. Vera Haliday, it turned out, had been born Vera Hale. Said so right on her Wikipedia page.

Nice.

I switched back to my original search page and typed in "Jessica Hale." After a moment, my laptop flickered and went black.

"What the hell—?"

"Forgive me, Eva."

I looked up to see Jonathan, the Protector Guide of the estate and Jonah's mentor, standing on the other side of my desk. He looked so dapper. So out of place in my California office. But I grinned when I stood to hug him.

"Jonathan! Forgive you? Are you kidding? I'm thrilled to see you!"

"As I am you." He gave me a smile that reminded me so much of a grandfatherly figure, I couldn't help but grin wider. "Yet, you cannot be doing what you are doing."

Jonathan gave me a look of concern and I winced. I looked like a mess, though I couldn't tell Jonathan what happened. I didn't dare after Cyrus' actions last night. And Joey had sworn not to tell another living soul. He spun a tale for me so that I was covered if I was asked about my injuries. I'd gotten into a fight at the office. An attempted mugging in the parking garage.

I hoped I wouldn't have to tell anyone, but it took

weeks to heal up after an attack from Cyrus. It always had.

"I'm fine," I answered his silent question without having to go into the lie. I pulled back to gesture to the set of chairs. "Now, what are you talking about? Let's go sit down."

He followed me over and took in the L.A. view before he joined me. Jonathan tapped his fingers on the chair arm before he spoke.

"The spirits have whispered your interest in our enemies."

"Jonathan, your enemies are mine. It is the least I can do —"

"No, my dear." He shook his head. "As admirable as your loyalty is to Jonah, we cannot allow you to interfere."

"Ok. I don't understand." I leaned forward to clasp his hand. "Jonathan, we fought together against Hera. You know that I can protect myself. And you know I will fight to my death, which is moot since I'm immortal —"

"And that is why you cannot fight, dear Eva." Jonathan clutched my hand tight in his grasp. "Your immortality isn't as moot as you might believe. You would perish. And we will lose our Jonah forever."

I stared at him. "What?"

"Close your eyes, Eva."

I took a breath and did as he requested. I felt Jonathan's hand go over my eyes.

I wasn't in L.A. anymore. I was at the estate. Or, at least, what had been the estate. It was a wrecked and ruined mess of its former self. I could see a wicked, truly evil-looking man and Jonah fighting tooth and nail.

I felt my heart stop when he got the upper hand. I

shoved past the assholes fighting around me. I had to get to him. I couldn't let him lose.

I willed a dagger into my hand and slammed it to the hilt into the bastard's back. Right at the top of his spine. He released Jonah before he turned to me.

"Come on, asshole," I snarled. "Let's go."

The resulting fight was one I would have been proud of. We both got our hits in. And I was successful in getting him away from Jonah. He needed time to recover. He would have it.

As I said, I did exceedingly well. I cut my opponent often enough to make him stumble back. I thrust myself upwards to deal the final blow. Knocked him flat on his ass.

The fucker grabbed me by the sides of my face and focused. I screamed when it felt as if my head was going to explode from the pressure he caused.

It was the last sound I would ever make. My view shifted as if I were outside of my body. I watched in horror as Jonah screamed my name before he went after my opponent. He was enraged. Horrifyingly alluring in his rage. His aura no longer the bright blue I adored, but so dark, it matched the being he savagely slaughtered with his bare hands.

Jonah was the victor, but not a single person around was celebrating. They looked as shocked as Jonah as he moved over to me.

He knelt, shaking as he gathered me up in his arms. He pressed his forehead to mine as he whispered words I would never know. I whimpered when Reena slid to a stop beside him. She was beat all to hell, but she went white at the sight of me.

"Jonah, let me help—"

"Don't," he choked out the word as he held my body tighter against him. "Don't touch her, Reena."

I moved over to them. I could see the gold in my

eyes fading. Eyes that looked like marble. There was no life in them. Not anymore.

Jonah stood up with me in his arms. He passed through me as he headed to the door. I heard the others calling out to him, but I knew that they wouldn't get through to him. And they never would again.

I gasped when Jonathan released me. He nodded once when I stared at him for confirmation of what I had seen.

"You, my dear child, are far too important for us to lose. Not only because you are Apollo's daughter, but because you have caught hold of something quite precious. And we cannot risk losing Jonah to dark ethereality."

"Why?" I swallowed when my voice cracked. "Why would he react by going dark? Surely—"

"You will see in time. 'Tis not my place to say." Jonathan squeezed my hand. "For now, promise me you won't fight against our enemies. Not just for your sake. But for Jonah's."

I remembered Cyrus' threat against Jonah's life. I wasn't supposed to see him or any of the Elevenths ever again. But I also knew I couldn't do that. Not even with Cyrus' threat. The dread I felt after witnessing the vision Jonathan showed me confirmed it. I had to see Jonah. I needed him in my life desperately.

"Jonathan, if he needs me—"

"Our Jonah needs you physically alive." He stood. "He needs you to be here once the battles are over, Eva. Please."

I studied him for a minute as I swallowed down the lump in my throat. I clasped my hand around my bandaged wrist and wondered exactly what had prompted Jonathan's visit today. Did he know?

No. That was impossible. There was no way for him to know.

"I promise, Jonathan," I whispered. "I promise."

The Protector Guide patted my knee then stood. "I need to return to North Carolina. Please do not mention what I have shown you to Jonah. It would be most upsetting to him."

"I won't. It's too upsetting for me, too."

I hugged him goodbye before he vanished. I went back over to my desk then picked up my phone. I needed to call Jonah. It was crazy, but after what I had seen, I just wanted to hear his voice. I wanted to reassure myself that he was ok. At that moment, Joey decided to barge in with an envelope in his hand.

"Guess who just got nominated for an Emmy?"

"Another one?" I faked a sigh. "I'm gonna need a bigger shelf."

Joey smacked me on the arm with the envelope, and I winced. He gave me a look of pure horror.

"Oh, God, sorry, Evie! Are you alright?"

"Fine." I cradled my wrapped wrist against my chest. "Which episode?"

"Covington." His smile could have lit the room. "Told you we were a shoo in. You gonna call Jonah to break the news or do you want me to do it?"

I swallowed down the knot in my throat as it tried to form there. Don't get me wrong. I wanted to see Jonah again as soon as possible, but I wasn't sure if he was going to go for it. Plus, I didn't know how I was going to explain my face. My bandaged wrist.

"Yeah. I was just about to call him anyway."

I swiped my thumb over the screen of my cell phone and watched the screen go back to black no less than ten times before Joey sighed and snatched the phone out of my hands.

"Stop punkin' out, Evie," he said as he shook his

head. "What would all the bad guys think if they knew you were afraid of making a simple phone call?"

"Joey Lawson, you give me that back." I reached for my phone that he held just over his head. "I'm going to call him, dammit. I'm just trying to figure out what I'm going to say."

"Right." My friend clicked his tongue against the front of his teeth. "What is there to say? How about just 'Hey, J! Come help me celebrate my Emmy nomination!'"

"Oh, be quiet." I reached out my hand. "Jonah's got a full plate right now. I'm just trying to figure out the best way to approach the subject and not seem like a burden."

Joey rolled his eyes. "I'd buy that if you two hadn't snuck off to play in Santa Fe the other day."

I ignored him and held out my hand. "Phone. Now."

"No go, Chicken." Joey grinned as he pressed a single finger against the screen. Within moments, I could hear it ringing.

"Look, I'm just not up to being laughed at. And Jonah is going to laugh." I crossed my arms over my chest. "Besides, when did you turn into such a traitor?"

"Hey, J!" Joey grinned as the call connected. "Listen, Evie wants to ask you something. Hang on."

"Thanks, Joey," I grumbled when he handed me the phone. I pressed it up against my ear with a sigh. "Hey, Blueberry. What's up?"

"Same shit, different day," Jonah responded. "Wishing we were back in the desert."

I couldn't help but smile at that. I started to tell him to come get me. But that wasn't the reason I had called.

"Same," I admitted. "I wish you would go out on the road with me. We'd have a great time."

"Evie's a wimp!" Joey called out from behind me and I picked up a pen and chunked it at him. "Alright, alright. I'm out. Don't forget to ask him!"

"Ask me what?" Jonah still sounded anxious despite my attempts to reassure him that I was fine. "You need a temporary co-host or something?"

"No," I frowned. "Wait. Does that mean you'd actually consider being on *Grave* with me and not just work behind the scenes?"

"Evie-"

"Ok, ok," I laughed a little. "So, Covington is up for an Emmy. You, Reena, and Terrence are cordially invited to be my dates for the ceremony. You down?"

"A date. To the Emmys." Jonah sounded distant, which was good. Maybe he wasn't really listening. "And you didn't want to ask me for what reason?"

Ok. So, he was listening. I tapped my fingers against the glass top of my desk as I stared out the window. "It's not that I didn't want to ask you, Blueberry. You should come visit me sometime. Take a week, and we'll hit up L.A., let me show you life outside of the desert. But I know how you are. Visiting me is one thing, but I knew that showcasing your talents at some Hollywood venue might be a bit of a stretch."

Jonah laughed. "You know me too well. And for that reason, I'll do something you won't expect for a change and take you up on the offer. When do we need to be there?"

I was relieved that Jonah took that stance, but I was even more surprised by the rustling I heard on his end.

"How did you manage to sneak in potato chips

past Reena?" I asked shrewdly. "Don't deny it. I can hear the bag in the background."

"We all have our secrets, Superstar," Jonah chuckled again. "I'll never tell. Now answer my question. When do we need to be there?"

I tilted my head to the side as I pulled out the letter and accompanying schedule that Joey had left on my desk. "Theia wants you here by Tuesday to get fitted. Appointments for hair and makeup start Saturday morning at nine, and we have to be on the red carpet by eight that night."

Jonah got quiet for a second, and I silently prayed to Apollo that he would hang up on me. Don't get me wrong. I wanted to see them all again.

Especially Jonah. I was drawn to him. I couldn't help it. But I also knew how much trouble we tended to get into when we got together. I closed my eyes as I remembered our first meeting back in North Carolina. We had all become targets of Hera, who had pulled us onto the Astral Plane to strike me down. But her plot flopped, and she got punished by her husband, Zeus, to remain in the mortal form of Juno Helakos, a billionaire heiress identity she used as her mortal cover on Earth. Despite her oath on the Styx that she'd leave us be, she'd promised me that she'd have her revenge. But that was a while ago. I hadn't heard a peep out of her since that time. I didn't know whether to be relieved or worried.

I studied the poster hanging up on the wall across from my desk. It was the first poster used to promote my television show, *Grave Messages*. I was standing in front of my former co-host, Elliot Lancaster, by a gravestone with Joey balancing his camera over his shoulder just to the right of us. It seemed as if we had shot that picture just days ago, but the truth was, it had been nearly five years since we started. And so much had changed since then.

I was brought out of my thoughts when the phone in my hand made a loud buzzing noise.

"Jesus, Jonah." I put the phone back by my ear when he stopped pressing the button. "I'm here. What did you say?"

"I said, will Cyrus be there?" Jonah asked. "Cause I don't want to be around him."

That made two of us. I cradled my wrist against my stomach. I should have told Jonah. He'd ask questions when he got here on Thursday. I couldn't do it.

"He shouldn't be."

"Hang on. Let me go get Reena and Terrence. They have a say in this, too."

"Alright. I'm putting you on the speaker." I heard a strange buzzing noise and pulled the phone away from my ear. "Hang on. My phone is messing—"

I didn't get a chance to finish my sentence as the shadows cast by the late California sun shifted into human forms around me. I ignored the clatter my phone made against the desk as I shoved my chair back.

"Who are you?" I willed my short sword into my hand as the dark forms inched closer. There were six of them total, each identical to the other.

"Shades? Stalkers? Tourists who took a wrong turn at Sunset?"

They responded by simultaneously launching themselves towards me. I grunted as the first one slammed me back into the desk, which sent my phone and the nasty pomegranate juice I'd been drinking to curb my wine consumption flying. Even the papers from the file I had been working on scattered across my rug. I went down beneath the bastard hellbent on ripping me apart.

I had seconds to react. I knew that. I slammed the palm of my hand into his throat then shoved him as hard as I could. He gagged and, in the sunlight, I saw blood on his teeth.

His blood? Or someone else's?

I could hear Jonah yelling my name through the phone, but I couldn't answer as beings that could loosely be classified as men surrounded me in the small space before they all launched at once.

I rolled over as the rest of them scrambled towards me. I tucked my broken wrist against my side to protect it then charged headfirst back into the fight at hand.

I'll admit that my thoughts flew at a hundred miles an hour as I dodged one blow after the other. They couldn't have been sent by Hera. She had sworn on the Styx, after all. Yeah, she'd vowed revenge and all that, but she couldn't buck her oath. Who else could it be, though? The Erinyes? Athena?

Cyrus in an attempt to teach me a lesson?

But I couldn't think about that now.

I did the only thing I could do. I fought. I stabbed the first man with my sword, then shoved him back. I brought my elbow back and cracked a bone, but I wasn't quick enough. Teeth began to tear at my arms, and I gasped from the sharp bite of pain.

I may have gasped, but the asshole who bit me began to scream. He erupted in a flash of fire, and I knew at once what he was. A vampire. I'd encountered only one before in Romania, and he had met his demise the same way.

"Jonah!" I yelled over the screeching as the group began their assault again. "Vamp—"

My words were cut off when something hard

cracked against my skull. I released a scream that was cut off as they converged onto me. Each one ripping at me with their teeth, and each one experiencing a horrifying death as the result.

By the time the last vampire was nothing more than a pile of ash, I couldn't move. I couldn't think about anything except the fire that raced across my skin from the gashes they had made. I had buried my face into the crook of my arm at some point, but the echo of boots across the hardwood floor made me lift my head.

"Perfect."

The shadow of a man said before he stepped on my phone. I heard it crack beneath his weight as he lifted me and threw me over his shoulder like a rag doll. I wanted to fight him. I needed to fight him.

I didn't have the strength to do either of those things as he stepped into the shadows and my office vanished.

TWO

JONAH ROWE

"JONAH?"

Jonah barely heard Reena calling his name as he stared at the phone in his hand. Maybe if he stared hard enough, he could see something. He got nothing except a dial tone.

"Jonah." Reena snapped her fingers in front of his nose. "What the hell is wrong? You look like something's happened."

"Eva," he whispered before he stared up at Reena, still horrified. "That was Eva. She got into a fight and—"

"Sit down."

"I can't sit down! I gotta get to E—"

"Ok. Start from the beginning. We can't do shit without information."

Jonah forced himself to calm. "Eva called to invite us to the Emmys. I heard a fight. She started to yell out vampires, and I heard more fighting before it just...it went silent."

"The phone died?"

"I don't know. The last hing I heard was a man's voice. Did he say perfect? Yeah. That was it."

"Ok. So right now, all we know is that Eva got into a fight."

"With vampires, Re!"

"You don't know that for sure." Reena gave him a stern look. "Eva has never encountered a vampire before. She wouldn't know them. So, it's possible she made a mistake. Right?"

"She's encountered vampires once before, in Romania," Jonah told her. "The damn thing bit her and exploded."

"You didn't tell us about that before, Jonah," Reena remarked.

"Sue me, Reena," Jonah said. "That's beside the point now! Eva's blood should keep her immune, but I don't know what multiple bites would do. Would they simply burn out or what?"

Terrence's face creased, and Jonah realized he had come up with Reena.

"How do you know there were multiple bites, J?" he demanded. "Maybe it was just the one. Call her back. She'll probably answer."

"Guys, she got attacked at home. We gotta go."

"Jesus," Reena tightened her black and scarlet ponytail with a sigh. "You know as well as I do how stubborn Eva can be. The last time I talked to her, she was in Scotland waiting for the fans to clear the streets so she could get to the airport. I tried to talk her into hiring a security team who could flush that shit out. No luck. She said Cyrus had been bad enough."

"Where was Cyrus when all of this was happening, huh?" Terrence wanted to know.

"Don't know. Tartarus, maybe," answered Jonah, and he shook his head, still not quite sure of how he felt about the existence of Tartarus. "Eva told me he hasn't been around since Hoia-Baciu, which would be great if he hadn't been assigned to guard her."

"But wouldn't somebody there have known shit was going on, like Apollo, or whoever?" persisted Terrence. "I mean, ain't the gods supposed to be all-seeing and all-knowing, or some shit like that?"

"No," said Reena. "I was curious about that myself, so I had a few conversations with Jonathan about it. The complexities and intricacies of life and nature are far too varied and random for predestination. The myths about gods and goddesses knowing and seeing all are just that—myths. They can't see the broad future any more than Spirit and Protector Guides. Apollo's prophecies in the old days dealt more with probabilities and likelihoods based on the behavioral patterns of the individuals who sought counsel. He didn't have advanced knowledge of every action they'd ever perform."

Terrence closed his eyes. "Next time, Reena? Stop at 'no' and save all that breath, 'kay?"

Jonah silently agreed but refocused on the task at hand. "We're wasting time. We have to go."

He purposely let that hang there. Reena gave him an appraising gaze, but it was Terrence who said it.

"You're actually going to L.A. to help her."

"Damn straight," Jonah responded. "I want you guys to come along."

"But Jonah, why?" Reena asked. "Apollo and all the Olympian agents, or whatever they are, can help Eva. You know how things are in our world now; why add this to your plate?"

"Eva needs us, Re," Jonah replied. "There's nothing else to say about it."

"Poor Joey." Terrence shook his head. "Was he there? Was he—"

"No." Jonah shook his head. "I heard him leave

before the fight started. We're going to use the Astral-imes to Eva's place."

Reena asked the inevitable question. "What will Jonathan have to say about all this?"

Jonah slipped his phone back into his pocket. "I don't see fit to bother him with it."

Reena's eyes widened, but Jonah raised a hand.

"Reena, I've got more respect for Jonathan than anyone, but I don't have time for the speeches or the riddles at the moment," He said. "I don't have a full grasp on Eva's world, but hell, I don't have a full grasp on our world, either. If we get going, she will have at least three people looking out for her. Im-proves the odds a bit, don't you think?"

Mercifully, Reena didn't argue with him. Ter-rence, who'd been seated at the foot of Jonah's bed, rose and looked Jonah over with a new interest.

"You ain't even thinking about it," he commented. "I'm cool with it and everything; Eva's my friend, too. But what about this has got you so wound up, Jonah?"

Jonah took a deep breath. He knew that his plan was rash. He knew that there might be consequences for the unauthorized Astralimes travel to Los Angeles he was about to do. But what Terrence and Reena didn't understand was that over the course of the time he'd known her, he'd come to care very much for Eva.

Maybe too much.

They had become good friends despite the dis-tance between them. Jonah didn't know when it hap-pened, but things about Eva began to stick with him. He could still smell the lavender oil she wore. He re-membered all too well how she had fit against him when they hugged that first time. How, for a fleeting moment when the Lancaster bastard had threatened them, he was overwhelmed by the desire to protect her. That she needed him to protect her. Not the Keeper.

It hadn't been a full two days since they ran off to Santa Fe. Their perfect day had ended with the two of them wrapped up in each other. He'd stayed awake as long as possible to relish in how she felt against him.

He shook his head to clear his thoughts. They didn't help matters now. Not in the least.

"I just think that more hands on deck will improve the chances of helping Eva. That's all."

Terrence, not as scrutinizing as Reena, simply shrugged. "Works for me. I was on board, anyway. Eva's our pal."

"How about it, Reena?" Jonah asked her. "Or do you want to wait for Jonathan to return from off-plane for a conference?"

Reena's eyes narrowed. "I look to Jonathan for advice, Jonah," she told him. "I need no one's permission to do what I want. Let's get to it."

And with no more preparation than that, the three of them took the two steps necessary to necessitate Astralimes travel and were in Eva's office in seconds. Joey jumped up when he saw them, but Cyrus didn't even look up. He had Eva's phone in one hand and a shard of broken glass in the other. Jonah had no idea what Cyrus hoped to glean because the objects looked about as useless as shit.

In all honesty, Jonah was just surprised to see the Keeper there in the first place.

"We got to stop meeting like this!" Joey looked so welcoming and hearty as he high-fived everyone, but Reena didn't oblige him.

"Cancel the smile, Joey," She told him. "The front is unbecoming. I know you feel guilty, and you have no reason to."

The false grin instantly fell off Joey's face. It was

as if he needed permission to drop the act. "I shouldn't have left," he said. "If I hadn't had to go to the office to file my paperwork since I'm heading out in a few hours for *House and Homes—*"

"Then her kidnappers would have had two hostages, Joseph." Cyrus broke his silence as he looked up at last. "It wasn't your responsibility to protect her."

"Kidnappers?"

"Yes. Kidnappers. She isn't here."

"Look, can you home in on her location?" Reena crossed her arms over her chest. "Like some Sibyl search pigeon?"

"I could, but I won't."

"Are you refusing to help Eva?" Jonah forced his eyes away from the bloodstained rug to gape at the Keeper. "Isn't that your job?"

"Not anymore. I don't give a damn what happens to her. Perhaps now, she will learn her lesson on the importance of my position."

Jonah felt anger, frustration, and rage join the worry in his head. Cyrus was a piece of work. A piece of something else, too.

"I knew it," he said quietly. "I knew this bastard would be of no use at all. Eva could be anywhere… anywhere right now…and he's found a way to make it about him."

"You have the audacity—"

"I'm going to step in here." Reena came up to stand next to Jonah. "What is your position to the Olympian Council?"

Cyrus narrowed his eyes as he stood upright. "Keeper of the Sibyl. Commander of Apollo's Keepers."

"And you took an oath to protect those in your care, correct?"

"Eva is no longer in my care."

"Yet, you still tout the title."

"I am bound to the role, not the bitch who inhabits it."

Jonah started forward, but Reena lifted her arm to keep him back.

"Then don't consider Eva, consider the role. How do you find Sibyls when they have run from you?" Reena smiled a little when Cyrus looked surprised. "That is the true purpose of your tracking ability, is it not? In case they run?"

"By their blood," Cyrus answered begrudgingly. "I can track a Sibyl because I can pinpoint where their blood is at any given moment."

"Alright," Reena nodded. "And this is the only blood you sense right now?"

"Yes."

"Then what do we know, and what have you found?"

"Um, Jonah?" Joey shifted on his heels. "Can I talk to you for a second alone?"

"Yeah, man."

The two of them walked out of Eva's office and into the hallway. Joey ran his hand through his hair as he glanced at the door Jonah had closed behind him.

"I don't know how to say this, but I might know something important."

"What?"

"Evie got attacked last night when she got home." He swallowed. "She didn't go into detail, but it was bad, man. Bad enough that I found her trying to open her veins in the bathroom."

Jonah didn't think he heard Joey right. Was that some sort of California lingo for drug use or something?

"You found Eva doing what?"

Joey crossed his arms over his chest then looked down for a minute. Finally, he met Jonah's eyes.

"You know Eva attempted suicide before, right?"

"In Charleston? Elliott shoved her out a window. Damn Cyrus probably helped him do it. That's not a suicide attempt."

"No, back in Georgia. She slit her wrists before she joined up with *Grave*."

A cold feeling curled up in Jonah's gut. He remembered the vision of Eva that Hera had tortured her with. That shit was real? He had played it off like his vision of Vera and Terrence.

"So what are you telling me, Joey?"

"I don't know. I know she was beat all to hell before she began to cut herself up. She wouldn't tell me what was wrong. Just that she isn't strong enough to deal with pain anymore. And now this?"

"You think the attack last night was related?"

Joey's eyes wandered to the door behind Jonah. He turned as well then stormed back inside the office where Cyrus was still talking with Reena and Terrence.

"What the fuck did you do to her?"

Cyrus raised an eyebrow as Jonah crossed the room.

"I have no idea what you are talking about and until you have proof of your words, I would take care with your accusations, Blue Aura."

"Save the Alpha shit for someone who's intimidated by it, bastard," Jonah snapped. "What did you do to Eva? I know it was you!"

"Then you know nothing."

"Wait," Reena stepped forward. "Eva was attacked last night? Where were you?"

"Since I was relieved from my post, thanks to your incessant meddling, I was on a different assignment."

"Then why are you here now?"

"Because Joseph called me in a panic. He was unsure if Eva had created this mess and ran off or if she had been taken." Cyrus crossed his arms over his chest. "Allow me to ask, but why are you here? I was under the impression that your time with Olympus was done."

"And I was under the impression *you* were useful," Jonah countered, "but I see that the only thing you ever do is lambast Eva and then blame her for your actions. You're guilty, asshole. What did you do?"

"As I said-"

"Did you have anything to do with her disappearance?" Reena placed a hand on Jonah's arm as she focused on Cyrus. "Start there."

"No."

"Ok," Reena glanced at Jonah. "What did Joey tell you that's riled you up so?"

"The whole damn situation has riled me up, Reena!"

"Uh huh. Be more specific."

"Eva was attacked last night when she got home. Then Joey found her in the bathroom carving up her arms." Jonah kept his eyes trained on Cyrus. "Eva wasn't suicidal when I brought her home."

"Ah, so she was with you?" Cyrus' eyebrows shot up. "Then one must pose the question. What did you do?"

"I didn't hit her, bruise her, or make her feel like shit," Jonah snapped. "That's all *your* wheelhouse, Pumpkin."

"This arguing is helping nothing, Jonah," Joey groaned.

43

"Neither is Cyrus," Jonah replied, "Yet, you called him."

"I didn't know what else to do."

"Ok. I think we need to all back up," Terrence interrupted the next round of arguing. "Joey, you're the only one who admits to seeing Eva after Jonah dropped her off. What time was that?"

"Around ten."

"What did you see?"

Joey ran his hand through his hair. It took a minute for him to answer.

"Eva had broken a razor. She was cutting herself. I realized what was going on and grabbed her. She begged me to let her go because she didn't want to live anymore. I couldn't do it."

"Then what happened?"

"She broke down for awhile. When I calmed her down, I took her in the kitchen."

"How do you know she got attacked beforehand?" Reena, this time. "Did she tell you that?"

"No. Eva's mouth was busted up. She had a wicked bruise across her left cheekbone. And her wrist was broken. I asked her what happened and she said it was nothing worth talking about."

"Who did you call after that?"

"What?"

"Who did you call?" Reena asked again. "To help her with the injuries and her mental state? Apollo? The cops?"

"Um, no. Nobody. I bandaged her up myself and helped her get to bed. I was hoping she would feel better if she got some sleep."

Reena narrowed her eyes. "You didn't call any Tenth authorities or medics? Joey, she could've had injuries that required more attention than you could give. Surely Apollo would want to know that her daughter was suicidal. Out of *everyone*, you called Cyrus. Why was that?"

"What are you implying by saying that, Katoa?"

"I'm not talking to you," Reena threw at Cyrus, her eyes still on Joey. "I asked you a question, Joey."

"I didn't call Cyrus either. Not last night." Joey threw his eyes over at Cyrus. "I didn't think that was such a good idea given the state Eva was in."

"And what are *you* implying, Lawson?"

"Eva is afraid of you, man. You know that. You remind her too much of her mom."

"Why didn't you call me?" Jonah glared at Joey. "If you didn't know how to handle the situation, I sure as hell would have."

"Would you?" Joey studied him. "No offense, Jonah, but I don't see how you would have been good in that situation either."

"So you were the brains of the operation, then, Joey?" Jonah said. "Eva was suicidal, so you clean her up, and leave her alone? You know she has a dagger she can pull out of thin air, and a .22 and in her nightstand. But you left her in the room alone."

Joey blinked. "But I didn't-"

"Don't you dare quail under these people, Lawson," Cyrus ordered. "They are nothing to us and never have been. They don't own anything here."

"Neither do you," Terrence muttered. "And where do *you* get off talking about ownership...ain't you a slave?"

"I didn't leave her alone, alright?"

Joey once again cut his eyes over at Cyrus and Jonah wondered exactly what that meant. Were the two of them working together? Were they getting the whole truth?

"I stayed in her bed with her. Nothing happened."

"You did what?" Cyrus said the words slow. Careful.

"I didn't do anything, man. I just didn't want her to be alone. No, I didn't think she would try again. But I didn't think she needed to be reminded that everyone has abandoned her. So I stayed with her."

"Cyrus, what *if* Joey did something?" Reena asked suddenly. "First you rise like a snake when you hear of Jonah being with her, now you throw that same voice at Joey. Last time, I checked, Eva's father is in spirit. But you seem to be usurping that role. Are you planning to...slap up Jonah and Joey, too?"

"I'd love to see him try," Jonah grumbled.

"Eva doesn't need to be petted and consoled like a child," Cyrus threw those cold eyes onto Reena. "She needs to be hardened. Molded. She does not need people in her ear whispering meaningless words. She has to learn that the only savior she will ever have is herself. That includes Joseph."

"Mmm hmm." Jonah folded his arms. "Once again, *you* know what's best for Eva. Fuck her own mind. You will tell her what to do and how to think."

"Boy." Cyrus's voice was dangerously calm. "You have no say in *anything* here."

"Neither do you, *boy*."

Cyrus jumped and turned in shock. Apollo stood at the door, stern and angry.

"My lord," Cyrus said, clearing not expecting to see Apollo, "I didn't know you'd be here."

"I took the liberty." Reena raised her phone. "I figured since you just wanted to be an ass and Joey just wanted to listen to whatever *you* said to do, I would do the right thing on behalf of Eva myself."

"What is going on here?" Apollo strolled into the room. "Where is Eva?"

"She has vanished, milord," Cyrus crossed his arms over his chest. "Apparently, she was taken."

"Taken? Explain."

"Eva called me this morning." Jonah tightened his hands into fists by his side. "I overheard a fight before the phone cut out. When we got here to check shit out, Cyrus was here. No Eva. Then Joey tells us that Eva was attacked the night before which led her to becoming suicidal."

"Why would Eva be suicidal?" Reena asked. "After a fight?"

Apollo stared at Cyrus then focused on Reena.

"There was a time when Eva attempted to take her own life prior to her immortality. This was due to memories of her mother. I would wager that whoever attacked her brought forth those same memories."

Jonah looked directly at Cyrus. The Cretan bristled.

"Why do you stare at me?" The keeper demanded.

"Because you're cruel, abusive, and have a history of trying to rule over people," Jonah answered. "Much like Janet."

"Once again, you insult my honor, Blue Aura-"

"Joseph," Apollo turned to Joey. "Do you know something? I feel familiarity within you."

"No, sir. Nothing more than I have already said." Joey cleared his throat. "Why do you ask?"

"Tell me. Where were you this morning when Eva was taken?"

"I had to go to the office. I came back and she was gone."

"And last night?"

"I went downtown to grab dinner. I knew Eva was with Jonah, so I didn't see a reason to wait for her to get back."

"You were fortunate then to avoid not one attack at your home, but two."

"If you think I had something to do with this, you're wrong, sir."

"I do not think you laid violent hands upon her, Joseph," Apollo said quietly, "but I sense you imbibed and were in vices yourself at some point yesterday evening."

Joey paled. "Um...fine. I had a few drinks and entertained a few partners last night. I was a little indisposed, but I helped Eva. I did a good thing man, I promise."

"Partners?"

"Yeah."

"I get it," Reena nodded. "That would also explain why Eva had no problems sharing a bed with you last night. You're gay."

Joey shrugged and stuffed his hands in his pockets. "Yeah, well. It's not something I advertise. I'd rather keep my preferences private."

"I can't imagine why," Reena said. "No one here would judge you; look who you're talking to. But you might need to have a conversation with your girlfriend back in Wyoming. The one you've been hiding behind all these years."

"You know about her then?"

"Of course I do," Reena said. "Your information is on social media and Wikipedia just like everyone else on *Grave Messages*."

"That's done on purpose." Joey gave Reena a sad smile. "Jennifer had been a friend for ages. Long enough to help me craft the arrangement to hide the truth from my folks. There's no need to talk to her. She knows."

"You won't come out to your folks?"

"My parents are Catholic. They find out the truth

and I won't be able to see my sisters anymore. I won't do that to them."

"That is sad, Joseph," Apollo said. "I myself have had male lovers and no-one has shunned me from my offspring or siblings. Your family needs to be informed that their absurd outdated binaries of sexuality are bullshit fed to the impressionable masses by hypocritical Titans. But that conversation will need to happen another day. The salient point here and now is what's happened with Eva."

"What can we do?"

"Jonah, you said you heard the fight where Eva was taken?"

"Yes, sir. She started to yell out 'vampires' but got cut off."

"Then Hades is involved."

"What? How do you figure that?"

"One, his sister is my daughter's greatest enemy. Two, in our world, he lords over them. He created the first vampire not long after the humans began to branch out on their own. You may have heard of her. Lilith?"

"Lilith?" Jonah gaped. "Adam's first wife?"

"Indeed. She is one of Hades' consorts. Lovely woman despite her desire for human blood."

"Holy fuck," Jonah breathed, stunned at this newest revelation. "I can't believe she's real. But the question is why is *she* helping out Hades? What's in it for her?"

"You all know that Persephone is Hades' wife, yes?"

"Of course."

"Well, Lilith is his consort and advisor. Persephone was a trophy. My uncle's true affection lies with Lilith. She is his actual wife in all but name."

"Huh." Jonah thought about that. That was some

messed up shit. Hades kidnapped and violated Persephone just to treat her like a side piece? "So Hades flaunts his whore in Persephone's face, and she's just...there? I feel for her."

"Don't pity Persephone. She has her fair share of lovers." Apollo scoffed. "At any rate, I will work on confirmation that Eva is actually in the Underworld. I want you to speak with Ares in regards to the location of the entrance."

"Why Ares?"

"He is the only god on the earthplane who knows the location. Cyrus, you will have to accompany them."

"I was under the impression you removed me from assisting the Sibyl."

"I removed you since you were unable to control your senses around her," Apollo snapped. "It should not be a problem if the Elevenths are around. Am I clear?"

Cyrus regarded Apollo before cutting his eye at Jonah. "I don't believe Rowe would consider it prudent working with me."

"And you'd be right," Jonah said, "but I'm thinking about Eva. Not you."

"Are you certain of that, Rowe? Or are you thinking of the accolades you will receive if you are successful?"

"That's the difference between the two of us, Cyrus," Jonah cracked his knuckles. "One of us cares about people and doesn't have an ulterior motive. The other one is you. Now can we get started, Apollo?"

"The first step is a parley between the two of you." Apollo crossed his arms. "I will not have Eva rescued only to be caught in the crossfire of your arguments."

Cyrus stiffened. "I do not believe that is necessary."

"Say the words, Keeper."

Cyrus struggled with himself before he spoke.

"I agree to a temporary parley with the Blue Aura."

Apollo looked at Jonah. "Jonah?"

"What he said," Jonah muttered. "Now, shall we begin?"

"Indeed. My daughter is far too precious to lose."

"Daughter?" Reena looked between Jonah and Terrence. "You mean that in the symbolic sense, right?"

"No. The literal."

Everyone stared at him. Jonah couldn't believe what he'd just heard. Eva was Apollo's kid? Seriously?

"Get over here." Apollo's voice was level, but it sounded dangerous as he focused on Cyrus. "Are you not assigned to the Sibyl?"

"I am."

"And yet, she has been stolen from us?"

"I believe you told me yourself that I was not to be within twenty feet of Eva."

Apollo's eyes narrowed. If possible, the shadows seemed to grow even darker.

"I will forgive such insolence only once, slave. Tell me what you know of this matter."

"Absolutely nothing, my lord. I came here as soon as I received a call from Joseph regarding Eva's disappearance."

"If she is in the Underworld, we need to retrieve her immediately." Apollo kept his gaze trained on the Keeper instead of the mess around them. "I would tell you to go to Ares alone to get the location, but your actions have been most disturbing as of late. Thus, I ask that the Ghostly Ones accompany you."

"Ghostly Ones?"

"An ancient term for ethereal beings, dear Reena." Apollo studied the group. "Will you assist us?"

"Of course," Reena said. "Eva means the world to us too."

"Of course, I'm in," Terrence said. "I'd do anything for Evie."

"The question isn't whether *we* will help, Apollo," Jonah said. "It's Cyrus here. His indifference is written all over his face."

"Forgive me if I am not excited about helping the Sibyl who tarnished my honor."

"You tarnished your own honor," Apollo glared at Cyrus. "And you continue to do so by not remembering your place. Your participation is not voluntary."

Cyrus breathed out through his nose before he spoke through gritted teeth. "Yes, Lord Apollo."

"So, what happens now, man?" Jonah asked Apollo. "I'd rather hear from you than Cyrus."

"Only four gods know the location of the Underworld since the entrance is constantly changing," Apollo began. "Hades, Persephone, Hermes, and Ares."

"Ares?"

"Yes. He has to know due to the number of souls lost in warfare." Apollo willed a notepad in his hand. "He is currently masquerading on the earthplane under the guise of the owner of a security firm in Van Nuys, California."

"Why isn't Hermes an option?" Terrence wondered aloud. "He seems cool. Might be more approachable than the God of War."

"Hermes is unavailable for the time being. My brother has squirreled himself away to mourn a recent heartbreak," Apollo responded drily. "So, until he tells us where he is, Hermes isn't an option."

"Hades rarely, if ever, walks the Earth," Cyrus added. "Persephone is amid her allotted time away from the Underworld, but she could be anywhere. She likes exploring as much as possible in her time away from Hades. So, the only option is Ares. He goes by the alias of Damien Bates."

"Where is this place?"

"You can't use the Astralimes, Jonah. The closest you will be able to go is Los Angeles. The rest is a road trip."

"We don't have that kind of time! It's already been half an hour since I talked to her. There's no tellin' what she is going through."

"If Hades is smart, he is treating my Eva as an esteemed guest."

"If he is not?"

Apollo's eyes darkened. "Then that would be cause for war amongst us."

"Even in war, there are invaluable lessons," Cyrus said. "These experiences could very well toughen Eva. Make her shed certain...deleterious pursuits and endeavors."

Jonah sneered. "You're stuck on isolating her."

"It has nothing to do with isolation, Rowe. It has everything to do with not making decisions that will harm her wellbeing."

Jonah bit back his response to that when another being stepped into the room. The woman was tiny. Delicate. In her hands, she held a tablet.

"You have a missive from Lord Hades, sire."

"Thank you, Delia." Apollo took the tablet and raised his eyebrow. "It appears I was correct then."

Apollo pressed *Play* as the others gathered around him. The video was grainy. Shitty quality at best. But a cell of stone could be made out. As well as the figure of a large man in black standing over a figure hunched down on the floor.

No, not someone. Jonah saw Eva raise her head long enough to glare at the man before her head was shoved back down.

"Do not insult my intelligence, nephew." A cold voice broke through the sounds of the beating. "Give me the mirror, or else."

"What?" Jonah asked, worried. "This is all about Eva's mirror?"

"It appears so."

"What does the end of that mean?" Reena asked from over Apollo's shoulder. "The 'or else' part?"

"It could mean anything, Reena," Apollo dropped the tablet and stomped on it, the broken pieces mixing with Eva's crushed phone. "It all depends on Hades' mood."

"We both know differently." Cyrus shrugged when Apollo glared at him. "Tis true, m'lord."

"What? Eternal damnation or something?"

"Worse," Cyrus continued. "Those that Hades wishes to torture the most are sent to the Incubus if they are women. The Succubus if they are men."

"What?" Reena croaked. "How can you say something like that so conversationally? You'd think we were talking about the weather!"

"'Tis only a fact." Cyrus kept his eyes on Apollo as he spoke. "The tortures were set long before the modern era. They have not – nor will they ever – change."

"Yeah," Jonah snapped. "A time you'd love to go back to. Who would have guessed strong women and men knowing their boundaries was too much for you, Cy?"

"My name is Cyrus, boy."

"My mistake," Jonah scoffed. "Who would have

guessed strong women and men knowing their boundaries was too much for you, Cyrus Boy?"

"You will respect—"

"Both of you, cease this at once. You agreed upon a parley."

"He's not going to help us." Reena shook her head. "Why would he? He is still stuck on the fact he got called out as an abuser."

"I did not abuse Eva," Cyrus snapped. "I trained her. If you hadn't been so damned determined to step into my place, I could have."

"And if *you* hadn't felt the need to overcompensate, we wouldn't have had to!" Reena growled.

Cyrus stepped forward, but Jonah and Terrence formed a wall in front of her. Jonah sneered and willed ethereality to his fists.

"Go ahead, dude," Terrence whispered. "If you wanna go there, like Spader would say, roll the dice and take your chances."

The sight of both men standing there seemed to snap Cyrus out of it. The Keeper sneered at both before he turned back to Apollo, who beckoned Cyrus closer. When the Keeper closed the distance, Apollo grabbed him by the collar of his suit and shoved Cyrus to his knees.

"One more show of insolence and I will replace you with Ulysses, do you understand me?"

"We both know why you haven't done that already, milord." Cyrus's expression was stoic. Completely cold. "But alas, I will continue to follow orders."

"Then follow them." Apollo released him. "If you weren't needed to gain an audience with Ares, I would have thrown you in Tartarus for abandoning your duty."

"My fault, my Lord," Cyrus murmured. "I will do better."

"My God," Terrence remarked. "If he backpedals any further, he'll blow through the wall."

Despite the situation, Reena cracked up.

"Sorry, sorry," She waved her hand at them. "But I think we should focus on the good news."

"The good news?" Jonah stared at her. "What good news?"

"One, we know where Eva is. Two, she's still alive. Both are bonuses in my book." Reena patted his arm. "The sooner we can get to the Underworld, the sooner you two can get back to lying to yourselves."

"The only lie here is that Cyrus thinks he's useful," Jonah snapped. "Now, let's go."

"Wait. Before you go, come here, Jonah."

Jonah tightened his hands into fists then relaxed them when Apollo drew a symbol over his head. The resulting buzz made it feel as if there was caffeine in his blood.

"You blessed me. Why?"

"Because you have the most to lose if Eva isn't returned to us."

"Huh?" Jonah stared at Apollo in confusion. "What? What do you mean?"

"'Tis not my place to say. I only ask that you and yours do not fail in this task."

"I'll...um...I'll put my best foot forward like I always try to do."

Apollo nodded, then bowed to the others.

"I will bless each of you when the task is done." Apollo addressed them once more. "If there are any problems with Cyrus, do not hesitate to contact me."

Apollo vanished, and Terrence whistled.

"What do you think he meant by that, J.?"

"No clue."

"Apollo is the god of prophecy. He knows something. Something big."

"I don't buy into that prophecy stuff, man. Not after Reena buried it in logic," Jonah said. "No disrespect to Apollo, but I think he just knows how to read the room."

Cyrus snorted before he headed out of the office. He left the door open, and Jonah could see him ascending the stairs.

"Where in the hell are you going?" Jonah called out to him. "We got to go."

"Eva is not going anywhere. I'll return shortly."

"Was Reena right, dude?" Jonah leered at Cyrus. "Is your dick so tiny that you have to control *something* to function?"

Cyrus kept walking up and disappeared around the corner. Joey ran his hand through his hair as he cleared his throat. Jonah had damn near forgotten he was even there.

"Guys, I want to help, but I leave for the airport in two hours. I can't cancel this shoot."

"Go do your thing, brother." Jonah felt a nerve twitch in his jaw. Better that Joey is out of the way in case the kidnappers came back. "We'll bring Eva home. No problem."

Joey nodded, then slipped out of the office. Reena shook her head in disbelief.

"One would think that Joey could cancel his gig since his meal ticket is in danger."

"Let's check the kitchen for snacks." Terrence headed out of the room as he tried to change the subject. Between the three of them, he was the one who had gotten close to the cameraman. Maybe he didn't want them to see his friend in a bad light or something. "We'll need them if we are doing a drive."

"You know you're not going to find anything."

Reena shook her head before she turned to Jonah. "Maybe you should sit down."

"I don't need to sit down. I need Commander Jackass to hurry the hell up."

"Jonah, just relax. Eva is going to be fine."

"I know she can handle herself, but it wasn't one on one," Jonah responded with more heat than he meant to. He took a breath and tried again. "This was fucking Hades. And if what asshole in there said was right, there is a damn Incubus, too?"

"We are talking about the girl who defeated Hera, Jonah."

"With our help." He finally sat down and put his head in his hands for a moment. Jonah rubbed his hands over his face then looked over at Reena when she sat next to him. "I shouldn't have left her here. I should have come to L.A. the second she told me she had been attacked last night."

"Don't play that game with yourself, J," Reena rubbed his back as Cyrus returned. "About time. What did you go do?"

"Refilled my flask, if you truly want to know."

Cyrus went out of the room, and they followed him. Jonah gritted his teeth when he saw how casually the bastard took Eva's keys from the hook by the door.

"Since we have a damn caravan, we'll have to take the Land Rover."

"Let me drive."

"No." Cyrus hit the button, and the doors unlocked. "Get in."

Jonah turned one-eighty and bumped Cyrus' shoulder with enough force to make him step back.

"Oops," he muttered. "You gonna drive now, yes?"

Cyrus released a low growl. Jonah was thoroughly indifferent about it as he climbed into the front seat.

"Get in, pumpkin. We've wasted enough time."

The sound of the doors opening and closing filled the garage space. Cyrus said nothing as he backed out of the garage and got onto the main street.

Jonah heard Reena and Terrence whispering as the city of angels flew past them. There was plenty to see, but Jonah's mind went back to the afternoon he'd spent teaching Eva how to drive. They'd gone to lunch at one of her investment restaurants afterward. Cyrus had been there with another Keeper.

"Tell us what to expect in the Underworld, Cyrus," Reena broke the silence. "Or have you never been?"

"Never had a reason to go."

"Do you mean to say that you know dick about the Underworld?" Jonah sneered. "Why am I not surprised?"

"I know what I have read in the accounts that have surfaced. Persephone herself has detailed the tortures numerous times."

"Like what? Aside from the Incubus?"

"Hades enjoys psychological torture as much as physical. I suspect he is using both Eva's past and her abilities as the Sibyl against her."

"How the hell can he do that?" Reena asked.

"You do realize that Janet and Martin McRayne are both residents of the Underworld, correct?" Cyrus glanced up into the rearview. "And the Underworld is full of restless spirits who can easily drive a medium mad."

"So, what can we do to help her once we're there?" Jonah demanded.

"That's your problem, Rowe. You are always trying to help," Cyrus leered as he pulled onto the freeway. "Has it ever crossed your mind that help may not be needed? That Eva should come to terms with her abuses on her own?"

"Has it crossed your mind that you were given a job to do by Apollo?" Jonah shot back. "Because right now, you are the only problem we have."

"One of these days, you will push me too far, Rowe."

"Not all that worried about pushing you, pumpkin."

Cyrus growled a little in his throat but did not respond.

"How long have you been assigned to Eva?" Reena asked from the back. "Two, three years?"

"Five."

"And you've done this job for every Sibyl?"

"Yes."

"Did you treat every Sibyl like you treat Eva?" Terrence asked bluntly. "Weren't you married to one?"

"I was married to Delphine, the first Sibyl. And to answer your question, no. I treated Eva as one should treat a soldier because that is what the role has evolved into. Strangely enough, none of you seem to realize that."

"Cyrus, I have been a fighter all of my life," Reena said, "and speaking as a trainer, you're an abuser, and you need to check that."

"Your definition of abuse and mine are two very different things. But it doesn't matter now, does it? I am the Sibyl's Keeper in name only."

Cyrus said nothing else as he switched lanes. The air in the car was thick with the tension between the Keeper and the rest of them.

"Why do we need you again?" Reena broke the

silence again. "Apollo knows good and well we can handle everything."

"Because Ares will only see members of Olympus, which none of you are."

The silence returned for a good half-hour before Cyrus spoke again.

"Why are you doing this?" He kept his eyes forward. "Reena and Terrence, you were both put on the backburner during Covington. And you, Rowe. *You,* I don't understand in the slightest."

"Caring for a loved one's wellbeing, Cyrus," Jonah said without hesitation. "Being helpful because you have the power to do so, without ulterior motive. Of course, you don't understand in the slightest. You're not a hero."

"I never claimed to be."

"Here's what I don't understand." Terrence leaned forward in his seat. "How in the hell did you and Eva ever get together in the first place?"

"Do you want the truth? Or do you want a horrific story that you're more likely to believe?"

"I want the answer, sans the dramatics."

"Convenience, for both our sakes. Eva believed that if we were in a relationship, she wouldn't get hounded by the press about who she was going to sleep with. And I was allowed certain liberties for my cooperation."

"What liberties?"

"Times of freedom."

Jonah's phone vibrated before he could respond. He checked out a small message from Reena:

Jonah, he's lying. That's TOTAL bullshit. I didn't even need my essence reading for it.

Jonah put the phone away. Cyrus had already been revealed to be an asshole, but this confession meant he was even worse than they already knew.

Jonah didn't need to be a brain surgeon to figure that out.

But why exactly would Cyrus, whose indifference was nigh palpable, feel the need to lie?

"No response, Rowe?" Cyrus said quietly. "No sarcastic impertinence?"

Jonah looked out over the city. "Let's just get to Eva," he said at last. 'I, um...I don't have anything else to say to you, man. Let's just get to Van Nuys."

THREE

EVA MCRAYNE

I CAN'T DESCRIBE the place I had been taken to. It was dark. Dank. And the cell they had thrown me in looked like something out of a bad Mel Gibson movie. I sat up to rub a grubby arm over my eyes to clear them, but it didn't do any good. The only thing I got was a slimy mixture of muck across my forehead.

Despite the darkness, I could make out the two shadowy figures that stood on each side of my cell door. They didn't look like much, but without my sword, I knew I didn't stand a chance against them.

"Hey." I shook the chains clamped down on my wrists. "Dude, the least you can do is loosen these damn things. I'm going to have marks for weeks if you don't."

Silence. Not that I expected an answer. I sighed as I recounted the fight which had gotten me here in the first place. The vampires. Their screams as they ripped into my flesh that became gargled and strangled as the fire from my paternal bloodline sent them all to Hell. The phone call where Jonah heard everything.

I groaned at the thought of my friend. I knew exactly what he would be up to right now. Trying to piece things together so that he could find me. Blaming himself for leaving me in the first place. Jonah didn't fancy himself to be a hero, but I'd known him long enough to know that was classic Jonah, modest to a fault. If something happened to someone he cared about, then he would try like hell to fix it. And I knew he cared about me.

The trip to Santa Fe had been proof of that. I frowned as I examined the cuffs in the darkness. Surely there was a way I could get myself out of this mess without Jonah rushing in. I'd gotten out of worse situations.

Ok. That was a lie. I'd been pulled into a mirror. I'd been possessed. Fought more battles against monsters than I cared to admit. But snatched? Never.

I heard a heavy door open somewhere just before a bright orange light flashed through the room. I stayed seated as the man who had grabbed me approached the doors.

"Stand for your new master."

"Yeah, I'm good." I folded my legs under me in an act of defiance. "Last time I checked, I only had one master. And he doesn't throw me in dungeons."

"Ah, but such actions aren't above your father, believe me," said the man. "You would have benefitted from it. It only serves to toughen you."

I rolled my eyes. A pep talk from my kidnapper? Pass. Sounded too much like Cyrus.

The orange light was replaced by a bright blue one. It reminded me of Jonah, and my heart skipped at the thought of him. But where my friend was warm, the man responsible for the newest light show was cold. He approached my cell with an expression of stone.

"This is the Sibyl?" He turned to my captor. "Are you certain?"

"Allow me to prove it," the other stranger barked as the guards opened my cell door. They stepped aside to allow him to enter. When he faced me, he held out a single mirror before my face.

I gritted my teeth as the whispers of the departed spirits filled my ears. Yet, they weren't whispers here. The voices I heard were screams of pain. Anguish. I turned my head away and tried to raise my hands to my ears to no avail.

"Ok," I gasped. "You've made your point. Put that damned thing away."

"For once, Ares, you have done your job well." The one by the door tapped his fingers together before his face. "Sibyl, do you know why you are here?"

"I'm guessing it's not for the free continental breakfast."

That quip earned me a fresh strike. I didn't see the next hit coming, but the only thing that kept me in place was the chains attached to the floor. I spat out the blood that filled up my mouth and awarded my captor with a grin.

"There," I murmured. "Made me bleed. Happy?"

"Bitch," the man growled as he grabbed the front of my shirt to lift me to my feet. "I'll beat you into submission yet."

"Stop."

Ares released my shirt to stand aside. The man at the door snapped his fingers, and the guards pulled me out as far as I could go.

"I will repeat my question only once more, Sibyl. Do you know why you are here?"

"No clue," I replied. "I'm sure you're just clamoring to tell me."

I raised my chin. He was thin. His face was dark.

Gaunt. The only thing that would mark him as significant was his strange blue eyes. They were hypnotic. "Let's start with introductions, shall we?" Maybe another track might be useful. "Who are you?"

"Ah, yes. Introductions. How rude of me." The man chuckled. "I'm known by many names, girl. Satan. Anubis. However, I would prefer for you to address me as Hades."

Hades. The chthonic god of departed spirits. The god famous for snatching people away from their lives to reside in the Underworld.

"So, we're in the Underworld, then?" I raised an eyebrow. "I'm surprised. This place seems more like a spooky cavern than a fiery pit."

Hades grinned. "As for why you are here, well. There are many reasons for your capture. For now, we will focus on your lack of appreciation for what I do."

"And what is that, exactly?" I asked him. "Cause you look like a cheap car salesman to me."

I knew I probably shouldn't be running off at the mouth like I was, but I couldn't help it. My opinions and viewpoints got me in trouble all the time. Apollo said it was because I had brio. Jonah said that it was because I was a brat.

I expected another strike, but Hades didn't touch me. He didn't need to. He waved his long fingers before my face, and an icy chill ran through my bones. I felt my hands start to shake. I clenched my teeth together to keep them from clattering. I groaned as images filled my mind.

I saw images of war. Images of murder and violence. Suicide victims swung from trees or closets. Gunshot victims who bled out on the pavement. Images of victims mutilated and brutalized flashed so quick, I couldn't see much, but what I did see was enough to make me gag.

"Death. Passing into Spirit. Whatever you want to call it. That is my business, Sibyl. You will do well to remember that it is me that you serve through the gift my wife has granted you."

"Your wife." I gasped as the scenes continued to play behind my eyes. "Your stolen prize, you mean."

"What of the others?" Hades turned his focus back to Ares. "Are they aware of your deed?"

"Yeah." Ares nodded as he grabbed my arm and leaned down to sneer into my face. "Would you care to experience the fear threatening to overwhelm your new friend?"

Hades snapped his fingers, and I whimpered as I fell against Ares from the weight of the emotions rushing through me. I felt as if my heart would break as the death scenes playing in my mind shifted to the sight of Jonah knelt by a pile of ash and a puddle of blood. I could see the Elevenths all in conversation as a knot rose into my throat that threatened to choke me.

"Stop," I managed. "What's the real reason behind this, Hades? Surely you didn't go to all this trouble for mind games."

"Games?" Hades looked surprised at my response. "You see this as a game?"

"No, but you are enjoying this as if it were one."

Hades took a measured breath and then turned on his heel. "Do what you wish, Ares. The Blue Aura will arrive sooner rather than later."

"So, this is about Jonah?" I shook Ares' grip off my arm with a frown. "What does he have to do with you?"

"That is no concern of yours, girl," said Hades. "No concern at all."

Hades called over his shoulder as the door clanged shut behind him. I didn't have a single moment to respond as Ares growled beside me. He grabbed my throat and shoved me against the wall with a grin.

"You're immortal," he whispered. "That means that these attacks will heal. It makes it that much more fun."

Apollo, help me, I managed before the massive man flung his fist my way. I tried to block his punches, but it was no use. Ares was known for his bloodlust, and he was determined to fulfill it with me.

I had been knocked to the floor when I caught sight of the one thing I should have noticed in the beginning. The massive iron loop attached to the floor held my chains in place. I cried out as my attacker slammed his boot against my side, but before he could lower his foot a second time, I twisted beneath him to wrap the length of the chain around his ankle. I ignored the sharp pains that ran through my wrist when I jerked against the metal.

With a yell, Ares crashed onto his back. I unwrapped the length as I straddled him. As he struggled to throw me off of him, I managed to loop the chain around his throat once.

"I think I owe you one," I hissed as I tightened the lengths around his throat. The god bellowed as he clawed at the chain. I held on, but my assault didn't last long. The man disappeared from his place beneath me.

"Dammit!"

I slammed the now empty links against the stone floor in anger. I started to stand when a small figure appeared before the doors. A woman this time; her long dark hair crowned with flowers. She studied me with an interest I found completely unwarranted.

"Great," I snarled, "another visitor?"

I tried to stand, but Ares had done some damage. I collapsed back to my knees and stayed there.

"If I must suffer, can't I do it in silence? All this chitchat is killing me."

"Your father has been made aware of your predicament, child." The woman reached through the bars, but she didn't touch me. "Your torment has only just begun, but I can be of assistance."

"Let me guess." This rigmarole would drive me insane faster than Hades and Ares. "You're Persephone. You're the whole reason I can't look into a mirror without the whole damned Underworld trying to pull me down here. Thanks for that, by the way. Putting on eyeliner is a bitch, thanks to you."

The woman chuckled as she dropped a single rose into my cell. "I can't be caught here, Sibyl. My assistance is this."

"A rose?" I didn't bother to shroud my sarcasm. "Wow. That will come in handy next time Ares decides I make a good punching bag."

"It is not the flower, silly girl." Impatience colored Persephone's words, but only a little. "It's what it represents. Beauty and grace can hide the sharpest of thorns."

She stepped back and pressed her fingers against her lips as she faded into the darkness.

"And that was as clear as mud," I mumbled to myself.

I winced as I tried to take in my injuries but gave up after a few minutes. It was too dark to see anything in here unless one of the Underworld's reigning deities decided to pay me a visit. So, I did the only thing I could do. I sat back against the bars and waited. I knew it wouldn't be long before Hades made his appearance again.

"So physical attacks have not broken your spirit." Hades pressed his fingers together just before the tip of his nose. "Nor did the fates of the souls who live with me now. What will it take, little Sibyl, to make you fear me?"

I stared at the stone wall behind him. I had been pulled out of the cell and presented to the god in his throne room. Maybe it was the beatings by Ares or the hours of silence I had endured, but I wasn't impressed. The room was much too gothic for my tastes. As for Hades, I refused to respond to him.

"No sharp wit? No harsh words?" Hades chuckled. "I am surprised. Perhaps another round with Ares is in order then."

Again, I refused to answer him. The man jumped up from his chair to circle me. He stopped in front of me to study my face.

"I have been in contact with Apollo, who is less than pleased that you were taken from him," Hades went on. "It must make you feel special to be so adored by your father. Yet, we both know that adoration is based solely on how useful you are to him. The moment you stop granting him followers, you will be cast aside for another favorite."

I shrugged. I mean, really. What was he expecting? For me to burst into tears at the thought of losing Apollo's favor? But I will admit that there was a pang of pain when Hades said what he said. Apollo was the only one I had who I knew held some affection for me. No. That wasn't true. Jonah cared for me a little. Joey, too, in his own way.

"Alas, that is of little matter to me." Hades' grin brought my attention back to him. "Perhaps it is time to push your mind to the limits, girl. We shall see how strong you truly are."

He turned to the guard standing to my left. "Take her to the chambers, but do not leave her unattended."

The two who flanked me nodded as one of them grabbed the chain attached to my neck.

Yeah. A leash. I thought it was cute, too.

The two led me down a set of stairs just outside of the throne room. I was sure they would return me to my cell. Perhaps that is what Hades called it. But when they stopped before a small door, I knew better. The larger guard pressed his hand against the metal before us to shove it open.

Inside, the walls, the floor, even the ceiling was covered with mirrors. I took a step back as I felt the blood rushing from my face.

"No," I begged. "You can't put me in there. Don't—"

The guards gave me the same silent treatment I had used against Hades. The man jerked the chain forward as the screams I had heard through Ares' mirror filled my mind. I struggled. I tried to fight them. But in the end, the guard attached my leash to the floor.

I barely heard the door slam shut as my screams mixed in with those around me.

———

I could still hear the screams long after my guards returned me to my cell. I had tried to block them out. I put up the barriers that Hecate had taught me to use at the Academy. But what I could do was good against a few spirits, not the onslaught Hades had ordered for me.

It took a while for me to stop shaking. I had to think. I had to figure out how I was going to get out of the hell I'd been thrown into.

The problem was I didn't know how to escape. I mean, it was the Underworld, for gods' sake. Running seemed pointless. And my attempts to pray to Apollo had resulted in nothing.

I refused to believe he had abandoned me. I was too important to the Olympian Council. *Grave Messages* had resulted in their resurgence in power. I knew Apollo wouldn't give up on me so easily.

I was his daughter. Surely, that meant something if none of the other things were enough.

So, I laid still and stared at the stone ceiling as if it were the most fascinating thing in the world.

"Do not respond to me."

I frowned as I heard the whisper in my right ear. Maybe Hades had been successful, after all. Maybe his wretched room of mirrors had made me crazy.

"No, your mind isn't broken. Not yet." The voice was replaced by a hand that pulled the hair matted to my forehead free. "Your father has heard your plea. He sent me to be a comfort to you."

Right. I closed my eyes and hissed my next words despite the order not to speak.

"Comfort, huh? Well, unless you brought an entire winery full of alcohol or the key out of this place, I don't think you're going to be much help."

"Shut up. You will expose us both."

"Oh, ok. Like they don't know I'm already in here." I frowned. "Who are you?"

"A friend, stupid girl," the voice hissed. "Now listen and do not speak. I can guide you through the maze of this place. I can get you to the entrance. But only if you follow my instructions to the letter."

"I'm listening."

The mystery whisperer detailed the escape plan. They described the path I would have to take to the entrance. When the voice finally went silent, I smiled.

"When?"

"Soon. Bide your time, Sibyl. The moment they come to take you to Hades, we will strike."

What else could I do? I rolled my eyes at the ceiling as the cell went back to the cold silence I had become accustomed to. I re-ran the conversation with my new "friend" through my head repeatedly to memorize the route they spoke of. Just before I repeated it for the fiftieth time, I saw a bright orange light fill the room as the wooden door opened.

Ares. Yay.

"Open the cell," barked the god.

My guards rushed to comply with his orders. I didn't move until he stood over top of me. Even then, I simply sighed and locked my fingers together over my chest.

"You are to come with me."

"What will it be this time?" I asked, cutting my eyes over at him. "Physical torture? Psychological torment? I'd like to know before I decide if I am going to make this easy on you or not."

"I'd prefer it if you didn't," sneered Ares. "I am known as a savage, girl. Do not make me prove it to you."

"Is that what you told Aphrodite?" I widened my eyes in mock innocence. "Why, I'm surprised that she could refuse such a charming brute as you. Poor Adonis shouldn't have stood a chance."

Ares gritted his teeth as he grabbed the hair from the top of my head then slammed it down against the stone. I had hoped to piss him off. It looked as if my plan had succeeded. I closed my eyes against the pain that shot across my forehead as he pulled me to my feet.

"Fuckin' half-breed," he spat. "You are not fit to speak of her." He turned back to the guards. "Release the chain. Now."

I watched as the shadowed figures unhooked the chain, but before they could attach it to anything, I grabbed it with both hands and snapped it downward. Both guards jumped back as I spun it around me like a lasso. I knew Ares was my greatest threat, so I focused my attention on him.

I managed to catch him across the jaw as I struck out. The god snarled as he fell back, but the distance was all I needed. I ran out the open cell door and slammed it shut behind me. I wanted to laugh. It had been far too easy to get out of the bars they had put me in. I didn't dare stop long enough to do so.

So, I ran, repeating the instructions under my breath as the very walls around me came alive with the faces and whispers that haunted my dreams as the Sibyl. I was so preoccupied with my escape that I didn't notice the dark figure that had appeared at the end of the hallway that led to the entrance of this damnable place. I slammed into it with a grunt.

"Evie?" The figure grabbed my arms. "Evie, help me."

Elliot? I blinked twice. No. That was impossible. He hated me. He had done everything in his power to destroy me. Just as he was doing now, slowing me down to let my captors catch up with me.

"Get out of the way." I wrenched myself free. "Damn you, Elliot. Move!"

"Evie, I'm a slave." The dark figure shifted into the Elliot I had once known. His handsome face streaked with tears as he reached for me. "Hera—"

The name of his patron goddess snapped me back

to the situation at hand. I lashed out with the chain, wrapping it around his waist to pull him aside. He stumbled forward as I freed myself from the weight he caused. I shook away the image of his tears as I pushed forward.

"Bravo!" Hades appeared in front of the door. He took two steps forward, clapping his hands slowly. "What a lovely escape attempt on your part."

I crouched down, ready to spring forward when I felt someone grab me around the waist from behind. No, not someone. Ares. I gritted my teeth as he shoved me down to the floor until my forehead was pressed against the smooth stone.

"You will learn to kneel, girl," he grumbled. "One way or the other. I will ensure it."

He kept his grip tight around the back of my throat.

"Ares, dear nephew," Hades said as he made a strange clicking noise, "the spirit of this girl is strong. You know as well as I that physical assaults have not been successful."

"Release the Incubus on her," Ares said instantly. "He has a special talent in breaking even the strongest—"

"No, no. Not yet." Hades knelt before me. "Lift her head. I have a much better idea."

Ares forced my head upward as I struggled beneath him. I expected to have my face slammed back against the stone. Hades gave me a cold smile as he flicked his fingers before my eyes. The chill I had experienced when I first encountered him returned, but that was by far the best part of the entire experience.

With the snap of his fingers, I was back in Charleston. I was supposed to perform at a recital in less than two hours. I was supposed to get ready.

Moma had given thirty minutes, and all I wanted to do was curl up on the couch against the wall.

I whimpered as I recognized this vision. I knew exactly what was coming next. I saw my fourteen-year-old self staring blankly in the mirror as Janet yanked out the knots in my hair. I experienced this memory too much lately. I couldn't watch this. Not again.

I didn't have a choice. I felt myself freeze into place as the room was filled with a clattering of broken bottles. I had lost my voice to the fear I felt Janet slammed a hand mirror across the side of my head. She had beaten me so badly; I'd spent that night in the hospital as the doctors removed shards of glass from my head. I still had the scars that ran just past my hairline.

"Your father abandoned you to a monster," Hades reached out, and the memory began to fade. He twirled a strand of my hair around his finger. "Tell me. How long did it take before you could cover those scars with your natural hair?"

I said nothing as I stared at Hades. There was nothing I could say. He grinned as if he knew he had already won.

"Take her back to the cell, Ares. I believe our work is done. I have agents working in Olympus now to retrieve the mirror. Once that is done, she'll willingly relinquish her role."

"How can you be so sure?" Ares grabbed my arm to pull me to my feet. "This could be a ploy for her to attempt to escape again."

"Perhaps. But to make sure, we will ensure she sleeps as the departed do." Hades brushed his hand over my tear-streaked face. "She will wake only when we wish for her to. And Ares," Hades grinned in a way that almost made me nauseous, "give her the sweetest dreams you can muster."

I felt my eyes grow heavy as my body slumped back against Ares. But as the heavy sleep overcame me, new memories came to my mind. They weren't of Janet or her past abuses. Far worse. I saw beautiful marble in pieces on grounds that were once beautiful but now were thick with ash and swathed by fire. I saw pockets of fighting as far as the eye could see. Palaces were in flames. Thrones lay in heaps in a town square. Chariots ran off course, their horses fleeing in agony because they, too, were on fire. I had never seen such unmitigated carnage in my life. Just when I thought things couldn't deteriorate further, the battle elevated in inconceivable ways.

Then, as if on a hunch, I looked down. At my feet lay a man. He must have fallen in this battle. He was unrecognizable due to the sheer amount of blood obscuring his face. The scene was grisly, but I couldn't look away. I felt like I should care about this. Care about him. But why?

Just then, Ares detached himself from some skirmish and approached me on a horse as black as a country-dark sky. He was in full battle gear and looked even more menacing than he did in Hades' throne room. Before I could even gauge the situation, before I could even move, he hopped from the horse and smiled.

"You have my thanks for the carnage you have wrought, Sibyl!" he said in a jovial tone that did not match this setting. "The ethereal world is not so grateful, I'm afraid, since you slaughtered their most prized soul."

I looked down again. No.

I nearly slid down in the blood in my attempt to

reach the broken form. I turned him over, and my worst fears were confirmed.

The bloody, defeated body was that of Jonah.

The sight of his blood-covered face and empty eyes brought a dreadful scream out of my mouth that no one except the god laughing next to me in my dream could hear.

FOUR

JONAH ROWE

THE REST of the drive from L.A. to Van Nuys was taken in total silence. By the time Cyrus parked the Land Rover and the group piled out, it was nearly five, so Jonah was surprised to still see a slew of Beamers and Audis in the parking spaces.

"Let me do the talking."

Cyrus adjusted his suit jacket and led the way inside. Jonah heard someone behind him whistle as they entered a large lobby of steel and glass. Large letters made of pressed metal lined the back wall to announce that they had arrived at Bates Security.

"Mr. Bates has already seen his last client for the day," The large woman with nails as long as talons spoke without looking up. "You will have to schedule an appointment."

"It is lovely to see you again, Griselda."

The woman's head snapped around, and she grinned. "Cyrus Alexius! My stars, is that you?"

"Indeed. I was in town and hoped to speak with the god himself. Is he in?"

"Of course, he is in. Are these…people…with you?"

"Yes. May we be buzzed in?"

"No need."

Reena latched onto Jonah's arm when Ares approached them. There was no denying who he was. The god looked nothing like the lily-white marble statues Jonah had seen online. Instead, Ares was large. Built like a linebacker whose ebony skin gleamed beneath the soft fluorescent lighting.

"Cyrus, you and your party shall follow me. You can tell me what this is about in private."

"Is that fucker for real?" Terrence breathed under his breath. "Dude is huge."

Jonah didn't respond as they followed Ares down a long hallway dotted with awards. He led them into a conference room and removed his jacket before he pushed up the sleeves of his pristine button-down.

"Um, sir," Jonah eyed the welts and bruises on the god's arms. They had the shape of chains. "Are you alright?"

"Never better. Now, what can I do for you?"

Jonah regarded those bruises all over Ares' arms and steeled himself. The guy was a legit force. "Our friend has been kidnapped and has been taken to the Underworld," he said. "We've also been told that you are one of the few who know where the shifting entrance to the Underworld is. We need that location."

"Explain."

Jonah simply brought him up to speed. He told him everything. A vein worked in Cyrus's temple during Jonah's story, which meant he probably didn't appreciate being shunted like that. Ares didn't move a muscle the entire time. He almost looked detached. But when Jonah ceased, he spoke, terse and to the point.

"So, Apollo knows how to reach Eva's location but cannot gain access to the Underworld without my assistance."

"We need the newest location of the Underworld." Jonah tightened his hand into a fist before he relaxed it flat against the table. "There is no telling what Eva is being subjected to this very moment. All other Olympians with knowledge of the entrance are otherwise indisposed. So, we came to you."

"I'm glad that you came to me. In a situation such as this, you'll need a little more than gold." Ares snickered at his joke. "The new location to the Underworld is a nightclub in Burbank. It is called The Den of Wayward Souls."

Jonah stared at him. "A club?"

"Yes." Ares turned his gaze to him. "Were you expecting a graveyard? A funeral home? You Ghostly Ones are too surrounded by death."

"Death isn't real." It was Jonah's automatic response whenever he heard that damnable word.

"Of course," Ares inclined his head. "My apologies, Blue Aura. Cyrus, when you've reached the domain of Hades, you had better be prepared for anything. You will have a short window at best, and you will have one shot. Blue Aura? Well—" He looked him over. "You are carrying a spiritual endowment, which is in accordance with the benefits of your realm. You also have Apollo's blessing. I will not pile too much on top of what you already have. It could very well stop your heart. However, a little something is in order."

When Apollo gave Jonah his blessing, he made a circle in the air. Ares, on the other hand, made a horizontal slash across the air, which left red flames for several seconds. When the flames faded, Jonah felt absolutely nothing. There was no change whatsoever.

"What did you do?"

Ares shrugged. "Let's just say that you'll have

what you need when you need it. Our business here is done."

He rose, and the group around the table did as well.

"I will expect a proper offering at my temple when this is done, Cyrus."

"Of course, milord."

"I hope this was the right move." Reena jogged up next to Jonah once they were back in the parking lot. "Ares gave me the creeps."

"Maybe not the right one," Jonah admitted, "but it was the only one. Now, we go to The Den of Wayward Souls."

Jonah got into the passenger seat of the Range Rover as everyone piled back in. He knew Ares' voice from somewhere. He knew it. But he'd have to address that at a later time.

Eva needed him.

———

The Den of Wayward Souls looked like the biggest dump Jonah had ever seen. The place looked condemned, which must have been part of the appeal. He didn't know.

All he knew was that he couldn't believe that the Underworld was linked to this shithole.

Jonah watched all manner of dregs of society come in and out of the place, but he barely saw them. He was ready to do something. Anything.

Reena kept trying to get his attention. He ignored her. The last thing he needed was for Reena to lecture him on not being careful. He didn't need to hear her misgivings when they were about to stage a rescue.

"The Den of Wayward Souls may be a new venue to the Underworld, but the rules never change,"

Cyrus explained. "As with every other place, the front door is ridiculous, so the back door is where we'll go. Once we are in the club, it shouldn't be hard to reach the Underworld, which, of course, isn't in the club itself. It will be underneath it."

"Makes sense," said Jonah. "Well, more sense than anything else right now, anyway."

"We should get in there now." Terrence clapped Jonah on the shoulder. "Can't let Goldie have all the fun."

"Yeah, we should."

Jonah was out of the Land Rover before Cyrus was, but his friends were at his side in seconds. Jonah's nerves, remarkably, weren't bothering him. Maybe it was the fact that the end was in sight. Maybe his patience was gone. Maybe he was done with the maybes.

"You can't use your batons just yet," Cyrus warned. "It would reveal to everyone that you don't belong there."

"It's cool." Jonah shrugged. "I'll just use my bare hands for as long as possible. When the shit hits the fan, then the batons come out. Won't matter if people know who I am at that point."

They stopped speaking when they reached the back of the club, but they didn't break stride. The bouncer in the back had dozed off, but when he heard footsteps, he jerked awake and rose.

"Go around the front," he said in a drowsy voice, "you can't be back—"

Terrence tagged him right across the face. It was safe to say that he was asleep once more when he hit the ground.

"That was too easy," Terrence snorted as he opened the heavy door and swung it open. "Way too easy."

"Guys, stay here." Jonah turned to his people. "Keep an eye out in case somebody tries to ambush us from behind. Cyrus, lead the way."

The Keeper narrowed his eyes at Jonah. Jonah glared right back. Finally, Cyrus went through the door. Jonah followed Cyrus down a set of obsidian stairs. A guy sat in the shadows, where he polished off a bottle of liquor.

"You're in the wrong spot," he murmured. "Go back up the stairs and in through the front."

"We need to talk," Cyrus said.

"Talk about what?" The man looked agitated like something was being interrupted. "I've got nothing to —Cyrus?"

Cyrus nodded. "Charon. It's been a while."

Jonah did a double-take. This was Charon, the ferryman of spirits? But he looked like he'd mixed the goth look with *Duck Dynasty*!

Charon hadn't missed the look on Jonah's face, and he shook his head.

"New blood, eh? Are you disappointed that I'm not a skeleton in a robe with a ferry full of spirits on black waters?"

"No time for any further pleasantries, Charon." Cyrus's patience had waned, and honestly, Jonah's had as well. "We need passage into the Underworld. I know that the venue has changed, but do the same protocols and fares apply?"

He dropped a pouch into Charon's hands that must have been gold. Charon looked at it sadly.

"What's wrong, Charon?" Cyrus frowned. "We have to go down there, now."

Charon shook his head. "You shouldn't have come, Cyrus. Everything has changed."

He flung the pouch of coins into Cyrus's face, which caused him to drop his sword and bring his hands up to his face. Jonah shouted, but Charon had him by the throat in seconds. Jonah grabbed at his hand, but the grip was like an iron vise.

"I wish you had stayed away, Cyrus," he said. "Lord Hades told me that help would come for the Sibyl. I am under orders to take the pair of you in chains to the Succubus. It's not personal. I'm merely honor-bound to my master."

Though he gasped for air, Jonah heard every word Charon said. So, since he was honor-bound, he was a victim, huh? Then why was he the one with one man subdued and another by the throat?

Suddenly, a disproportionate level of rage engulfed Jonah's consciousness. It was an instant switch.

"Let—go—of me—Goddammit!"

Jonah grabbed the hand that throttled him. Instantly, the flesh on Charon's arm began to hiss as Apollo's blessing flowed in his fingers.

Charon released Jonah, but Jonah didn't release him. He fell to a knee, crying out in shock and agony.

"Who are you?" he cried. "What are you?"

"Fuck you!" Jonah's voice almost sounded maniacal in his ears. "Tell me where Eva is!"

"I—I can't! My master will—!"

Jonah conjured blue flames in the hand that wasn't burning Charon's arm, which he blew in Charon's face. Charon used his free hand to cover his now-burning face. His muffled screams infuriated Jonah. How could he be so weak after trying to stop them? Where were his balls now?

"Tell me where Eva is, or I will barbecue your sorry ass, bitch!" he snarled. "Where is she?"

"She's with the Incubus!" Charon shrieked. "I swear on the Styx! Please release me!"

Jonah had a better idea. He pulled out a baton,

struck Charon's forearm, and snapped it like dry wood. Charon howled as he removed his hand from his steaming face to his new injury.

Cyrus eyed Jonah with alarm. "What's gotten into you, boy?"

Jonah didn't understand Cyrus's shock. "He was in our way, wasn't he? If the dumbass had just taken your gold and hadn't throttled me, he wouldn't be hurt. Fuck him. Fuck *you,* too, while we're at it. We have to find Eva."

Cyrus still looked shocked at what Jonah had done, but at that moment, an inhuman voice raised to a bellow.

"They're upstairs! You know our orders! Follow them!"

FIVE

EVA MCRAYNE

I HAD GROWN numb to the horrific images of my dreams which scared me. The fear and sadness I had felt shifted into a casing of ice. I watched and re-watched this war a hundred times.

Yeah, I'd become numb.

But each time I rolled over Jonah's corpse, there was fresh pain that wounded me down to my very core. It was during this latest replay that a man appeared beside me. He didn't say anything, nor could I turn to look at him. But I felt his presence next to me. It was calm. Soothing.

Or maybe, I'd gone too numb to feel anything else again. I had sunk to my knees at some point, but I couldn't remember when. I couldn't think of anything other than the blood that made my beloved's face unrecognizable. Or the beautiful craftsmanship of palaces and thrones which lay in ruins amid this horrible battle.

"Grim stuff, this." The man tapped a cane against the stone floor I was sitting on. "What could you have done to elicit such punishment, girl?"

"Nothing," I responded, but I didn't recognize my own voice. It was vacant. Hollow. "Everything. I was to be broken. Ares was ordered to give me this dream, and now Hades has succeeded in breaking me. I'm done."

"Oh, I wouldn't go that far." The old man chuckled. "Let's break this enchantment, shall we?"

"Can you do that?" I frowned. "Won't they know?"

"Who? Ares and Hades?" The man laughed. "Their games are of little consequence to me, child."

The man waved his cane in front of himself, and the images of war faded into a darkness I welcomed. Then he tapped me twice on the head. I lurched forward with a gasp.

"There. Now we can have a proper conversation."

"Who—what—are you?" I managed as I stole a glance over my shoulder at him. I had been right. The man was old. His beard reminded me of old Father Christmas pictures from the Victorian Era. He wore a robe decked out in tiny stars made with silver thread. The man grinned as he plopped down beside me on the stone.

"I am Morpheus. Keeper of Dreams. I heard your dreams were in dire need of change, and thus, I am here."

"How?" I demanded before I shook my head. "Look, I'm sorry. I just—it's been too much."

"Yes," agreed Morpheus. "Your torment seems unjustified. Yet, I am tasked with giving you a message."

"Please don't give me a way out of here. Somebody already tried that and it failed. Miserably."

"Persephone, and her nymphs. They mean well, but no. My message does not concern your escape. You must maintain your strength a little longer. Do not give in to Hades' demands."

"Oh, ok." The irritation that poked through my numbness seemed foreign to me.

"So—what? More rounds with Ares? More memories of what happened to me as a kid? Or that damned war for another continuous loop?" I shook my head. "No. I can't. I won't go through any of that again."

"You have no choice." Morpheus graced me with a look of abject pity. "You see, Apollo's mirror has been stolen from Olympus. Hades wishes to see you usurped."

"Dammit!" I snapped. "I'm nothing. Why can't they see that?"

Morpheus tilted his head to the side, and I resisted the bizarre urge to giggle as his beard flopped over his robe.

"No, child. You are everything. You hold the secret to the very power of the gods. You are the pivotal piece that affects two extremes."

There it was yet again. I might be the reason for something big. Hera even said I would bring about the "decimation of Olympus." But I didn't believe a word that drama queen said. Why was Morpheus saying similar things, though?

"I hold no secrets," I said. "I don't know a damn thing about them!"

"No. You are knowledgeable. And you are quite the fighter. But you ignore your heart." Morpheus tapped a long white finger against my chest. "Many who become Hallowed by the gods are happy to live their posh lifestyles. You are different. You use your abilities to aid your father, not take advantage of him."

"And so, one of the gifts bestowed upon me was this secret knowledge." I rolled my eyes. "Look, I appreciate what you have done. I appreciate you attempting to save my sanity, but—"

"Hades will replace you with another. One who will cause havoc in your world if you do not refuse him. Apollo has made it quite clear that you are to follow his orders and no other. No matter how you are made to suffer."

Ah, so the truth had come out at last. Apollo had sent me this messenger. I swallowed the knot rising in my throat. I'd cried enough to last a lifetime. I refused to do so now. "What will he have me do, milord? Fight against Ares? Destroy the Incubus they have threatened to unleash upon me? Or better yet, invite those two to dinner so we can all have a big family meal with minimal bickering?"

Morpheus laughed. He threw his head back and laughed. When he had regained his composure, he smiled. "No, child. No family dinners. Both Hades and Ares have broken the protocol for how the Hallowed is to be treated. Deep down, you know this. Yet how can you use that knowledge to your advantage?"

"I can't." I shrugged. "I mean, telling them 'no' works just about as well as pouring water down a drain. It gets you nowhere."

"But if you take away the only instrument they can use against you, that will lead to success, no?"

"You mean the mirror?" I raised an eyebrow. "I've already broken it once."

"Then do so again." The old man winked at me. "Look into your heart, dear Sibyl. You have the answers there."

He tapped my arm twice, and my head became clearer. I saw my memories of victory. Of success. I looked happy. Relaxed. I looked like Eva, not Evangelina.

"I am sorry, Morpheus." I didn't mean to burst his bubble. Truly, I didn't. "But the girl you are showing me? I don't believe she exists anymore. I'm not sure she ever did."

"Perhaps not. Or perhaps you will use that girl's

wretched experiences to make yourself a better version of her. Stronger. More determined."

I closed my eyes as I thought about what he said. It sounded like cheap lines from a greeting card. But what choice did I have?

Give up the mirror. Give up myself to remain here forever. Or fight.

"I will do what I can." I opened my eyes to see him watching me. "I can promise no more."

Morpheus smiled, and once more, I fell back into a deep slumber.

I sat up with a gasp to find myself once again in Hades' throne room. I started to jump to my feet but stopped when Ares pressed a silver blade to my throat.

"Ah, so she wakes." He turned his head towards the throne. "Are you certain she has been broken, Uncle?"

"There is only one way to find out."

Hades strolled over to us, and I didn't miss the glint of gold in his hand. Apollo's mirror. The relic which had granted me the role of Sibyl. The mirror itself was ancient but intact even though I had smashed it against a gravestone a few years before. As Hades knelt beside me, I caught a whiff of what smelled like roses.

Beauty hides the sharpest of thorns.

I swallowed back my grin as I remembered Persephone's words. Instead, I cried out with fear and attempted to scramble backward. Ares pressed the blade harder against my throat with a look of surprise.

"Don't," I begged as I tried to ignore the blood

running down my skin. "Please. I'll be good. A good girl. Just—please—"

Hades looked to his conspirator and laughed with triumph. "You see, Ares? My exacerbation of the vision you gave her did the job. I told you that there would be no need for the Incubus. The fact that you brought him here today only proves how little faith you have in me."

The lord of the Underworld reached out to stroke my cheek. "Poor child. Your own mind has been your very undoing. If only you could forget all that has happened to you. I can offer you the peace you crave."

"How?" I started to tremble beneath his touch. "Lord Hades, help me."

Another smug look crossed his face, and it took every ounce of strength I had not to smash him in the nose.

"Do you recognize this?"

He held up the mirror. I winced as the screams of the dead filled my ears, but they meant nothing to me now. I wasn't afraid they would drive me mad. I'd been on the brink of insanity, and it was by the grace of Apollo that I'd been pulled back from it.

Not that I would tell Hades that. He could go screw himself for all I cared.

So, I nodded. "Of course. It is Apollo's mirror."

"It will be the instrument of your peace, dear girl." Hades brushed my grimy hair away from my face. I stole a glance of my reflection in the glass and held back a groan. Ares had done more than enough damage. I was almost unrecognizable. "You will relinquish your role as Sibyl, and no more harm will come to you."

"None?" I asked in my most timid voice. Under normal circumstances, I would have made myself sick before I wilted beneath such a bully. But things were not normal. And if Hades found beauty through submission, then dammit, he would have it. I cut my eyes over to Ares. "Not even from him?"

"No," promised Hades. "Once you are a resident here, I will place you under my protection. You will serve Persephone. Won't that be nice?"

Yeah. Nice. I bit back a snarky comment as Ares slowly removed the knife from my throat. I bowed my head in Hades' direction.

"My will is yours, milord," I whispered while mentally apologizing to my own patron god. "But I don't understand. Why are you being so kind to someone as lowly as me?"

"Because you are mine." He tugged my hair to force me to face him. "Or you will be. The moment you relinquish your powers as the Sibyl and restore peace."

I remained silent and waited for my next orders. Turns out, I didn't have to wait for long.

"Stand, Sibyl." Hades pulled me to my feet and put the mirror into my shaky hands. I saw him nod to Ares, who had stood up behind me. "Repeat what I tell you to say."

I closed my eyes as I felt the power of Apollo's relic flow through me. It had been some time since I'd touched it, much less held it. But here, in this dark and desolate hell, I welcomed the warmth of the sun. I welcomed the feeling of adoration. I silently rejoiced at the feeling of absolute power that ran through me.

Hades started speaking, but I wasn't listening. Instead, I forced my body to start shaking harder. I loosened my grip on the mirror and watched as it dropped face down on the stone. This time, it didn't just crack. It shattered into tiny little pieces that hissed as they made contact with Hades' domain.

I spun around to snatch the blade out of Ares' hands. I ducked as the god grabbed for me, slamming my foot against his knee before thrusting the blade into his chest. I didn't stop to think of the consequences of my actions as I turned onto Hades himself.

"Release me," I growled as I took a step towards him. "Now. Or I swear to all that is sacred that—"

I lost my ability to speak as Ares snaked his arm around my throat and began to squeeze. I kicked backward. I tried to bite his arm. But he simply sighed and faced my other opponent.

"I tried to warn you. The girl was too strong. She won't be broken by your means, milord. Even after you bolstered my vision's power."

The icy friendliness that Hades had used when he thought he had won was replaced by the look of stone that I had come to associate with him. He narrowed his eyes as he wrenched the blade from my hand. With a single flick of his wrist, the god thrust it into my thigh.

"Let us see how she attempts to flee now, Ares. Throw her to the Incubus. I care not what happens to her now."

"Wait, my love."

I barely saw the tall woman who approached us. I blinked back the spots of black in my vision to take her in. My love? But this wasn't Persephone. This woman reminded me of a snake. Sleek, beautiful, and deadly. Her alabaster skin gleamed against the black gown she wore.

"Leave us, Lilith."

Lilith? I started to struggle against Ares as I recognized the name. Her tale was one of the few I had actually read from the ancient texts at the Academy. The mother of vampires.

"Come now. You've had the toy for days now and

I have yet to play with her." The woman frowned. "Tis only right I get a taste."

"Hers is the blood of Apollo. It is far too dangerous for you."

Lilith didn't walk so much as she glided towards me. I began to fight even harder against Ares' grasp until she wrapped her cold fingers around my chin and forced me to stare into her sharp blue eyes.

I was mesmerized within seconds. I couldn't breath when I realized her pupils were slits. When she grinned, her canines were sharpened to points.

"Let go-"

"Are you certain that this poor creature should be thrown to the beast?" She kept those monstrous eyes locked on mine. "Tis such a waste."

"Nothing else has worked." Hades snapped. "Release her so we can continue."

"Very well. Then allow me to say goodbye.The woman stared at me. "You know who I am."

"Yes."

"Say my name then."

"Lilith."

I felt her power slam into me the second she kissed me. I was so enamoured by her power, I relaxed against Ares' grasp. Flashes of her mind raced through mine. The independence she had craved. The battles she had fought to obtain it. How she used the seduction of snakes to weaken her prey before she struck out. I felt my teeth grow longer. Sharper. I released a low moan when she released me.

"Your enemies are mine, Sibyl." She whispered against me. "Use the gift I have given you to destroy them."

"What did you say to her?"

"Secrets only women should know. Ones that will make her time with the Incubus easier."

As Ares dragged me away from Hades' throne, I was filled with a rage I didn't understand. I didn't know if it was Lilith's anger or my own when I started cussing him with every breath left in my body. He only laughed as we came to a stop just down the hallway from the room we had left. I struggled. I clawed at his arms despite the chains the guards had clamped back down on my wrists. It wasn't until he forced my chin back that he responded at all to my latest tirade.

"Have you heard of the horrors that reside behind that very door, girl?" He whispered. "The Incubus will suck the very soul from your body before you have had time to resist him."

"Damn you!" I hissed as he tightened his hold. "If you wish for me to suffer, Ares, then just keep talking. Listening to you is torture all on its own."

The god yanked open the door and thrust me inside. "A toy for you, demon. Consider this one a gift of the highest order."

I slammed the full weight of my body against the metal door as Ares jerked it shut. But it was no use. If I was going to get out of this, I had to think. I wasn't stupid. Granted, I depended on Cyrus to tell me everything I needed to know about the creatures we fought. But I knew enough to know the sort of demon I had been thrown to.

The Incubus. Known throughout history as a being that raped and ravaged women until their souls had been absorbed. Most perished under the being's attack. Others suffered for months depending on how long it took for their life to be drained from their bodies.

I couldn't panic. I wouldn't panic. I'd managed to overcome every obstacle Hades had thrown my way. This would be no different.

I hoped.

I narrowed my eyes as I heard the strike of a match, and a candle came to life across the room from me. The light was welcomed, but it surprised me. So too did the man who stepped into view. Tall. Chiseled features. Thick dark hair. The only things he possessed that were even remotely alarming were his ruby-red eyes.

"At long last, a guest!" The man proclaimed as he strolled towards me. "And a lovely one at that. Tell me your name at once so that I may worship the newest goddess of this realm."

"Leave me alone," I snapped when he stopped within inches of me. "I know what you are. Ares was quite boastful about this newest torture."

"Torture?" chuckled the man. "Darling girl, no. I am the light. Refuge in a world filled with hate and anger." He reached for my hands. "Now allow me to get these wretched chains off of you. The iron looks as if it is quite painful for you."

The man hummed as he worked the chains off of my hands. When he was done, he tossed the links aside as if they were nothing.

"That is much better. Would you care to join me? I have the finest vintage wines and no one to share them with."

Wine? I rubbed at the raw skin of my wrists as I eyed the man with suspicion. It was entirely possible that he knew my weakness for the stuff. I watched as he took out a bottle, inspected it, and then poured the liquid into two glasses. He held one out for me with a smile.

"Dear One, you must be frightened." His tone was soothing. Almost reassuring. "Please. Take a seat and enjoy the beverage. It is the least I can do to apologize for the actions of such a brute."

CYNTHIA D. WITHERSPOON & T.H. MORRIS

I used the wall as a crutch to make my way over to the table. Heat raced up my leg with each agonizing step, but I didn't dare show it. Hades had been stupid enough to leave the knife buried into my skin. I had to keep it hidden in case I needed it. I ran my tongue over my sharpened teeth. Could I bite him and take him out?

The man must have noticed despite my efforts to stay in the shadows. He made a strange "tsk, tsk" sound and swept me up in his arms. I didn't miss how he brushed his nose against the top of my head as if to smell me. He lowered me down into the chair and handed me the glass.

"Here. Drink this. I will free the knife from your leg."

"No, I can't —" I started, but he interrupted me.

"If you do not, then this will be far more painful than you realize." He offered me the glass once more with a smile. "Despite the stories about my kind, we are not all dangerous villains. You can trust me."

"I doubt that very much," I muttered.

The demon clasped my chin and lifted my head up to the light. He frowned as he turned me this way and that.

"Why do you have a serpent's eyes? Open your mouth?"

I grinned and he jerked when he saw my teeth.

"Of course, Hades would allow his favorite to play with you first. Where are the bite marks? Your skin is unblemished!"

The incubus tore at the neck of the blouse I wore as he prodded around on my throat. When he found nothing, he passed me the glass of wine he poured.

"Your blood is not tainted. Perhaps, just your soul. No matter."

"What does that mean?"

The demon took hold of the hilt and jerked it free without answering my question. I tossed the wine back despite myself. I was willing to do anything to get my mind off the fire that had returned to my leg.

"Now we can speak in peace." The man awarded me with a dazzling smile as he stood and plucked the glass from my hand. All concern about my interaction with Lilith must have been forgotten then. "Shall I start the introductions? I am known as Ian."

"Eva." I studied the man as he refilled my glass. "Why are you here?"

"To serve." He shrugged as he placed my drink on the table. "It was my destiny to reside here in the Underworld. Though I call it home, I can roam free whenever I wish it. What of you, Eva? Are you a wayward soul?"

"I'm...sorry," I slurred as my head began to spin. Or was it the room going in circles. "I'm sorry. Can't...focus."

He circled around my chair and placed his hands on my shoulders. I felt my head fall forward at his touch just before I felt his nose brush against my skin.

"There is such life about you, Daughter of Apollo." Ian trailed his fingers up the sides of my neck until he found my chin. He tilted my head back until I was staring into his strange eyes. "A true prize for any man lucky enough to claim you."

"Wait," I groaned just before he kissed me. If the wine had slowed me down, the embrace from this stranger brought me to a complete standstill. I forced my head to the side as much as I could to break contact with him. "This isn't right."

The world has already forgotten about your existence." Ian trailed faint kisses down my neck as he tugged my shoulder free from the ruined shirt I wore.

"Relax, darling girl. Enjoy what pleasures I can offer. Wine. Conversation—"

"Conversation is not what you have in mind." I swallowed down the fear threatening to overwhelm me despite my mental confusion. "Ian—"

He didn't respond as I felt the skin he had touched begin to go numb. I may have been drunk, but as I heard a series of loud shouts down the hallway, I knew the words this man had spoken were false.

Jonah was here. Thank Apollo, Jonah was here. He'd set me back to rights.

"Ian—" I tried again as I rested my arm against the table. I was going numb. My eyes were once again heavy with sleep. "We have company."

"What?"

The demon rose, and I grabbed the knife he had placed on the table. I had seconds to react, but my reactions were slow. I pushed myself up from my seat to stumble towards the door.

Ian growled as he wrapped his arm around my waist to throw me down to the floor. He was on top of me within seconds. He wrenched the knife from my sluggish fingers then threw me against the farthest wall. I grunted when I hit it. I wanted to scream when I felt another iron being latched around my wrist.

"We will resume this shortly, my dear." Ian knelt before me. "But first—"

He grabbed my chin and forced his kiss on me. I felt my eyes roll back into my head as what little energy I had left vanished.

SIX

JONAH ROWE

JONAH WAS thankful that the shouts they heard made Cyrus stop staring at him like a lab rat. What was his deal, anyway? Charon got exactly what he deserved. The bastard had been in the way. He had tried to stop them from getting to Eva. He was lucky Jonah hadn't blown his ass up on that fact alone.

"We need to get down those stairs!" Cyrus led the way. "The lair of the Incubus is always on the first level of the Underworld. It makes it easier for the women to have false hope for escaping because freedom is so near. And yet so far."

Jonah whipped around and struck an enemy who'd tried to grab him through the wall. It vanished in a wave of black shadow. "Shut up, Cyrus."

Without conscious thought, Jonah sailed over Cyrus's head and tackled a guard. A grisly swipe of a baton later, and the thing was gone in a hazy shadow as well.

"Jonah, what has come over you?" Cyrus demanded. "If that had been a mortal Tenth, that blow would have surely turned you into a murderer!"

"Don't talk to me about murder." Jonah wasn't even shocked at his indifference. "It's not even a matter of murder because these things aren't mortal. They're no different from minions we've had to vanquish in Rome. Now come on! Eva may not have much time!"

Jonah ran down the corridor without a response Cyrus. Guards came left and right, but Jonah dispatched them with either blue batons or blue-handed flames. He struck, he kicked, he moved on.

He turned here and there. There wasn't anyone else. It was just him and Cyrus.

"Yes!" Jonah couldn't believe that they'd cleared the corridor. "Double team for the win."

Cyrus regarded Jonah with something like alarm. "There was no teamwork," he muttered. "You didn't give me a chance to attack anyone. See?" His golden sword was nowhere in sight. "My weapon disappeared from lack of use."

Jonah frowned. "Huh. Well, if that's the best they've got, the Underworld both sucks and blows at the same time."

"Those were some of the vilest creatures in existence, Jonah."

"Maybe I'm stronger than I thought."

"I don't think that's—"

"Fuck what you think, Cyrus. We're here to rescue Eva, not listen to you judge how I fight. Speaking of Eva—"

Jonah smelled blood. It was freshly spilled and still warm. It put him in mind of war. Vicious, glorious war. The kind of war that could result in that kind of blood being spilled all over the place, with the smell of it akin to that of a home-cooked meal—

He kicked in the door. Cyrus shoved past him to get inside. It looked like a swanky apartment. Completely in order and completely out of place in the Underworld.

"Eva?" Jonah stepped into the room. "You here?"

"Shit."

Cyrus snapped as he headed to the other side of the room. Jonah turned to see Eva sitting back against the wall. No. Not sitting. Chained with a shackle around her left wrist. When Cyrus shook her shoulder, she slumped against him.

"Goddammit." Jonah started towards them. "Move. I'll get—"

"What is this?" A man appeared in the doorway. He grinned to show off a row of razor-sharp teeth. "Is Hades so generous he brought me more toys to play with?"

"We're no one's toys, creeper," Jonah snapped. "Least of all yours. What have you done to her?"

"Immortals have such...life...about them."

"What did you do?" Jonah snapped again. He bounced his batons in his hand. "If you touched—"

"Touched? By the god's gate, I did nothing improper." The demon actually looked insulted. "Who do you take me for, a monster?"

"Then why—"

"Despite my reputation, I did not attack the girl. Apollo would have me strung up by my balls. I had only just begun to feed on her energy."

"You did what?"

Jonah was so inundated with fury it was almost dizzying. He grabbed a bottle of Merlot, shoved past Cyrus, and bashed the red-eyed guy in the face. The thing yelped and crashed to the floor. Jonah kicked him in the gut once he was down.

"You wanna drain someone?" he roared. "Drain me!"

When Jonah kicked him in the ribs, the demon snarled. He grabbed Jonah's ankle and jerked him down. He crashed on his back as the demon lunged at him.

Jonah rolled back to his feet as the demon snarled at him. The thing lunged at him a second time, latching onto his throat.

"You wish to give me your energy, boy?" The bastard laughed. "I will gladly take it."

Jonah growled an unearthly sound that would've scared him were he not so angry, and he clutched the demon's arm.

"Get...off...me."

He wrenched the guy's arm, hyperextending his elbow. He snapped his wrist like kindling. The monster cried out and clutched the injury. Jonah drew up his feet and drove his feet into the demon's chest and shoved him across clear across the room.

"Am I supposed to be afraid?" Jonah whispered. "You're fucking failing, Pumpkin. Miserably."

The demon stood slowly as Jonah approached. Jonah had been in enough fights to know a trap when he saw one, so he didn't get too close.

"You gonna try to drain me?" Jonah laughed as the demon turned. "Please. The only reason you were able to do that to Eva is because she was already hurt."

"Hurt? Weakened? Yes." The demon grinned. "Yes, she was. Between the daily beatings and the room of mirrors, it was easy to break her even further."

"Bastard—"

"Just as it is easy to break you, hero," the demon sneered again. "You think that all this posturing hides what you really are? Do you think that being a hero changes what you will always be? A worthless, useless excuse for a human being?"

Jonah's blood roared in his ears. "Classic. You realize you had no power over me, so you resort to sarcasm. One would assume that would be amusing. But unfortunately for you, it just pisses me off."

Jonah manipulated the winds and pulled another liquor bottle his way. He popped the cork and took a drink.

"Everclear," he muttered. "Ninety-proof. Sucks for you, once again."

Jonah broke the bottle over the demon's head, then used blue fire to ignite him.

The demon's entire body went up, and he began shrieking. The sounds incensed Jonah even more, so he wrenched a leg from a nearby table and proceeded to bash the demon with it.

"Shut up!" he shouted. "Where is that monster? Where are your balls? I was waiting for a fight, and you just scream like a little bitch! Fight me! I'm right here—!"

"Jonah! Goddammit, *Jonah*!"

Jonah snapped his head around towards Cyrus, who looked almost afraid.

"He's dead. You've won."

Jonah took a minute to catch his breath before he tossed the table leg away.

"You get her free yet?"

"Yes. Found the key while you kept the Incubus occupied."

Cyrus lifted Eva and threw her over his shoulder. Jonah sneered at him.

"You can't stand it, can you? Even touching Eva to save her is enough to turn you green. You really like them pleasure boys, don't you?"

"My disdain for Eva has nothing to do with my sexuality." Cyrus snapped back. "I have no use for a bag of weak bones—"

"Watch it," Jonah snagged another bottle of Everclear from the shelf. He popped the cork and took another swig. "That's my friend you're talking about."

"Friend. Please. You are acquaintances at best. And even you balked at the idea of having physical contact with her." Cyrus shifted Eva over his shoulder. "Now, if you don't mind, it is time for us to leave."

"You'd better watch that mouth," Jonah told him. "Don't pretend that you know my mind. If you try, you'll be wrong one hundred percent of the time. Per usual."

Cyrus sneered. "You look here, boy —"

Jonah spat Everclear into his palm and then lit it. Blue flames rose almost two feet in his hands.

"What was that, Pumpkin?" he whispered. "I'm all ears."

Cyrus eyed the flames and swallowed. "Let's just go."

Jonah let the flame fade in his hand. "That's what I thought you said. Now cradle Eva's head. She might have a concussion."

"She's immortal. She's fine."

Jonah started to argue when a growl caught his attention. He walked out the door to see the biggest fucking dog he'd ever laid eyes on. Its three heads turned towards him and it snapped in his direction.

"So you are real."

The dog turned and rushed towards him, snarling and barking from all three heads. Jonah whirled around in time for a long snake whipped out to smack him across the chest. Oh, hell no. Jonah rolled to the side then jumped to his feet within seconds.

"That was your one and only shot, Fido."

Jonah took off like a bullet towards the demon dog. His blue batons were flying, but the monster was not to be deterred. He snapped his jaws. He growled.

He swiped at his opponent with claws larger than anything he'd ever seen. But Jonah was just as determined. The massive dog began to yelp when Jonah got his hands around one of the being's snouts, and they glowed bluish gold. The dog wrenched itself free before charging at Jonah again.

"Enough."

Everything stopped. Cerberus and Jonah were frozen as if their fight had been immortalized in stone; Jonah's hands extended as the mouths of the dog were ready to go in for the kill. Hades stepped forward, applauding as he circled them.

"You've done well, Cyrus of Crete." He approached Jonah and turned back towards us with a wicked grin. "Turning men into monsters."

Hades pressed his fingers together on his chin and studied us for a moment.

"The girl will be destroyed," he said in a matter-of-fact tone. "There are too many in Olympus who wish to see her fall, Blue Aura. You are merely delaying the inevitable. I was hoping to take her in. Give her a new purpose that didn't culminate with destruction. I had such high hopes for her." Hades sighed as he continued his monologue. "But, alas. It was not meant to be. But perhaps, you can serve me like no other. Your time is limited, Jonah Rowe." Hades turned away from him. "I will see you leading my armies before the next pansalene has risen."

Hades snapped his fingers twice, and the wretched hell he reigned over faded away as the unearthly silence shifted into a mixture of heavy metal music and pitch-black darkness. But Jonah didn't have to see the world around him to know that he was back in it.

"Come on."

"What the hell just happened?" Jonah snarled as

he ran up the stairs past Cyrus. "I had Cerberus—Cerberus—right where I wanted him!"

Cyrus cut his eyes over at Jonah as he unlocked the Rover. He lowered Eva across the backseat. Jonah barely heard Reena and Terrence join them.

"Oh, my god—"

"Take the Astralimes. Meet us at Eva's condo."

"Jonah, what—"

"Just do it. We won't all fit in the Rover."

His friends all began to fade. Reena was the last.

"See you soon, J."

"See you."

Cyrus sneered as Reena vanished. "You comin', sweetcakes?"

"Oh, I get it." Jonah snorted. "You don't like pumpkin, so you gotta find a word for me? Nice."

"Just get in the car."

Jonah went around to the backseat and climbed in. He lifted Eva's head and put it in his lap. Her skin was like marble. Cold and smooth. Jonah rested two fingers against the side of her throat before his shoulders slumped with relief. She had a pulse. They weren't too late.

"What the hell are you doing?"

"Checking her injuries, pumpkin," Jonah replied. "Now do what you are told and damn drive."

"I don't know who the fuck you think you are, but I answer to no one save Apollo." Cyrus glared at him from outside the car. "She can sleep it off. Your assistance in her healing is not necessary."

"Your assistance is not necessary at all," Jonah said. "You didn't lift a damn finger in there. Your sword vanished. That was a testament to how pointless you are. You know, maybe I shouldn't call you 'Pumpkin.' Pumpkins are actually useful."

"Rowe," Cyrus growled out his name. "You will insult me one time too many."

"And then what? You'll run home to Daddy Gold and cry?" Jonah snorted. "Get in the damn car and drive."

Cyrus must have decided not to push the issue. Jonah kinda wanted him to. Instead, the Keeper got in the driver's seat and started up the car.

Jonah took the time on the road to examine Eva's injuries. She'd been beaten, alright, but the farther they got away from the shithole, the more the bruises faded. The cuts healed. She was still pale, but that couldn't be helped. Jonah examined her skin under the streetlights, but he couldn't find any evidence of vampire bites. He lifted up her wrist that still had bits of wrapping around it. The bruising had turned black, but there were thin scars that raised up.

God dammit. Why hadn't she called him? Why hadn't Joey called him? He would have been there in two seconds.

Jonah lowered her wrist across her stomach and ran his thumb along her lower lip. If there were no bites on her skin, they could have healed. But if she had been turned, her teeth would tell him everything he needed to know.

Jonah tugged at her bottom lip. Another flood of relief filled him. Her canines were normal. The vampires who attacked her hadn't been able to turn her after all.

Fuckers. Jonah brushed her matted hair away from her face. He'd go back and burn the Underworld to the ground for what they did to her. He should have done it anyway.

She's just a friend. Jonah told himself. *Nothing more.*

Wasn't she? He reached down to stroke the curve of her cheek. The black bruise that had been there before was now a pale yellow. Why couldn't he have Eva if he wanted her? He deserved the best, after all. And there was no one better.

"Stop doing that." Cyrus barked from the front seat. "Stop coddling her. It does her no fucking good."

"Right now, *you* are no fucking good," Jonah mumbled. "Speed up. I can get out and run faster than this."

"I'm serious, Rowe. Don't give her any false hopes. She does not react well to disappointment. The scars on her wrists are evidence of that."

"Will you shut up?"

"No. You are looking at her like some lovesick puppy, and I won't stand for it."

"Stop pushing our parley and get Eva home."

Cyrus snorted, but he pressed the gas and turned up the stereo. Some old rock station that Jonah knew Eva would never listen to in a million years.

Jonah glared at the back of his head for a good five minutes before he heard a whisper come from his lap.

"Jonah?" Eva opened one eye and peered up at him. "What...what happened?"

Jonah peered down at Eva's eye. The gold was there, but her pupils seemed to be slits. Like a snake. She closed them then opened her eyes again. The slits were gone. Hell, he was imagining things. Happens when the world goes insane in less than twelve hours.

"Hell on Earth happened," Jonah said. "But Cyrus and I saved you. Well, I saved you. Cyrus was practically a three thousand years old driver."

"You and Cyrus...together?" Eva whispered. "Did Hell...freeze over?"

"No." Jonah snorted. "We agreed on parley. A shaky one."

Cyrus looked in the rearview with eyes that could

match lasers. Jonah felt the gaze but barely looked up from Eva.

"Eyes on the road, Pumpkin," he said. "This is L.A."

Cyrus narrowed his eyes but didn't acknowledge Jonah.

"You care to tell us how you ended up in the gods damn Underworld, Eva? Of all the things you could have done—"

"I don't know." She closed her eyes and swallowed. Jonah kept his hand on her shoulder in case she tried to sit up. She didn't. "One minute I was in a fight with vampires. The next, I was passing out."

"Who took you?" Cyrus growled. "Dammit, girl. I need answers so that I can give them to Apollo when we see him. I am already going to catch actual hell for you getting snatched in the first place."

"What Cyrus means is that everyone was worried sick, but it was worth it for you," Jonah said coolly. "No pressure on you right now. Rest. And as the thoughts come back to you, share them with us. Deal?"

"That is *not* what I mean. Don't put words in my mouth."

"You stretchin' that parley pretty fucking thin."

"Thank you both." Eva broke in as she pressed her hand to her forehead. "For saving me. I mean that. I'll talk to Apollo. It's my fault. I'll make sure he knows that."

"Good." Cyrus turned the radio back up with a snap of his wrist. "As you should. After all the training I have given you, you should have been able to fight off whoever it was who attacked you."

"Eva, the only thing faster than Cyrus' mouth is his capacity for failing," Jonah said. "So if his training didn't get you out of there, that says more about him than you. It's alright."

Eva didn't respond. Instead, she kept her arm over her eyes. Jonah felt the second she passed back out. Not because her breathing changed. It was something different. Something internal. Primal.

When they reached the L.A. city limits sign, Jonah reached over her and smacked Cyrus across the back of the head.

"Mother—"

"Talk to her like that again, and I'll fuck you up, understand me?" Jonah hissed. "You think what I did to the demon was bad—"

Cyrus started laughing, but there was no mirth in his tone. "I don't know what has gotten into you, Rowe, but you touch me again, and you won't live to regret it."

Jonah smacked Cyrus again. "Touch."

Cyrus growled, and it was Jonah who laughed this time.

"That's what I thought. Cyrus, your threats are like baked beans. They give you gas, and little else."

Cyrus jerked the car to the right, damn near dumping Eva from Jonah's lap.

"What the hell!"

"I can run this vehicle off the freeway," Cyrus seethed. "I'll survive it, sweetcakes. Will you?"

"Do that again," Jonah snapped, "I'll put my foot so far up your ass that you'll be rolling down Rodeo with a toe for a toothpick. And you'll feel every inch of it since you're immortal and all."

Cyrus jerked the Rover again, harder this time. Jonah held onto the handle over the door with one hand, Eva with the other as he braced for impact.

The impact never came. Cyrus jerked the car back

on the road hard enough for Jonah to smack his head against the glass.

"You wanna keep running that mouth, boy? Or can you keep it shut long enough for us to get back to the condo?"

Eva shot up from Jonah's lap before he could stop her. She reached past the headrest and grabbed Cyrus by the back of the throat.

"Unhand me!" Cyrus barked. "Now!"

"Drive," Her voice was no louder than a whisper as she dug her nails into the keepers throat. "Or I will rip your spine out by each individual vertebrae. Do you understand me?"

Cyrus jerked the car again, but Eva held on to him. Trails of blood were running through her fingers as she whispered again in a language Jonah didn't understand.

Cyrus straightened the car then punched the gas. Jonah stared at Eva. He stared at the blood now pooling around the collar of Cyrus' shirt.

"Eva?"

She didn't respond. She didn't let Cyrus go either until they were off the interstate. She dropped her hand and slumped back against the seat.

"Um, Eva?"

"Tired. So tired."

Jonah gathered her up to put her head back in his lap. He was unnerved, but hell, Cyrus had that coming to him. The keeper remained silent until they pulled into Eva's garage. He shook his head then clasped the back of his neck with a growl.

"How dare you?" He seethed as he forced open the driver's door. He jerked open the rear door and grabbed at Eva. "How dare you place a single hand-"

Jonah was ready to level Cyrus if he touched Eva again, but Eva surprised him.

Surprised them both.

When Cyrus grabbed for her, Eva caught his hand with reflexes Jonah hadn't yet seen from her. The fatigue in her expression vanished in that moment.

"Don't touch me, Cyrus," She said in a menacing tone. "Don't fucking touch me."

She swatted the stunned Keeper's hand aside and exited the vehicle. Jonah looked at Eva with shock, but Cyrus regarded her with fury.

"Your attitude has been a problem for awhile," Cyrus stepped up to her. "Is it because of Rowe then? You feel you can act out because he will step in to protect you?"

Eva met him face to face. Jonah barely heard her when she responded. "Right now, my problem is you. You touch Jonah, and there will be hell to pay."

"Oh, shit!" Jonah laughed "I fucking *love* this."

Cyrus ignored Jonah completely, gaping at Eva with shock and fury.

"Have you forgotten your place?" he whispered. "Who do you think you are?"

Eva leered at Cyrus, and Jonah swore he saw those slits again. "For the first time, Cyrus, I think I've *remembered* my place, and it's not sitting here kowtowing to you. As for who I think I am, well, right now, I think I'm someone who has neither the patience nor the time for your bullshit. If it makes you feel like a man to lord over someone, go find a whore on Sunset and pay her. I'm not the one."

Cyrus nearly choked on his rage, but Eva turned her back on him and faced Jonah.

"Can you help me, Blueberry? My adrenaline is fading fast."

Jonah swept Eva in his arms without hesitation. That was fucking hot.

"With pleasure, Superstar."

Jonah freed one hand up enough to give him the finger, then raised his voice.

"Guys, I'm coming in! I got Eva!"

At that moment, Apollo jerked open the garage door. His stern expression softened when he saw Eva.

"My poor darling." He stood aside. "Jonah, will you take her to the couch? I'll take a look at her injuries."

"On it."

Jonah didn't miss the glare that Apollo gave Cyrus as he passed him. When Jonah lowered Eva onto the couch, Apollo turned to them.

"Where did you find her?"

"She was with Hades' Incubus, milord."

Apollo hissed as Cyrus continued.

"Nothing occurred between them. He did admit to feeding off her energies."

"And the beast? Did you do your duty to slaughter him?"

"Wait, I got this part," Jonah took a seat then put Eva's head back in his lap. He clasped her hand against her stomach when she groaned. "Cyrus did nothing. I got us in. I got us out. I did, in fact, beat the demon bastard to death."

"You are pushing it, Rowe," Cyrus snapped. "Had I not got us in, you wouldn't be posturing now."

"I owned Charon, I battered the Incubus, and I tamed Cerberus." Jonah ticked his deeds off with his fingers. "All you did, Cookie-Puss, was run your mouth."

"Jonah?"

Reena and Terrence came into the room. Apollo held up his hand to keep them back.

"I need to examine my daughter. Once she is well, then we will discuss those orders."

Jonah tensed up as Apollo approached them. He

forced himself to relax. Where the hell was this new possessiveness over Eva coming from?

"Jonah, allies, please leave the room." Apollo gave him an appraising look. "You can return to Eva's side when I am done."

Jonah worked his way free of Eva and followed the others into the kitchen. The second the door shut, Cyrus rounded on him.

"What is wrong with you?" he snapped. "Do you not understand the position you are putting me in?"

"You're just mad that the position I'm putting you in isn't the same position your boys at the whorehouse do," Jonah stated. "Now get out of my way, I'm thirsty."

Cyrus stopped Jonah with a hand to the chest as he tried to get to the fridge. Jonah growled in his throat.

"Cyrus! Jonah!" Reena snapped. "What the hell is wrong with you? Cut it out!"

"You better move that hand before you lose it, pumpkin," Jonah met Cyrus nose to nose. "You might just lose it anyway."

""You want to give it a shot, sweetcakes?" Cyrus snarled back. "Or you and your friends want to go hide behind Apollo again?"

"Reena called Apollo because *you* were trying to delay us with circular arguments," Jonah spat. "Now get away from me."

"Cyrus, move your hand. Now."

Terrence came up behind Jonah. Reena, too.

"You want to take on all three of us? Or you gonna back down?" Reena added.

Cyrus looked at the three of them then dropped his hand. He pushed past them and headed into the foyer without another word.

"Yeah. That's what I thought. Walk away."

"Jonah, you aren't helping." Reena grabbed him a water and tossed it to him.

"Details." Terrence leaned against the kitchen island. "What was the Underworld like?"

"It was a joke." Jonah shrugged. "I got worse bruises shopping on Black Friday. I don't know what the big deal was."

"Jonah?"

"What?"

"Why did your eyes just flash?" Reena frowned at him. "That was the weirdest thing."

"What are you talking about?"

"They flashed orange. Did you get a spiritual endowment or something?"

"Nope," Jonah shook his head. "Nothing out of the ordinary except Apollo's upgrade."

"Weird." Reena stopped when she realized Apollo was opening the door.

"Eva is physically well."

Jonah grabbed an extra bottle of water and headed back to the living room. He bristled when he saw Cyrus standing just off to the side. Eva was sitting up with her face buried in her hands.

Jonah met the Keeper's glare with one of his own before he sat his water down and opened Eva's.

"Here, Superstar." He sat down beside her as she lowered her hands. "You need this."

"Thank you."

She cleared her throat as she took it. Apollo had followed them back in, and he sat across from her in the armchair.

"I don't know where to start."

"Take your time, Eva." Apollo kept his eyes trained on her. "We are in no rush for answers."

"I..." Eva must have noticed Cyrus standing off to the side. She took a sip of water then tried again. "I fought and I lost. If you are going to be upset, be upset with me."

"I am *very* upset—"

"If I screwed up the way you did, then let my sword disappear, I'd be very upset, too," Jonah interrupted Cyrus. "Now, let her speak. Go on, Superstar."

"You have no right—"

"Cyrus. Silence."

Eva cut her eyes up at Cyrus then focused on her lap. Jonah took the water bottle from her hands when he saw how bad they were shaking. She glanced up at him then took a breath.

"Alright. I was on the phone with Jonah. The Covington episode had been nominated for—"

"The abduction, Eva." Cyrus sighed. "Forgive me, Apollo. We must get the information to assess the dangers that may still be present."

"The abduction, Eva." Cyrus sighed. "Forgive me, Apollo. We must get the information to assess the dangers that may still be present."

"I can't tell the damn story if you are interrupting me every two seconds," Eva snapped at Cyrus. "Shut up and sit down."

The group went completely silent. Jonah felt a pride he wasn't used to feeling with Eva. He was feeling something else, too, but that could wait.

"Pardon my interruption." Cyrus seethed. "Please. Continue."

"Anyway," Eva glared at the keeper. "I got jumped by a group of vampires. I thought I got them all, but someone picked me up and I blacked out. When I came to, I was in a cell. I met Hades. He wanted me to give up my Sibyl abilities and stay in the Underworld as a maid for his wife."

"What the hell purpose would that serve him?" Jonah asked. "What did he hope to gain?"

"It would be a great insult to me." Apollo's eyes flashed as he leaned forward. "To have the daughter of a god as a servant is a slight against the other god. It is enough to create havoc in our ranks."

"Wait. Really?"

"Yes. Really. Hades barely avoided war with Demeter when he took Persephone. It was only avoided because he made her his wife."

"Why would he want war with you?" Jonah asked. "Your shrines are blazing. It'd be stupid."

"The Lord of the Dead shrines are volcanic, boy," Cyrus said. "People die every day. One would think you'd remember that."

"Death isn't real," Jonah snapped. "One would think you would know that."

"Physical death." Cyrus rolled his eyes. "Really. The distinction was quite obvious."

"The point is," Apollo cut in, "this was an act of war. When my envoys return from the Underworld, we will assess the state of things. Depending on his treatment of you, Eva, that state may be one of disaster."

Eva had been studying her hands. She snapped her head up at the sound of her name.

"Cyrus stated they found you with an Incubus. Can you tell us what happened?"

"No," she choked out. "No. I don't want to talk about it. I am fine. There is no need for all this talk about war. I am fine."

"The Incubus will never bother you again, Superstar," Jonah said. "I beat him into the ground. Literally. Ask Cyrus. He observed."

Eva looked over at Jonah, and her expression softened.

"I know."

Jonah took her hand and clasped it. He silently

dared Cyrus to say something. When he didn't, Jonah turned to Apollo.

"Let me take Eva to the estate. You know how safe she is there. She won't be left alone."

"No," Cyrus broke in. "No. Milord, you cannot allow this."

"I believe that Eva can make her own decision in that regard."

"Actually," She squeezed Jonah's hand. "Can I ask you to stay here? I understand if you don't want to do the Emmys with me, but I want to stay close to you."

"Eva—"

"Please just stop it, Cyrus," Eva said with a steely note that was never there. "But yes, Jonah, please stay. As for the Emmys—"

"Consider it done," Jonah said. "I'll feel better knowing that you have people like Terrence, Reena, and me at your back. We'd never leave you to rot."

Eva knew exactly who he was talking about. She cut her eyes over at Cyrus before she responded.

"You know you always have a room here. You guys, too." She swallowed as she looked at Cyrus. "Are you staying?"

"I can't imagine why I should," he responded with an icy tone. "'Tis obvious you have plenty of guards around you now."

"Cyrus, watch your tone." Apollo snapped his fingers. "Apologize."

Cyrus gritted his teeth, then relaxed his jaw. "My apologies, Eva. The stress of the day has overwhelmed my senses. I am not myself."

"You're right. You're not. Because Apollo is right here. Otherwise, you would have jerked me away by now to tear into me for getting you involved."

Eva's tone was sharp. Bitter. Jonah raised an eyebrow. He didn't know she had that in her.

"I tell you what. Apollo, take him somewhere else. I don't want him anywhere around me."

"Eva, Cyrus is your Keeper—"

"Who has done a horrible job in the role since I met him." She stood up on shaky legs. "When he isn't here, I am at peace."

The harsh tone shifted to pleading.

"Please, Daddy, just…just for a few days. I can't handle him right now. Please."

That tone ignited something in Jonah. He stood with her as if Cyrus would be stupid enough to attack her at that moment. Apollo seemed taken back as well. His expression softened before he stood.

"Very well. I will contact you before I return Cyrus to your side."

"Am I no longer the Sibyl's Keeper, milord?" Cyrus spoke between clenched teeth. "Does my role mean so little that it can change at the whimper of an inexperienced girl?"

"Aw, don't be hurt, pumpkin," Jonah said. "Apollo is just responding to the actions of an inexperienced Keeper."

"You dare—"

"You were absent for nearly a year, Cyrus," Jonah said, "so a handful of days will make zero difference."

"That was before Hades decided to start a war!"

"Cyrus, my office. Now."

Cyrus stared at Eva with eyes of pure hatred before he vanished. She sagged a little when Apollo approached her. He clasped her arms with both hands and kissed her forehead.

"Rest, daughter mine." He squeezed her arms before he turned to Jonah, Reena, and Terrence.

"Thank you for your assistance in getting my Eva back."

"Always, man," Jonah said. "Now, go handle your boy. If he tries anything, give me a call."

Apollo frowned. "You do realize I'm a god, Jonah."

"Yeah," Jonah mumbled. "I hadn't forgotten."

Apollo went to shake Jonah's hand then froze. He narrowed his eyes at him.

"Jonah, are you feeling well?"

"Never better," He popped his neck. "Why?"

"Your eyes are different."

"What the hell do you mean, different?"

"They flashed orange." Apollo's frown deepened. "Tell me. Did you receive blessings from any god aside from me?"

"I've no other blessings except from you, man," Jonah told him. "I'm L.A. gold and Carolina Blue. Everything else is just organic awesome."

Apollo scrutinized him then nodded. "Very well. I will check on you tomorrow, Eva."

"Thanks again."

Apollo gave them all a small salute before he vanished. Eva waited for a moment before she turned to them.

"Please. Make yourself at home. I mean it. I'm going to take a bath."

"We'll come up, too." Reena gestured for Eva to go. "Just in case."

"Just in case?"

"Yeah. Hades might send someone back here since Jonah went all Rambo on the Underworld."

Eva said nothing. Jonah grinned at the memory. The sounds of the skulls crushing beneath his batons were sweeter than Eva's piano music.

Eva stumbled as she reached the stairs, and Jonah

took the opportunity to sweep her up again. He had to admit he liked doing that. He liked being able to hold her so close.

"Jonah, I'm fine."

"You and I have two very different definitions of fine, Superstar." He tightened his hold on her. "Besides, you don't want my help?"

"I do. Desperately," She threw her arms around his neck and buried her face into his shoulder as he went up the stairs. "I just don't want you to think I am taking advantage of your kindness, Jonah. You mean the world to me. I don't want to chase you away. Not now, not ever."

"Good," Jonah assured her, "because you ain't ever chasing me away. You're stuck with me until my very last breath."

Eva held onto him tighter before he sat her down at her bedroom door. He started to follow her in when Reena tapped his arm.

"We need to talk."

"Can we make sure there aren't any bad guys in her room first?"

Reena sighed and followed him in. Everything was as it should have been. So much so that Eva was already at her closet, pulling open drawers from her dresser.

Jonah checked the bathroom suite. A room that was larger than his old apartment. He caught sight of himself in the mirror and smirked.

He deserved a place like this. No. He deserved *this* place. He deserved to live the same way as Eva. Maybe even more so since he had saved her.

"Jonah?" Eva was leaning against the door frame with her robe thrown over her arms. "Everything ok?"

"Not a soul in here. I'm kinda disappointed." He

squeezed her arm. "Go. Relax. I'll be out here when you get done."

She nodded, and he shut the door behind him. No surprise, Reena was waiting for him. Terrence, too. When the water started running, Reena beckoned him to follow her downstairs. When they reached the media room, she whirled around on him.

"What was that about?"

"What are you talking about?"

"That…'stuck with me' line." Reena studied him. "Jonah, you said it yourself. You're not interested in Eva. Don't do this to yourself or her."

Jonah closed his eyes. His impatience ramped up. "Reena, listen carefully. And I mean carefully because I'm deliberately choosing my words and I'm not going to repeat them. You're my sister, and I love you. That said, I'm no longer tolerating words or monologues that try to deter me from my goals. I'm done with that. I never had a mother, and I don't need one now. I'm done with being controlled, corralled, shot down, and every damn thing in between. I won't take it from Cyrus, and I won't take it from you, either. Because, quite frankly, anything concerning Eva and me is none of your business."

Reena looked stunned. "Excuse me?"

Jonah grabbed a bottle from Eva's bar and downed half of it in one gulp. "I explicitly stated that I wasn't repeating myself, Reena. Mind your business. Good night."

"Jonah, wait —"

"Good night, Reena."

"Wait, dammit. This isn't like you." She moved in front of the door. "And now, you're drinking? You never drink!"

"One won't kill me, nor will it make me an alcoholic," Jonah said. "If you want to criticize someone, criticize Cyrus. He did nothing but watch me save Eva, then bitched about his role."

"Ok. Ok, just stop. Just for a second."

"What the hell do you want me to stop, Reena?"

"I want you to stop and think!" Reena clasped his arms. "Please. You have goals? Great. But you can't change your entire personality to achieve them!"

"All I said was for you to mind your own business, and now, I got a whole new personality?"

"Yes, because before? You would at least listen to what I have to say!"

"Fine. Spit it out. I'm listening."

Reena took a breath and released him.

"You aren't acting like yourself since you came back from the Underworld. Everything from your tone of voice to how you interact with people. I don't know what happened, but now, you're all about Eva? All about alcohol? Being snarky? I think you need to go home, J. Get your head on straight and come back when you're good."

"I'm not being off or even weird, Reena," Jonah said. Why couldn't they understand? "I'm not all about Eva. It's kinda troubling that she was just rescued from Hell, and you're indifferent about it. I don't need to go home, not while Hades and whoever else is after her. Go home by yourself if you want. But for the moment, I'm staying here."

Reena narrowed her eyes at him. "Why don't you want to go home?"

"I literally just gave you the reason."

"Ok." Reena crossed her arms over her chest. "At least let Jonathan check you out."

"No."

"What's it going to hurt, J? You said you got into fights, right? What if you hit your head or something?"

"Or maybe, I finally realize what I deserve, Re!"

She blinked when he snapped at her, but her expression remained calm.

"Explain that."

Jonah tossed back another drink. "When I was a kid, I was always told what I needed to be for popularity. College, I was told what to be to get a good job. Job, I was told the right amount of ass to kiss to make it. Well, I'm done, Reena. Done. Done with being told what to do. Who to be. How to go about my life. For once in my damn existence, I deserve more than to be fate's floozy or everybody's puppet. I'm worth more."

"Jonah, you are worth more, but do you think you're going about things the right way?"

"If I want it, Reena? I'm going to take it. No matter what it is."

Now, Reena was shocked. Her mouth dropped open. Jonah moved around her to go back upstairs.

"I'm staying here. You do whatever you have to do."

Reena turned on her heel. Jonah took another swig before he spoke again.

"You never answered my question."

"What question, Jonah?"

"Why you're so indifferent about Eva being saved from the Underworld."

"I'm not indifferent. I'm glad she is home and safe. But I am more worried about you than her. You're my family, J, not Eva. So you will always be my main concern."

"Fuck, Reena?" Jonah was stunned. "So now, Eva doesn't matter?"

"That's not what I said—"

"You didn't have to, Re. You've been to parties on her dime. Bunked in her house. Broke bread at her table. And *all* the while, she was just…nothing? You're fucking worse than Cyrus!"

"Take that back, Jonah!" Terrence was silent this whole time, mostly due to the utter shock at Jonah's words. But the Cyrus thing broke him out of his stupor. "You're crossing the line now, bro—"

"You know what, *you* go home," Jonah snapped. "Eva needs friends right now, and they're all M.I.A. That's fine. I'm here for her. Get on back to the estate."

Jonah grabbed a second bottle and headed upstairs without another word.

Jonah started to go to his room at the condo, but he stopped at Eva's door. He knocked before he pushed it open.

"Eva?"

"In here," she called from the bathroom. "I'm still good."

Jonah slipped in and saw the bathroom door cracked open. Eva was standing in front of the mirror, braiding her hair. She was dressed in a short nightdress and nothing else.

He took another swig of the liquor as he watched her. She was smaller than the women he was usually attracted to, but why had he always gravitated towards bigger women? He had earned the right to have a woman like Eva. The gorgeous television star. The one who was grabbing her robe to hide that stunning body because she had been told all her life that she was fucking repulsive.

Jonah had an image flash in his head. One where he gauged Cyrus' eyes out. The man didn't need 'em. He was obviously not using them.

Jesus, she moved like water. How had he never noticed that before? Every motion contained an element of grace that sent Jonah's mind right back to

127

where it had been when she damn near took Cyrus' head off.

Eva spotted the liquor bottle when she strolled out of the bathroom then tilted her head at him.

"Celebrating with vodka instead of weed?"

"Everclear," Jonah corrected her. "Nana loved this stuff. She rarely ever drank, just on her birthday, New Year's, and when she had her friends over for cards. But if and when she *did* drink, it was this. But I have my backup joints at the ready, should I wish to get baked."

"I don't know liquor as well as I do wine."

"Really?"

"Yeah." She gave him a small smile as she pushed a loose strand away from her eyes. "Wine is more easily obtainable. Dinner, lunch, the damn grocery store."

"Try it." Jonah extended the bottle to her. "Just a sip."

"Why not? Maybe it'll take the edge off."

Eva took the bottle from him, and he laughed at her expression as she took the drink. She made a face as she handed it back to him.

"By Olympus, it's like rubbing alcohol."

"Try it again." Jonah grinned as he took another swig. "It gets easier."

Eva grimaced, but she took the bottle and another drink of it. Her face flushed red as the alcohol went straight to her system.

"Better?"

"Not by much, but yeah. It's better."

"It's not bad at all. However, I won't subject you to a lot of this hard shit." Jonah capped it and pocketed it. "I was just checking on you to see how you were doing. Think you'll be able to rest?"

"Yes," Eva raised up and pressed a kiss against the

side of Jonah's mouth. He clenched his hands into fists when she licked the corner of his lips. Eva pulled back and he resisted the urge to grab her. "Everclear."

"Um, what?"

"You had a drop of Everclear on the corner of your mouth. No point in letting it go to waste."

"Hmm. Suppose not."

"I think I should pass out soon. I didn't sleep in the Underworld."

Jonah nodded, and she moved around him to pull back the comforter. He watched her slip the robe off her shoulders and climb into the bed. Once Eva got situated, she turned onto her side and looked up at him.

"Thank you again, Jonah, for saving me. For staying."

"I've got your back, Eva," Jonah said again. "If you need me at all, I'm just an intercom call away."

"Noted, Blueberry." Eva pulled up her covers. "Will you be going to sleep soon?"

"Nah, too wired." Jonah shook his head. "Do you have a deck of cards anywhere?"

"Check my sock drawer," Eva said. "Are you gonna play solitaire?"

"Hell no," Jonah scoffed. "Gonna do the Gotcha Bible."

"The Gotcha-what?"

Jonah allowed himself a smile. It didn't do to succumb to playfulness too often, as the world was too cold for that, but her response was truly amusing. "I'll tell you more about it in the morning. You need your rest."

"Have fun," she yawned. "See you in the morning."

"See you, Superstar."

Jonah headed out then stopped in the hallway,

leaving Eva's door open a crack until he heard her tell Alexa to turn off the lights. He went into his guest room and shuffled the cards.

Let the fuckers try to come, he silently prayed. *Let them come here now*.

Suddenly, a scent reached his nostrils. It wasn't a bad one, though; it was quite a remarkable smell. Familiar even.

Impatiens. He knew the plants well. But why did he smell flowers? Soldiers had no need for those kinds of things.

But then another flowery scent mingled with the impatiens. That particular one was roses. Roses—

He sat bolt upright and searched here and there.

"That was quite a challenge," said a soft voice.

Jonah trained his eyes on the direction that the voice came from. He didn't have to try too hard, though, because the owner of it came into view.

She was raven-haired; it fell well past her shoulders. She looked like a spiritess in the moonlight, but when she moved, Jonah heard a footfall. Her dark eyes bored into him, but Jonah couldn't sense her motives. She was unreadable, kind of like Reena. Kind of like Vera. But the smile she bestowed upon him was warm enough. He supposed that that counted for something. Still, he remained wary and alert.

"You are very hard to read, which is something I believe you have heard before." Her voice was quiet, but Jonah got every word. "But the flowers—that was an unexpected find in your consciousness. Either the impatiens or the roses. One was sure to grab you, and it turned out to be the latter. What pull do the roses have on you?"

Jonah ignored the question and focused on the flower shtick. "Flowers, huh?" He racked his brains for old mythology info. "So you're Demeter?"

The woman chuckled. "Very close, but no. I'm her daughter, Persephone."

"You're Hades' wife." He willed his hands to gleam blue, meaning that Apollo's blessing was ready to merge with his ethereality. "Back up, lady. I will blast the shit out of you; not even joking. I've got an endowment and Apollo's blessing—"

"Darling, darling." Persephone smiled and spread her hands. "I mean you no harm. Violence is not my way. Usually. And I am well aware of your capabilities. The spiritual endowment, the Golden blessing, and...ahhh." She looked him over, as though studying him. "I see that my half-sibling has improved you."

She smiled. Jonah frowned.

"Who are you talking about?" he demanded. "I remember that Zeus is your father, so when you say half-sibling, do you have any idea how little that narrows it down?"

"Indeed, I do," said Persephone, sincerity in her soft tone. "But unfortunately, that's all you're going to get."

She seated herself on the bed that Jonah vacated. "As I said, my intentions are not harmful. The windows? Unlocked. Same with the door. If you have no interest in what I have to say, you are free to leave if you wish."

Jonah didn't trust Persephone, but he didn't get an antagonistic vibe. So she wasn't lying—about not wanting to fight, anyway.

"What is the deal with you people?" He wanted to know. "What's up with all the mind games?"

Persephone's smile didn't fade. "Games only occur when someone is playing, Jonah," she said. "I am serious. Dead serious."

"Don't use that word around me," Jonah snapped.

Persephone shrugged. "I'm aware of your stance,

but it flowed better. I couldn't very well say *'In Spirit serious.'* That'd just be tacky."

Jonah rolled his eyes. The sweetness was starting to annoy him. "So did your husband send you? Is this like good cop, bad cop, or some shit?"

"Not at all," replied Persephone. "This period is part of my allotted time away from the Underworld. I won't see my husband again for several more months. I have come here to speak with you concerning your glorious opportunity."

Jonah raised an eyebrow. "Why you?" he queried. "I've never even met you."

"Simple," Persephone answered. "You have more respect for women than you do for men. Doubtless, that is because of your grandmother. Doreen, yes?"

Jonah's fists tightened. "Did you encounter her in the Underworld?"

"No, Jonah." That serene smile again. "Your grandmother didn't toil with such preliminaries. She went to your Other Side. I never had the pleasure of making her acquaintance."

Jonah was pleased to hear that. It was great to know that Nana had no dealings with these crazy bastards. "Let's stop the rigmarole, okay? You Olympians just love to be verbose. What is this opportunity?"

Persephone seemed pleased that Jonah cut right to the chase. "Tell me, Jonah, why does someone as powerful as you languish with a part-time job on a forgotten tract of land in North Carolina?"

"What's that to you?"

Persephone smiled again. The sweetness was annoying, but the smile was disarming. "You are a fan of modern professional wrestling, yes? So you are certainly familiar with Hulk Hogan?"

"Duh," scoffed Jonah. "But he isn't modern. He's been out of the ring for years."

Persephone shook her head. "When you have millennia behind you, Jonah, the concept of what is modern is vastly different," she said. "Anyway, let me tell you a small story about Hulk Hogan. Just one. Before he became a legend, he had a meaningless, nondescript job on the docks. He'd have been perfectly content doing that job forever, had he not been convinced by another legendary wrestler, Terry Funk, that he was allowing his gifts to go to waste. Now, imagine what the landscape of your beloved wrestling would be had he remained on those docks? Do you think it would be what it is now without his contributions?"

Admittedly, Jonah was taken aback by the fact that this sweet, serene goddess knew professional wrestling, but he pushed that aside. "So...are you trying to say that I can be the Hulk Hogan of Eleventh Percenters or something?"

"I'm saying that you can be a larger deal than you are now," said Persephone. "You should be. Look at the things you've done! Among Elevenths, you are already a legend. In certain ethereal circles, so I've discovered, Jonah Rowe is the story people tell to make potential Spirit Reapers reconsider their choices. You are a massive deal, Jonah. But you retire each evening to an unknown town, in an ignored part of the U.S. It isn't right. You aren't limited like the Sibyl—"

"I thought you were an ally of Eva's," Jonah interrupted.

"I *am* an ally of the Sybil," Persephone raised her hands before her in a surrendering gesture. "I'm merely pointing out that you are stronger. She is affected by the crossed lines, a flaw that is only kept in check by a bauble. A bauble from your world, as I understand it. But you, Jonah…you have no such restrictions. You can be an Eleventh Percenter anywhere."

Jonah regarded her suspiciously.

"You know, Hera promised me greatness, too," he said in a slow voice, "and there were heavy strings attached. If that's your game, Persephone, forget it. I'm not betraying anyone."

Persephone rose. "I am not Hera, Jonah, and I promise you nothing. Grandiosity means less than nothing if it is simply handed to you. What I am saying is that I know that you want to be great. But you don't need it to be given to you. You have a gift in you. A seed. Plus, you have been improved. So take what belongs to you. Forget Rome. Forget the other Elevenths. As a matter of fact, forget the Sibyl. She is headed for ruin, anyway. Just go and take the world by storm. With your ethereal talents and your current blessings, you wouldn't have to be as patient as mere mortals. Pardon me; *Tenths*. As I said, forget Rome. Look at where you are."

She pointed out of the window. Eva's condo had an impressive view of the Los Angeles skyline. It was a sprawling and sparkling puzzle of grids, streets, buildings, and God knew what else.

"It's the land of opportunity, Jonah," Persephone continues. "It's even far more burgeoning than Athens, Colchis, Troy—the list goes on and on. You spoke of betraying people? If you continue to sell yourself short, the only person you will have betrayed is yourself."

She vanished. Jonah thought about her words but then forcibly filed them away. He knew better than to try to hide Persephone's visit from Eva. He remembered all too well what happened last time. He checked the clock to see it was just after midnight, but it couldn't be helped.

Jonah threw on a t-shirt and went back into Eva's room. He sat on the edge of the bed and shook her shoulder.

"Eva? Eva, wake up."

She sat up quick then gave him a look of confusion. "Jonah? What's wrong?"

"Persephone was just here," he hissed. "I didn't want to keep it from you. She was just here, in your condo."

"Persephone was here?" Eva's eyes widened. She was completely awake now. "But...why? Was she alone? She wasn't coming to take me back, was she?"

"No," Jonah answered. "She was trying to... cheerlead me."

"What?"

"I'm serious. She ran over my accolades and told me the world was my oyster."

"That's good, though."

"It was."

"She must like you." Eva pulled her covers up around herself. "Maybe she saw you kicking all that ass on her home turf, and she wanted to meet you in person. You are pretty impressive, Blueberry."

"Think so?" Jonah snorted. "I am pretty awesome. Just wish l could recall how me and pumpkin knew to go to the Underworld in the first place."

"You don't remember?"

"No. Not in the slightest." He tucked his hands into his short pockets. "One minute we were on the freeway and the next, we were in the Underworld."

"Stress, maybe?"

"What do you mean?"

"It's not uncommon for people to lose sections of

their memories if they are in a stressful situation. It's like you blackout."

"That's probably it," Jonah decided. "I was worried about you. And I didn't even think to ask pumpkin."

"Why do you call him that?" Eva laughed. "Don't get me wrong, it's hilarious, I'm just curious."

"Because to me, Cyrus is a joke," Jonah said. "There is an old farm saying from back in Radner. 'All heads, but no cattle.' That's Cyrus. All smoke and mirrors, all mouth, and easily owned when he gets out of line. As inadequate as he is in the field, I can't help but wonder about his adequacy in other situations. But yeah. Pumpkin is the perfect name."

"I think it's hilarious, but I wouldn't dare."

"You've stood up to him pretty well recently."

"Only because he pissed me off," Eva admitted. "I know he wouldn't dare to do anything in front of Apollo. And you? I think that deep down, he's afraid of what you could do to him."

"He should be." Jonah was instantly serious. "Because if he tries anything, his ass is grass. And I'll smoke it."

"That's sweet, Jonah."

"It's the truth."

"Still sweet, though." Eva yawned behind her hand. "I like that about you. A badass who has his sweet moments."

"Well, I guess the sweet moments are connected to sweet people, like yourself." Jonah produced a smoke and lit it. He pulled once, then passed it to Eva. "But badass is equally as fun."

"Badass is fun." She took the joint and willed an ashtray. She put it on the bed between them as she passed it back. "Badass gets shit done."

"Damn straight," Jonah said. "And my weapons *don't* disappear. That's a sad oversight on his part."

"You want to know what I think?"

"What?"

"I think that Cyrus can't fight well," she whispered as if he could overhear them. "I think that's why he always has me fight for him. It isn't training. It's because he can't win. Same with you."

"Sounds about right," Jonah said. "My observation? The dude has been in the world so long that it's made him complacent. He fights one way. Very one-dimensional; he hopes to hamper you with bullying and then strike when you're psyched out. Might have worked a bazillion years ago, but now, it's as dead as the dinosaurs. Time has passed his ass by. If his immortality didn't correct everything, he'd probably look like a cross between John Goodman and Al Bundy, still talking about the days where he mattered."

"Jonah!" Eva laughed again. "Now, I'm never going to get that image out of my head!"

He grinned as they passed the joint back and forth. Eva took her hit then handed it to him.

"You ok?"

"Getting sleepy again." She turned her head and yawned. "The adrenaline spike from your Persephone visit must be wearing off."

"I can go—"

"No, stay." Eva shook her head. "I like having you close. You can even share my bed with me like the last time you were here."

"Nothing would make me happier," Jonah stubbed out the smoke then sat the ashtray aside. "But I need something hard underneath my back. Still healing from the fights. Tell you what. May I use your

137

rollaway? I'll push it close so I'm right next to your bed. Sounds good?"

Eva pushed her covers aside. "Let me get it."

"Where is it?"

"I store it in the closet." She stood then stretched. "Alexa, turn on the lights."

The room flooded with light, and Jonah followed as Eva went to her closet. Eva knelt and pulled the rollaway bed free.

"Let me get it."

"I don't mind." She looked up at him. "Seriously. You are doing me a favor."

"True, but you're still healing. Scoot."

"Scoot?"

Eva stood, and Jonah took her place. He wasn't kidding when he said she was still healing. But there was an underlying desire to do the work for her. He'd be damned if he let her put together a bed for him to sleep in.

"Got it. Where do you want me to put this, Superstar?"

"Right next to mine." Eva crossed her arms over her chest. "Full circle. Like that night Jonathan forced us to share the room for the night."

"Confidentially? Your rollaway looks a ton more comfortable than my sleeping bag."

"Don't tell your sleeping bag that. It might fall apart like your bookbag."

Eva grinned as she went to another closet and pulled out sheets, but Jonah stopped her.

"I'm good. Really."

"But—"

"It's ok, Superstar." He sat on the mattress. "If I wanted a blanket, I'd be sleeping in that bed with you."

Eva shook her head then put them back. "If you change your mind, you know where they are."

"Thank you." Jonah stretched out. "And for the record, don't knock the backpack. That's vintage."

"Does that mean you're vintage?" She leaned up on her elbow. "You know I'm just teasing you, right? No disrespect."

"Of course I do," Jonah said, "but yeah, I'm Vintage. Were I say, Bartesian, my age would make me damn near priceless."

"What does that mean?"

"What?"

"Bartesian."

"It's a cocktail machine," Jonah explained. "Makes damn good drinks. Runs about three grand, I guess?"

"I told you I was an awful alcoholic, right?" Eva chuckled as she got situated on her side. "I'm not good with things like that."

"Oh, not at all," Jonah said. "Not what I meant. I was referring to quality mixes and materials. Like my backpack."

"Or yourself?"

"What do you mean?"

"A mixture of quality materials," Eva smiled. "I know I said it earlier, but you really are awesome, Blueberry."

"I know." He settled on the cot and closed his eyes. "Good night, Superstar."

"Alexa, turn the lights off," Eva ordered through another yawn. "Good night, Blueberry."

Jonah listened as she got settled in. He listened for her breathing to change. He knew he needed to sleep. His body was exhausted. But he couldn't. Not yet.

What good was a guard who slept through their

duty? He threw his arm over his eyes as he attempted to shut off his mind. Images of the day flickered across the back of his eyelids.

Fighting in the Underworld until the monsters became nothing but crushed bones and blood beneath his batons. The image of his Eva in that short nightdress twisted up in sheets and a thin blanket.

His Eva. That in itself was a dangerous thought. The dreams he had been having of her escalated after Santa Fe. He had wanted to approach her the next day. Tell her to drop the Keeper for good, and he would take the steps necessary to put Vera out of his mind. He and Eva could do what they wanted. The rest of the world be damned.

The rest of the world be damned.

Jonah heard Eva's breathing slow as she fell into true slumber. Good. He stood up, wrapped her up to the shoulders, and then took a deep breath, centered himself, and raised both his hands. His fingers gleamed blue, and he focused until they stung. Then he stepped out of Eva's room, happy to hear the lock catch on her door. He turned to leave, and saw Cyrus inches away. The Keeper froze when he locked eyes with Jonah.

"What are you doing up here?" Cyrus demanded.

"Oh, I figured you'd come up here and try something after Eva handed you your balls earlier," Jonah replied. "So I saw to it that she sleeps peacefully tonight without having to worry about you."

"Do you truly believe your little tricks can stop me should I wish to harm her?" Cyrus took another step closer. "Perhaps it is true then. Perhaps Reena is the smartest one between the three of you."

"Yeah," Jonah replied, "Reena is the smartest of us all. I'll never dispute that. But I'm no idiot, either."

Cyrus focused, then frowned. He focused once

more, then his expression turned black. He rounded on Jonah.

"What did you do?"

"Just realized your shadow travel doesn't work?" Jonah gave Cyrus an evil grin. "Guess I'm not an idiot, huh?"

Cyrus swallowed down some rage. "I believe I told you once before that this is none of your business."

"And I believe I told you once before to kiss my ass," Jonah replied. "Yet here we are."

"What have you done?"

"None of your goddamn business, pumpkin."

Jonah started to head away from Cyrus when the keeper's voice stopped him.

"Hades was right. You are only delaying the inevitable. Eva will meet her end. It appears her preferred method is the blade if her enemies don't get to her first. And if you stand in their way, they will come after you."

Jonah stopped, but didn't turn around. That disproportionate anger began to well up inside him again. "Let them come. And I will be the end of days for every single one of them. And if you just so happen to be among them, pumpkin, the same rules apply."

Jonah meant every word. The keeper didn't respond as he continued to the garage. He could keep Eva home. Keep her from harming herself. Keep her safe.

Or be damned trying.

SEVEN

EVA MCRAYNE

I woke up with a start as the screams from my nightmare resounded in my ears. I stayed still for a moment as they faded and clutched at my pillow until my hands stopped shaking.

I was home. I was safe. Jonah was asleep in a cot right next to me.

I knew I shouldn't have, but I reached over to the rollaway bed. Maybe if I could feel him, then I would be convinced that everything was going to be alright.

Except, he wasn't there.

I turned on the lights to see that the rollaway bed was indeed empty. Where on earth could he have gone? It wasn't the bathroom. The door was still open, and the lights were off.

I groaned softly and fell back on the mattress as I remembered nearly kissing Jonah. I couldn't say what had come over me. I acted before I thought about what I was doing or the effects of my actions.

I grabbed my robe then got out of bed. I needed to find him. I needed to apologize. Maybe it was the liquor. Maybe I needed more of it.

I checked the balcony, in case he decided to smoke. I checked his room at the condo, too, in case he had decided that sleeping on the cot wasn't such a great idea.

By the time I reached the kitchen, I was convinced that he had left. Reena and Terrence were gone, too. I sagged against the kitchen counter and buried my face in my hands. What had I expected? What had I expected? Of course, Jonah would leave. We were friends, nothing else. He didn't want me all over him.

He promised to stay. I told myself. *Which means he is going to stay.*

I pushed myself away from the counter and headed to the garage. Jonah had said something about a Gotcha Bible, which had to be a workout thing. Maybe he had more options in the garage.

When I made it to the garage, it was dark. Just as quiet as the rest of the condo. I sighed in frustration as I moved between my Land Rover and the wall. I stepped away from my car when a hand grabbed my wrist. In one smooth move, my back was shoved against the Rover. I gasped in surprise when Jonah pressed his body against mine.

"Looking for me?"

His eyes searched mine, and I managed a nod despite the heat racing through my blood. I felt my skin flush as I tried to take my mind off the road it wanted to go down.

A road where our friendship was more. A road where nobody else existed.

"What," I cleared my throat. "What are you doing out here?"

"What are you doing out here, looking like Christmas morning?"

I swallowed before I found my voice. Jonah was hot. Not just in appearance, but his temperature. He felt like fire. A very dangerous one.

"I came to find you," I managed, though just barely. "I wanted to apologize for what I did upstairs."

"Apologize, huh?" Jonah smirked. "Why? Did you want to apologize for the fact that it didn't lead to me flipping you on that bed and giving you a night you would never forget?"

Oh, my.

I closed my eyes as I struggled against the images those words brought to the forefront of my mind.

"Yes, I mean, no," I opened my eyes as Jonah ran a single knuckle from the base of my throat to the top of my silk nightie. "I know we're just friends. I acted without thinking."

"Well, Superstar," Jonah ran that hand down to my torso. I felt my breath catch as the silk brushed against my skin. "Sometimes acting without thinking is good. Thoughts have a tendency to make us hesitate. Pause when all systems are on go. Know what I mean?"

"Are you thinking right now?"

"Oh, yes."

Jonah slipped his hands under the silk and my breath caught when I felt his palms stop on my ribcage.

"What," I managed. That same heat was spreading through me now. It took every ounce of willpower I had not to grab him. I wanted him. I wanted every inch of him. "What are you thinking about?"

Jonah examined my face in the low light. He had this look in his eyes like he'd devour me as he leaned in until his mouth was inches from mine. "I'm thinking that I need your permission."

"You have it." I said it without hesitation. "Yes. Whatever it is, yes."

I couldn't control myself when Jonah kissed me.

Hard. I returned his kiss with one of my own. Just as hard. Just as desperate. It took a second for my brain to register what was happening. His hands were on my skin. His mouth was on mine.

I nipped at his mouth with my teeth as I grabbed the shirt he wore. Jonah broke away long enough for me to rip it over his head before he freed me of the damn nightgown before we slammed back together again. I wrapped my arms around his neck and wrapped my legs around his waist before he pressed me against the side of the Rover. Not even the cold glass against my back was enough to bring me back to my senses.

Jonah grabbed the curve of my hip to hold onto me. Gods, the heat that I felt from Jonah now encompassed us both. What little restraint I still had was long gone now. I needed this man. He could do with me whatever he wanted, and I would let him.

"Well, now. What is this?"

Jonah and I broke apart in surprise as Cyrus emerged from the shadow. He raised his eyebrows as Jonah lowered me down to my feet. I grabbed my gown from the floor and slipped it back on as Cyrus continued.

"Why stop on my account? After all, she's been throwing herself at you since the two of you met. May as well get off while you can."

"You get bored trying to break through my shields, pumpkin?" Jonah didn't portray the slightest hint of fear. I, however, felt as if my heart was going to beat out of my chest. "Leave. You ain't wanted here."

"Oh, I don't think I will be leaving any time soon." Cyrus' eyes flashed with anger as he turned to me. "How dare you? Do you not know the alliance you are threatening by assaulting Jonah in this manner?"

"Now wait-" I started. Cyrus cut me off.

"Jonathan has been in contact with Apollo. He fears something is wrong with the Blue Aura. I see now that is correct."

"What the hell are you talking about?" Jonah snapped. "There is nothing wrong with me!"

"Oh, there is. Otherwise, you wouldn't have been seduced by the wannabe whore." Cyrus sneered at me. "Really, Eva. Are you so desperate that you would twist the mind of a damaged man?"

Jonah growled under his breath as he stepped to Cyrus.

"Don't you *ever* talk to Eva like that again, you little bitch," he spat. "Don't transfer your anger onto us because nobody wants you around."

"Or what, Blue Aura?" Cyrus met Jonah nose to nose. "Are you truly stupid enough to start this war with me? The bitch isn't worth your life. I can assure you of that."

"Cyrus, just leave. Please."

"Stay out of this, Eva." He snapped without taking his eyes off Jonah. "I will deal with you soon enough."

"War?" Jonah laughed. "You think I'm afraid of you, or impressed by you? None if the above, asshole. I've already warned that I would be the end of days for anyone who dared fuck with Eva, present company included. As for 'dealing' with her? Nah, pumpkin. You deal with me."

"Very well then."

Cyrus shoved Jonah hard in the chest. I was so stunned, I couldn't react as Cyrus struck out again. The keeper's punch caught Jonah right in the jaw.

"Cyrus! Stop it!"

I yelled as Jonah shook off the hit. He ran his hand under his mouth and gave Cyrus a bloody grin.

"Now, it's my turn."

Cyrus made it clear that he didn't view Jonah as a threat, and headed towards me with malice in his eyes.

He never reached me.

Cyrus was maybe five feet away when Jonah grabbed him. Jonah had subjected me to professional wrestling long enough for me to recognize the move as a half-nelson. Then, using strength I didn't know he had, Jonah flung Cyrus clear over his head.

Cyrus shouted in shock and pain as he slammed onto the hood of Joey's hybrid and then rolled into a heap on the concrete, where yard supplies collapsed on top of him. Jonah popped his neck.

"Who's the whore now, pumpkin?" he demanded. "Who's the whore now?"

Cyrus got to his feet and launched forward. He slammed Jonah so hard against the side of the Rover, the car shook. I wasn't thinking when I grabbed Cyrus from behind. I jerked him off of Jonah. The keeper stumbled back as I moved to stand in front of my friend.

"Don't you dare touch him, Cyrus," I heard the ice in my voice. "I swear upon the throne-"

Cyrus swung before I realized he had moved. My head snapped back from the force of the blow. I grabbed at my nose with both hands and doubled over as the shock of pain reverberated through my skull.

I dropped to my knees as I tried to stop the blood that gushed from my face. It felt warm and wet between my fingers.

"You fight for a man who sees you as nothing," Cyrus spat at me. "You will learn my words are true sooner rather than later, Eva."

Jonah grabbed Cyrus by the shoulder and spun him around. Cyrus sneered.

"Boy, I will destroy you-"

Jonah wrapped Cyrus's head and locked in a chokehold. Cyrus growled and snarled, but Jonah had him.

He then locked his legs around Cyrus's waist, and momentum pulled them down to the ground. Soon enough, Cyrus' growls became choked cries and yelps. Jonah simply tightened his grip. My friend was calm. Methodical. I saw the darkness his in eyes and memories of the vision Jonathan had shown me spurred me forward.

"Jonah, stop!" I yelled in an attempt to get through to him. "He's turning blue! He can't breathe!"

"That's the idea," Jonah said through gritted teeth. "Not such a big man now, are you pumpkin?"

"Jonah, stop."

I forced myself to ignore the pain in my face as I approached them. I dared to reach out and placed my hand on Jonah's shoulder.

"He's not worth this. Please. He's not worth your peace."

Jonah didn't move an inch. "He punched you, Eva," he whispered. "Just to spite *me*."

"Jonah, please," I whispered back so that he would be forced to listen to me. "Please."

Somehow, I got through his anger. Jonah made a grunt of frustration as he released Cyrus. The Keeper clutched his throat, taking in harsh, ragged gasps. He managed a look of the utmost loathing. Jonah raised a middle finger at him.

"Take a good look at that since you wanna stare at me," He sneered at Cyrus. "Don't ever think for a second that I'm scared of you, bitch. "

Cyrus vanished and I reached for Jonah, my

hands slipping against his skin as I checked him over for injuries.

"Are you alright? He didn't hurt you, did he?" I ran my palm over the large bruise forming on Jonah's jawline. "You need an ice pack. That's going to swell."

"You shouldn't have stopped me, Eva."

"I had to," I dropped to my ass next to him. "I did. I've never seen you so angry, Jonah. I didn't want Cyrus to be the cause of any trouble for you."

"Cyrus *is* trouble," Jonah told Eva. "He's a fucking disease. But if the situation demands it, I'll be the cure."

I didn't know what to say to that. Jonah reached out to brush his thumb under my eye.

"How's your nose?"

"Been better."

"Why did you do it, Superstar? Why get between us?"

"You had gotten the air knocked out of you and you were trying to get your breath back." I swallowed. "I wasn't going to let him hurt you. I wasn't. You mean too much to me, Jonah."

"You mean too much to me, too, Eva," Jonah said to her. "So much so that I never wanted you to take hits for me. What did he say to you, by the way? After he hit you?"

"I'll always take hits for you." I studied his face in the dim light. "You have to know that."

"What did he say?"

I didn't want to tell him, but I wasn't going to lie either.

"He said that I was fighting for a man who sees me as nothing. I know that's not true."

Jonah rolled his eyes. "Eva, don't you even worry about that shit. He became a bona fide bitch once he was in the guillotine. I swear, his balls dropped off.

CYNTHIA D. WITHERSPOON & T.H. MORRIS

Alpha when no one confronts him, but is a whimpering ass the *second* he gets punked."

"I'll admit it was hot seeing you take Cyrus down like that," I gave him a small smile when he turned his head back towards me. "What? It was."

"It was hot seeing you own him, earlier," Jonah confessed. "Told you that you had bigger balls than him."

A part of me wanted to lean forward and kiss Jonah as I had against the Rover. But his bruised face and my throbbing nose were enough to stop me.

"Let's go inside." I stood up and reached for his hand. "I want to put ice on your face and mine."

Jonah grumbled something under his breath but took my hand. He snagged his shirt from the floor and started to slip it on when I stopped him.

"You don't need to wear that."

"Why not?"

"Two reasons. One, my home is yours. Go shirtless. We're both adults. And two, I want to check your back out."

"Sure there's not a third reason?"

"Oh, there is."

I left it at that as we went back inside. Once we were in the kitchen, I grabbed two ice packs and turned around to see Jonah right behind me.

"Here-"

I groaned when he kissed me again. This one was slower. Deeper. Where Jonah had wanted to rip me apart before, it seemed now? He wanted to savor me.

"Wow." I breathed and he grinned as he took the ice pack from me.

"Wow not ow?"

"Definitely wow."

Jonah smirked again and put the ice to his face. "I would love to continue, Superstar, but I need to address this." He indicated his bruised jaw. "Wish I had *your* healing right now."

"I wish you did, too."

I hopped up on the counter and pressed the bag of ice to my nose.

"I'm sorry that he hurt you." I sounded muffled thanks to the ice. "I'll call Apollo."

"I don't need Apollo to fight my battles for me, Superstar." Jonah pulled the bag away from my nose. "You're going to look like hell tomorrow. I think it's a clean break though."

"Thank Olympus for the little things, right?"

"He better keep his distance when he shows back up here." Jonah put the bag back on my face. "That fucker had some nerve punching you."

I knew that my broken nose was meant to be a reminder of what he could do to me if I kept falling out of line. And I was well aware that I needed to distance myself from the keeper completely. A feat that was easier said than done since he could track me at any time. At any place.

"If Cyrus comes within five feet of you, he's dead, Eva."

I snapped my head up at his words. Jonah never said words like 'die' or 'death'. In the ethereal world, you just didn't use those words because they were vile. Words that went against everything the Elevenths believed to be true. Jonah must have noticed my shock because he waved it away.

""Yeah. I said it. The bastard would've been dead tonight if you hadn't talked me down."

I dropped the ice and reached for him. Jonah came to stand between my knees and I buried my head against his stomach. He felt so solid. He felt like home. A place I had never known but recognized in an instant.

"I'm sorry," I whispered. "I'm sorry that you keep getting involved. I'm sorry you had to defend me yet again. You got hurt because of me and I can't stand it."

"Eva, drop it," Jonah scoffed. "This is nothing. I've gotten hurt worse in the Glade. It's a sad, sad day when I can't take a sucker punch after everything I've gone through."

"Worse in the Glade, huh?"

"Much worse." He grouced at me. "How long does it usually take for you to heal from Cyrus' attacks?"

"Mortal healing times. Six weeks?"

"Uh huh," Jonah lifted up my hand so that the brace was in my line of sight. "Is that why this isn't healed yet? Even though Apollo healed everything you injury you got in the Underworld?"

"I don't want to talk about it." I pulled my hand free and kept it in my lap. "Let me see your back. You hit the Rover pretty hard."

"Pumpkin hit the hybrid harder," Jonah reminded me before he relented and turned around.

I didn't respond right away. Instead, I focused on the darkening skin along his spine. I pressed my ice pack against it and laughed a little when he jumped.

"Sorry, Blueberry, I should've warned you."

I kept the bag in place with one hand and trailed his exposed tattoos with the other. The art never ceased to amaze me. Jonah didn't either.

"That feels amazing, Superstar."

"The ice? Or me playing with your tattoos?"

"Both," Jonah replied. He relaxed under my touch. "You have an interest in body art?"

"You know I love your tattoos. Remember that night before Romania? I could have traced these all night if you had let me."

Jonah laughed and I felt him wince from the

movement. "The *only* reason I don't have twenty tats now is money."

"You can afford them just fine nowadays, right?"

"Oh yeah," Jonah answered, "I'm just not being frivolous with my funds is all."

"You should be. Gods know, you've earned it."

I ran my fingers down the dip in his spine then over to the cursive tattoo of his nana's name. *Doreen* spelled out for all time on his skin.

"I can't decide which one is my favorite." I muttered. "I think it's your grandma's name. It's such a sweet sentiment."

"I agree," Jonah smiled. "Still hope she is proud of me."

"I know she is."

"Superstar-"

"No, I don't want to hear anything to the contrary," I removed the ice pack to wrap my arms around his waist. "You are an amazing man, Jonah."

Jonah twisted his head enough to give me a small smile. I knew he didn't believe me. "You flatter me, Superstar. I'm thankful."

"I'm honest."

Jonah clasped my arm against his stomach then tapped me so that I would let up. I cleared my throat as he turned back around to face me.

"It's getting late. You should be in bed."

"You should, too," I clutched the edge of the counter as he stepped back. "I know you have the rollaway bed next to mine, and you suddenly hate mattresses, but will you lay down with me tonight? I swear, I'll keep my hands to myself."

Jonah didn't respond with words. Instead, he lifted me down from the counter and took my hand. I followed him back up to my bedroom.

"You're really going to stay with me tonight?"

"Yeah. Change and get in the bed."

I moved over to my closet and changed out of the nightgown that had ended up on the garage floor. When I came back out, I crawled under the covers.

Jonah eyed my mattress with disdain for a moment before he went around to the other side. He got in the bed and pulled me down so that my head was laying in his lap. Jonah began to stroke my forehead right between the eyes.

"Oh," I breathed. "That's even better than the ice pack."

"Because it's relaxing you?

"Yeah," I mumbled as my eyes fluttered closed. "Feels wonderful."

"Good, Superstar," Jonah grumbled. "Good. I want you to try to sleep now. Cyrus won't be a problem. I promise."

————

"Connor, I don't know what to tell you other than I am not addicted to cocaine."

I tapped my fingers against the granite countertop as I waited on my coffee to finish brewing. Connor Garrison, the producer over *Grave Messages*, had shown up at my door around noon, demanding to see me at once. So now he sat at my kitchen table with no less than five newspapers all carrying the headline of my supposed trip to rehab.

"Then where were you, Eva?" Connor shook the newspaper at me. "My star—the very centerpiece of Theia's top-rated show—goes missing! And look at you. You're a mess. I'm going to have to pay Makeup double their usual rate to make you presentable."

"You should do that anyway," I snorted. "I'm always a wreck when I go to them."

"Eva—"

"Ok. Fine. You want to know where I was?" I heard the final hiss and pulled out the cup. "The Underworld. Do you want to know why I've turned green? My bruises are healing. They will be gone in two or three weeks."

"Weeks?" Connor gaped at me. "No. You are going on the Emmys red carpet. I will not have *Grave* tainted by these—these—"

"Accusations," I pointed out. "Come on, Connor. You know that's exactly what this is. A play by the media to tear me down. The only thing they have on me is what the rumor mill can produce."

"Then it is up to you to put a stop to it." Connor waved away my silent invitation to fix him a cup of coffee as the anger left him. He rubbed his face as if he finally realized how ridiculous he was acting. "I'm sorry, Eva. I do know you better than to believe you are snorting up coke in hotel bathrooms. But promise me you'll do the awards show."

"It's the Emmys, I kinda have to be there." I gave him an exaggerated sigh. "What's the schedule going to be for Saturday?"

"Makeup will meet you here at four. Wardrobe by six, and you have to be at the theatre by eight."

I groaned. "Connor, I can't deal with the makeup witches. Can't I just do my own face?"

"No." Connor had his intractable look. "Not with a broken nose. You look awful."

"Oh, thank you," I responded drily. "Thank you so much."

Connor pushed the chair away from my table and stood. He crossed over to me then squeezed my arm with the first act of affection I'd ever received from him. My producer said nothing else as he nodded to Cyrus and Jonah, who had been standing just outside the door the entire time. Yet, before he could make it to the front door, I called out behind him.

"Connor, tell the witches to bring coffee. I won't let them in without it!"

Connor waved my threat away before shutting the door behind him. I took another sip of my coffee and gave my audience the most innocent look I could muster.

"What?"

"Eva, are you sure you are ready to be making appearances?" Cyrus glared at me as I sat down. He'd shown up not long after I'd gotten awake with news of the security Apollo wanted to put in place at the Emmys. "What if you break down on television?"

"Why would I break down? I haven't broken down yet."

"I don't think you realize the extent of the damage you suffered." Jonah took the chair next to mine, his eyes dark with concern. "Last night notwithstanding."

"I'm fine," I stressed the last word until my voice cracked. I downplayed it and took another drink of my coffee. "It will be fine."

"Right." Jonah frowned as he put his hand on top of mine. "Listen, Superstar. You are damn good at hiding behind that wall you've built. But I can see right through it."

I looked down at Jonah's hand so I didn't have to meet his eyes. I couldn't help but remember how good his hands felt against my skin. I resisted the urge to interlock our fingers together. "I'm good, Blueberry."

"Look, I'm just saying I'm here if you need anything. Chitchat, a bad joke, a good sparring partner —" He grinned when I gave him a small smile. "God knows, you need somebody to be here for you."

I saw Cyrus tense up just as I knew he was

watching Jonah like a hawk. But I didn't pull my hand away. I just couldn't.

"Right now, we've got more important things to worry about than me," I told them both in a clear, strong voice. "We've got the Emmys at the end of the week. I've got an appearance to do first thing tomorrow morning. And you, Reena, and Terrence each have a contract to sign."

"Contract?" asked Jonah blankly. "What the hell for? I already work for Theia."

"So, Theia can pay you for your participation in *Grave*, Blueberry." I pointed to the folders Connor left behind. "Forty grand each for the Covington episode. It's probably a little more now since they let it sit to generate a little interest before they doled them out."

I thought Jonah was going to fall out of his chair. "We've had forty-something thousand dollars for months now? But we didn't do anything!"

"You did more than you could ever imagine," I shrugged. "You helped me stop Hera. The money is nothing compared to what you accomplished."

"You know what?" Jonah cupped his hands together as he leaned forward on the table. "I want to stay here. In Los Angeles. I think Persephone was right. I think it's time to show the world what I'm really worth."

EIGHT

JONAH ROWE

CYRUS GLARED AT JONAH. He narrowed his eyes.

"What? You're staying?"

Eva pushed her mug aside. "Jonah, are you serious? You want to stay here and work on television?"

"That's what I said, isn't it?"

"Jonah, I don't understand. That's a complete one-eighty for you! You want to become a celebrity and you're drinking?"

"You are back to drinking again, too, " countered Jonah. "You got along with that Everclear pretty well last night."

"So that's how she did it, then?" Cyrus barked out a laugh. "She got you drunk. I told you that you weren't in your right mind, Rowe. This confirms it."

"Eva had a swallow, dumbass," Jonah snapped Cyrus' way. "One swallow. I had maybe one glass. The bottle isn't even finished. I'm in my right mind. You, on the other hand, are suspect because you happily break women's noses and don't hold yourself accountable."

"I did nothing wrong," Cyrus snorted. "Eva is a fighter. She knows how to block and when to get out of the way."

Eva looked a bit awkward; Jonah yawned.

"You know what, Cyrus? Just go back to fucking everything that moves. I'll take care of Eva from here on out."

"What exactly do you mean by that?"

"I'm gonna have a little talk with Daddy Gold. I'm going to take your place as Eva's Keeper."

Cyrus lunged, but Jonah was ready. He caught Cyrus's punching hand with his left, flung him off-balance, and finished it off with a graceful spin that culminated with him pinning Cyrus face down on the wet bar. Cyrus struggled, but Jonah had him at a disadvantage. Further struggle would make him hyperextend his shoulder.

"Both of you, stop it!" Eva cried.

With a shrug, Jonah released Cyrus and backed off.

"You know I'll do a damn good job. I won't beat Eva down like you do. She won't have to worry about her natural mind being altered—"

"It's already been altered," Eva blurted out.

Jonah tensed. Cyrus even abandoned his leering at him to focus on Eva in a slow, deliberate manner. "What did you say?"

Eva shut down. Jonah could sense it. He saw it in her face. "Nothing. It was nothing. Forget it."

"No." Cyrus stepped forward with his eyes trained on her. "What the hell do you mean, your mind has been altered?"

Jonah tightened his fists, instantly furious. "You need to back off, motherfucker. Now."

"Stay out of this, Rowe."

"I said back off," snarled Jonah. "You already hit Eva once. I'll be damned if I see you pushing her around on top of that."

"This is between me and Eva," Cyrus bristled.

"But since you're so damned insistent on getting in between us—"

"Last I heard, there ain't nothing to get in between, old man." Jonah took a step forward. "You made it crystal clear that Eva ain't your priority anymore. Don't go getting all pissed off when somebody else decides to right the wrongs you committed."

"Jonah, Cyrus, both of you...please." Eva stood and leaned forward against the table. "Please, just stop. Jonah, you want to make it in Hollywood? Fine. I'll do what I can to help you. Just tell me what you want to do."

"I thought you'd never ask." Jonah didn't take his eyes off of Cyrus. Just in case. "I want Elliott's old spot. I want to co-host with you."

"Are you serious? You want to be on *Grave* with me?"

"Yeah, I do. But I'm not finished." He glanced over at Eva. "In light of Cyrus' new ability to fuck off when you need him the most, I wasn't kidding about wanting his spot as well. I want double duty as your co-host and your new Keeper."

"What you are asking is absurd, boy. I will never relinquish my post—"

"Don't give a fuck what you will or won't relinquish. You have relinquished it, anyway; didn't you say you were her Keeper just in name only?" Jonah crossed his arms over his chest. How was he able to make the mental connections so quickly? Maybe it was the spiritual endowment. Maybe it was his own prodigious skill. Maybe both. "You weren't even around when Eva got dragged down to the Underworld."

"Neither were you," Cyrus snorted. "You care as little about Eva as I do, Rowe. The only reason you're acting all gallant now is because someone has screwed with your brain and you don't see reason anymore."

"Eva, do you see this?" Jonah looked her way. "This is proof positive that Cyrus is the scum of the earth. You need to know that he'd have left you in the Underworld had Apollo not ordered him to save you as part of your growth and development, or some shit. Moreover, he keeps wanting to say someone screwed with my brain. As though to insinuate that someone can only care about your well-being if they're crazy. What kind of so-called Protector thinks like that? Do you see why he needs to go?"

Cold steel touched Jonah's throat before she could respond. Eva hissed, "Cyrus, no!" but he ignored her.

"There is no way that your desires will be fulfilled, boy," Cyrus growled. "I've had more bathing time than you've had fighting time."

Eva, who wasn't dealing well with this at all, tried to put herself between them. "You two have got to stop—"

"Stay out of it, Eva," said Cyrus without looking at her, "You and I will have a discussion soon enough about your recent attachment to the Eleventh."

"Funny." Jonah's seething anger underwent marginal cooling due to amusement. "Do you plan on sticking around long enough to talk to her? Or are you just going to go off and find the first whore you come across, per usual?"

Cyrus gritted his teeth. "I will not step down, Jonah. And I will not take the insults you throw at me lightly. My honor will not allow it."

Jonah lowered his eyes to the golden sword at his throat. His resolution and consternation were as hard and sharp as the blade's metal.

"Shove your honor up your ass, Grandpa," he whispered. "I'm improved now. Whatever I want out of life, I will have it. Regardless if it's handed to me, or I have to grab it."

"Bold words to say with a sword at your throat," Cyrus reminded him. "You and this impertinent bitch had better learn your place. This is my final warning—"

"Bitch?"

Jonah grabbed Eva and pushed her to the side. He swatted Cyrus' sword away and shoved him back. Cyrus's eyes blazed, and Jonah felt the purest, most primal rage he'd ever felt in his life. This man thought he was dangerous. He was no threat. Not at all.

He head-butted Cyrus in his mouth, knocking one of his teeth out in the process. Cyrus yelled and struck out, but Jonah was ready. He dislocated Cyrus's wrist when he flung a punch. Cyrus doubled over, and Jonah grabbed the back of his neck and flung him down to the floor with such force that Eva's china rattled.

"Stop!" Eva cried. "Just stop it!"

Jonah ignored her entirely and glared at the Keeper. "Don't you *ever* call her that again, do you hear me?"

Cyrus writhed in agony, and Jonah noticed the sword. The sword he dared flash at him. He growled in his throat as the heat in his hands spiked. Cyrus's sword was in his hands in seconds. The metal was no match for his fire as he folded the thing in half, then balled it up like paper. He dropped the melted mass of steel on Cyrus' chest.

"This is why Eva needs a new Keeper," he whispered. "Because the only bitch in this room is you."

Jonah stood over Cyrus' writhing, pained form, staring down at him and his destroyed sword the same way someone might regard trash on the sidewalk.

"I know what was running in your head,"he continued. "You thought I got lucky, because I didn't beat you, I just choked you out. So you still didn't take me seriously. Thought it was a fluke."

He stepped on Cyrus's broken wrist. Cyrus cried out in pain.

"No fluke, pumpkin," Jonah went on. "I am your superior. I am your better. I am your master. So you better bow down, slave, because if you don't, hand to God, I will fucking kill you."

"Well, my word." a low voice said.

It was Jonathan. Terrence and Reena were a step behind him. Jonah hadn't even felt the sharp gust of wind that signified Astralimes travel.

"Terrence, Reena, you told me that something was wrong with Jonah," Jonathan continued. "I see now that that assessment was a gross understatement."

NINE

EVA MCRAYNE

I WAS CONVINCED that the world had gone crazy. Or that maybe, just maybe, I was still trapped in the Underworld and Hades was messing with my head again. I mean, that made a hell of a lot more sense than the events unfolding in my kitchen.

"Jonathan, you don't understand. Cyrus started —" I began before Jonah's mentor held out his hand and my best friend crumpled to a heap at my feet.

"Jonah!" I knelt beside him to shake his shoulder. I got nothing, so I looked up at the Elevenths who had appeared in my kitchen. "Jonathan, what did you do?"

"I need to properly assess him." The Protector Guide eyed me first with suspicion, then pity. "Is there anywhere I can take him for the time being?"

"His room." I was shaky as Terrence knelt across from me. "Is he going to be alright?"

"No worries, Goldie," Terrence focused his attention back on Jonathan. "Can I use the Astralimes? We can't carry him."

Jonathan nodded, then looked at Cyrus, who was sitting up. The Keeper's expression was one of rage.

"Your charge attacked me, Jonathan. Such a careless action will cause untold damage to the relations between Olympus and the Curiae."

"No." I stood on shaky knees as I faced Cyrus. "No. If there is any cause for damage, it was done by you."

Cyrus gave me such a cold look, I took a step back, but I wasn't going to let him throw Jonah under the bus like that. Not now, not ever.

"The truth is that Cyrus began a physical fight with Jonah last night, but I got in the way. That fight came back when Cyrus insulted Jonah and grabbed him first."

"Eva," Cyrus hissed at me. "Watch your words."

"I won't lie for you. Not for this."

I turned on my heel and followed the others upstairs. Jonathan met me at the door.

"Please, allow us time, Eva. You can check on Jonah when we are finished."

I nodded, then stood back as the door shut. I felt Cyrus appear behind me.

"You will regret the side you chose today." He studied me. "You betrayed me yet again, Sibyl."

"Cyrus—"

The Keeper vanished, and I leaned back against the adjoining wall. I pressed my fingers to my eyes as I willed my heart to stop pounding so fast. I prayed to my gods that Jonah would come out of this alright. That he hadn't turned into the cold man I had seen in Jonathan's vision.

I folded my arms around me as I waited. I wanted to help, but there was nothing I could do. I'd just be in the way while Jonathan did what he could to bring my Jonah back.

My Jonah. I had to be careful with those words. He already had my heart. And I had been seconds away from giving him more if Cyrus hadn't interrupted us.

I stayed that way until I heard the door open. Reena seemed surprised to find me still there, waiting.

"Eva? What are you doing?"

"I wanted to make sure Jonah was going to be alright." I pushed away from the wall. "What did Jonathan find?"

"I'm not at liberty to say." She placed her hand on the doorknob. "But only because we don't understand what's going on. When we have answers, I will share them with you."

"Can I see him?"

"Only for a moment. Jonathan knocked him out for a reason. It may not be safe to be around him for long periods of time."

I waited until she stepped aside then walked into the room that Jonah had claimed during his first brief stay at my condo. I knew why he picked it. There was a gorgeous view of L.A. from the windows. The decor was a mixture of whites and blues. It was calming. Peaceful.

Terrence and Jonathan both hugged me before they joined Reena in my hallway. I pulled a sitting chair up next to Jonah's bed and studied him. Even in his sleep, he seemed pensive. Hard. His expression was much tenser than the one I remembered back in New Mexico.

"Hey, Blueberry," I whispered. "You're one hell of a sight when you kick ass, you know that?"

Jonah didn't move. I didn't expect him to.

"Everyone is worried about you. I'm worried, too, but not like they are. They think that something in you is triggered. That you're dangerous right now. But I don't think so. I think you're no threat to your loved ones at all."

I reached out to stroke at the lines that creased his forehead. I shouldn't have taken such liberties, I knew that. But the more I caressed his skin, the more he seemed to relax. I stopped only when I felt his fingers wrap around the wrist I had resting on the mattress.

"Welcome back, Blueberry," I smiled when he opened one eye. "How ya feeling?"

Jonah took in his surroundings and grimaced. "Like Jonathan aggravated the hell out of me," he replied. "And I want to take it out on Cyrus. Did he threaten you anymore?"

"He's gone. Thank you for what you said. What you did. That means a lot to me, Jonah." I folded my fingers around his then squeezed them gently. "As for Jonathan, he knocked you out to assess you. I don't know what they found. Reena said that they didn't even know."

Jonah still seemed so irritated. I shifted in the chair and focused on him.

"Tell me what I can do to make you feel better. If you want television, I got every streaming service imaginable. If you want food or weed, I can get that for you, too. Bad jokes? I can come up with as many as you want."

"All good ideas," Jonah conceded. "But what I really want is for you to petition Zeus and Apollo to dissolve the binding between you and Cyrus. He's no good for you. He has a cushy job and takes it for granted. Takes *you* for granted. He's a fucking joke, Eva. You deserve more than a crusty old warlord who holds on to outdated principles and viewpoints."

"I agree."

"What?" Jonah leaned up on his elbows. "You agree with me about Cyrus?"

"I do," I released a slow breath. "I've been thinking and…and reading a lot since Romania. I think that the reason I haven't asked to have Cyrus removed as my Keeper is because of conditioning."

"Explain that."

I swallowed. This was not going to be easy for me to talk about.

"Jonah, there is something you need to understand. I was abused as a child. I won't go into detail now. Someday, maybe, but not now. Just know that nothing I ever did was good enough, so I became as perfect as possible. I accepted her hatefulness and harsh words as truth because it didn't hurt as bad when I questioned them. With Cyrus, I fell into that same survival mechanism. I recognize that it's become a cycle and I need to break it."

"Her who?" Jonah asked. "Your mother?"

"Yes, my mother."

"Is she the reason you changed your name? Why you quit piano?"

"I changed my name because I hated it. I hated the frail girl it belonged to," I admitted. "But she comes out from time to time, no matter how I try to keep her locked away."

"So what was your name? Were you named after your mother?"

"No. Her name was Janet. My birth name was Evangelina. It's long and pretentious and awful."

"And interesting."

"Why?"

"It's a Christian name," Jonah explained. "Religious. Evangelina is Latin for 'gospel.' Remember I know my Latin because of my friend Malcolm. Sweet name, and your stupid mother had to ruin it. No offense."

"She wasn't thinking about the gospel when she came up with that name. She was thinking about that model from the late 80s, early 90s."

"I don't follow."

"My mother wanted me to be famous or deceased." I began to pick at the comforter. "I told you how I began to play piano at three?"

"Yeah."

"I wasn't playing, I was practicing. Every single day for hours. As I got older, she added more things to my schedule. Cheerleading, ballet, soccer, and of course, school. Performances. By the time I quit piano, I had to quit something. I was sleeping three hours a night to fit it all in."

"And?"

"And Janet demanded perfection in everything. I had to be tiny and thin. I couldn't eat more than a thousand calories a day. She had locks installed on the cabinets to make sure I didn't sneak food. I wasn't allowed to eat anything two days before a performance. She would always say, 'No one likes a fat pianist, Evangelina.' Things like that."

"And you're saying that you see Janet's abusive tendencies in Cyrus?" Jonah has filled with that rage again. "That's not okay, Eva. That fucker's head needs to be stomped to the ground—"

"That's precisely the attitude we need to fix, Jonah," Jonathan said.

Jonah's temper flared. "Dude, did you just hear—"

Jonathan raised his hand again, and Jonah was once again out. Jonathan looked at Eva with pity.

"I'm sorry you had to see that," he said. "But Jonah is not well. We need to address it as soon as possible."

"But Jonathan, Jonah was only reacting to stories of my past." I kept my hand tight around Jonah's wrist. "Any decent person would be appalled."

"Very true," Jonathan said. "And Cyrus...he has

indeed behaved in ways that I didn't believe capable of him. But still, you can surely see why we can't have Jonah reacting to every slight by 'stomping heads to the ground,' yes?"

"I do." I rubbed my face with my hands with a wave of guilt. "Jonathan, you're right. I shouldn't have said anything. I was just trying to help Jonah understand."

"Eva, Jonah is not well. Remember the vision? We do not want to lose him to dark ethereality. We can't lose him."

I felt the panic overwhelm my guilt as I remembered the vision I'd seen thanks to Jonathan. I started to stand when Jonathan raised his hand.

"Stay, Eva. I am not advising you to leave. Jonah needs light, not darkness, from you. Do you understand?"

"I do, sir. I swear it. But can I ask, what is wrong with Jonah?"

"We do not know. There are irregularities in his aura, that much is true. He is imbalanced, child. We must put him back to rights."

"How can I help? What can I do?"

"Stay here. With Jonah. He is asleep, but speak of good things. Happy things. Nothing negative."

I nodded as Jonathan clasped my shoulder. He released me, examined Jonah once more, and I got an idea.

When Jonathan left us this time, I crawled into the bed and placed Jonah's head in my lap. I ran my fingers through his hair as I told him the stories he had told me about his beloved grandmother. I'd soaked them up. Memorized them. Even my actions mirrored his grandmother, for when he had a bad day, she would feed him, bake him his favorite cookies, and hold him. If he talked, great. If not? That was fine too.

So I recited those stories. I stroked his hair, his beard, his skin. I wanted to pour as much positivity into him as possible.

TEN

JONAH ROWE

JONAH WOKE UP CONFUSED. How the hell did he get to sleep in the first place? He was a soldier. A guard. And what the hell was he laying on?

No, not what. Who. He opened his eyes wide enough to make out the smooth skin of a woman's thigh. He felt fingers tangled in his hair. When he caught a whiff of lavender, he knew exactly who he had been asleep on.

Eva.

He didn't move. He didn't want to move. Jonah recalled the dreams of his grandmother. His best memories had shot to the forefront of his mind as he slept.

Jonah shifted off of Eva and examined her. She had fallen asleep against the headboard. She jerked awake and stared at him for a moment before she rubbed the sleep from her eyes.

"Are you ok?" She studied him. "How are you feeling? Better? Please say better."

"I'm not currently wanting to stomp heads to the ground, since that's what you mean," Jonah said. "That comes later. But my mind is full of some of my best memories, so there is that."

"Really?" Eva's smile was a mixture of pride and relief. "I'm so glad that helped."

"What helped?"

"The stories you told me of your grandmother." Eva tilted her head to the side. "I was retelling them to you as you slept. I didn't know if you would hear me. I'll admit, I focused on my favorite one, though."

"Which one was that?"

"The gingerbread. How she would always make you gingerbread no matter the holiday and the two of you would decorate them together while listening to the *Great American Songbook*. And how no matter how bad your day was, she would take care of you without you having to say a word. That's just the sweetest thing, Jonah."

"Wait. You remembered all of that? All of my stories?"

"Of course, I did. They are important to you, so that means they are important to me."

Jonah was touched by that but filed it away. A soldier had to stay cold, after all. Still, Eva was doing her damnedest to help, and he appreciated that hugely.

"Thank you. See? This is what is necessary for your life. People that fill your mind with goodness, not fear-mongering and bullying." Jonah saw the change in Eva's face and begrudgingly switched tacks. "But never mind that. One day, I'm gonna learn those damn gingerbreads, as well as the cookies. Be like a little piece of Nana lives on."

"She already does." Eva tapped his chest where his heart is. "Here and on the Other Side. She lives on through your goodness and your honor. Through the stories you shared with me so that I could know a piece of her, too."

Jonah snorted. "I wonder what she'd think of me now, to be honest. "

"I have an idea." Eva dropped her hand back to her lap. "She would be so proud of you. Of the hero you've become. She'd be proud of your accomplishments and the lives you've been able to save."

"I've been weak, Eva. Too fucking soft—"

"No." She shook her head. "Jonah, being kind and showing compassion in the worst circumstances is the strongest thing you can do. What makes a warrior isn't his skills or his hardness; it's the exact opposite. I've never known you to be weak or soft. In fact, you're my hero. My role model, though you don't realize it."

"I'm your hero, huh?" Jonah regarded her. Probably a little more than necessary. "That makes me feel pretty damn good. Heroes rescue those in need. People that need saving. Do you need me, Eva?"

Eva regarded him as well. Finally, she spoke.

"I need you desperately. But I need *you*. I need the Jonah that took me to Santa Fe. The one who helped me against Hera and who hiked to Tartarus with me. I want to know without a single doubt that you need me, too."

"Eva." Jonah took her hand. They were already close. He pulled her even closer. "I'm doing you one better. I'm that man, plus so much more. I haven't changed; my mind is just now clear of confusion. Of contradicting things that dull my edge and toss me off my game. V-12 Engine, Superstar. No more cruising off of three-and-a-half cylinders. To make matters even better, I'm not like that oily bastard, Cyrus. I'll take no liberties with you. No force. He's a sorry excuse for a Keeper and a soldier. A soldier knows that it's doubly important to be courteous to people in need of defense. So instead of trying to tell you what you want, I will simply ask you. Eva McRayne, what do you want? This day, this minute, right now?"

"I want you, Jonah," Eva tightened her grip on his hand. "I want all of you. I don't understand how I feel so dizzy around you. Or why I damn near ache around you. I think you've set me on fire without even lighting a match. But, Jonah, I need to know if you feel the same. I need to know that you want me, too."

Jonah smiled. That was the answer he was hoping for. "Of course I want you, Eva. Everyone wants you. I've been telling you that forever. But right now, I'm not talking about everyone, just me. You said once that you weren't a sexual person. Yeah, I remember that. But cards on the table, I dispute that. The garage made me do so. I believe that you aren't asexual at all."

Eva's breath quickened. "The garage made me question that, too. And so is how you're looking at me right now."

"How's that exactly?"

"Like you want to eat me alive. You just don't know where you want to start."

"You'd be right," Jonah admitted. "You hit the nail on the head. But I'm a good man before I'm a good soldier. I'm trying to do the right thing."

Eva's eyes sharpened, much as they did in her photoshoots. "Well, soldier, as you said, 'this day, this minute, right now?' The right thing to do is to kiss me."

Jonah grinned and leaned in. Eva's lavender scent was almost intoxicating at this point —

The door flew open, and Terrence and Reena walked in. Jonah and Eva backed from each other like an explosive was between them. Reena shook her head, and Terrence raised a hand to her and stepped forward.

"Put Mr. Happy back to sleep, bro," he said. "We need to talk."

Reena looked aghast. "Mr. Happy, Terrence?"

"Hey," Terrence said, unashamed, "I didn't hear you coming up with anything."

"Now is not the best time," Jonah glared at the two of them. "What the hell are you doing just barging in like this?"

"Eva, can you leave us for a while?" Reena kept her eyes trained on Jonah. "We need to speak with Jonah alone."

"Wait a damn minute—"

"Jonah, this sounds really important." Eva released a staggering breath. "I'll go."

"Eva—"

"It's fine. I am going to go crash in my bed. We'll talk later." She squeezed his hand. "I promise."

Eva slipped off the bed and headed out of the room. When she closed the door behind her, Reena nodded

"So you and Eva, huh? That's new."

"Better than the gaslighting asshole," Jonah spat. "But you said we needed to talk? Talk. And be quick about it."

"Oh, we're going to do more than talk." Reena crossed her arms over her chest. "Get up. We're going back to Rome for a little while. You are convinced that you're totally fine. We've got something that is guaranteed to show you that you are far from it."

"Does Jonathan know about this?"

"Nope," Terrence said. "It's gonna stay that way, too. We'll be back in L.A. soon enough. There is still that awards ceremony, plus we gotta get the paper-work for those checks."

"Never mind the money at the moment." Reena untied her black and scarlet hair and stood up. "We've got a surprise for you, Jonah. Now let's go."

ELEVEN

EVA MCRAYNE

I WOKE up to the feeling that someone was watching me. I opened one eye to see Cyrus sitting in the chair across the room. His dark suit blended in so well with the shadows, I wondered if I had imagined him.

"Hey." I cleared my throat as I sat up. "You're back."

"What are you doing, Eva?"

"Trying to wake up at the moment. And trying not to have a gods damn heart attack given how you were just sitting in the dark."

"You know damn well what I am talking about." He stood up then crossed the room. I ignored the flash of fear that flickered across my mind. "I saw you with Rowe. Had his friends not shown up, I would have dragged you out of that bed myself."

"Excuse me?" I narrowed my eyes at him when my fear gave way to anger. "You are making some heavy accusations, Cyrus."

"Am I?" The Keeper stopped beside my bed. "First, you spend the night with him in Santa Fe without telling me where you are going. Then, I walk in on the two of you making out in the garage. And tonight, I come back to find you in his bed. You tell me, Eva. Where am I wrong?"

"I haven't slept with him. Not in the biblical sense. That's where you're wrong. And that's exactly what you are implying!" I shoved the blankets aside to stand. "Move, Cyrus."

"I haven't slept with him. Not in the biblical sense. That's where you're wrong. And that's exactly what you are implying!" I shoved the blankets aside to stand. "Move, Cyrus."

Cyrus didn't move out of the way. He slammed his hand across my mouth to shove me back flat against the mattress. I saw him raise his fist seconds before he shifted into an image of my mother.

Janet as she raised her hand to strike me. Janet as she shoved a box of razor blades in my hand. Janet as she told me that death was the only way I would ever be free of her.

Something in my mind snapped. I felt a rage that I had never experienced before as Cyrus brought his fist down on my collarbone. He lifted his hand to do it again when I felt my canines elongate. I felt the power Lilith had given me rush through my veins.

I bit down on his hand as hard as I could. My fangs impaled his palm and he yelled out before he jerked his hand away. Cyrus stumbled back and clutched it against his chest.

"You are not to touch me again."

I rose up and he took another step back.

"What happened to your eyes?" Cyrus willed a dagger into his hand. "Who are you?"

I lunged forward to smack the dagger out of his hand. Cyrus' head cracked against the wall before he lashed out. He caught me by the throat.

I caught him by the balls. I tightened my grip as we glared at one another.

"Let. Me. Go."

"Demon!"

I gave him a cold grin as I squeezed harder. Cyrus grunted as he loosened his grip.

"I will see you dead, Sibyl."

"Too late." I released him and he collapsed against the wall. "I already am."

I strolled downstairs and heard the doorbell. That sound was enough to pull me out of the euphoria I felt from handling my former keeper.

Former. I didn't need Cyrus anymore. I would be sure to make that perfectly clear to Apollo the next time I saw him. I halfway expected Apollo to be standing there when I opened the front door as if my thoughts could bring him forth.

It wasn't Apollo. It was the people Theia sent to fit us for the Emmys.

"Ugh." I couldn't help it. This was never fun. "I thought you weren't coming until after two."

"Ms. McRayne." The woman looked me up and down over a pair of glasses. "I'm Betsy Whitner. I am here to fit you for—"

"Yes, yes." Whitner wasn't alone. Two others were with her, with racks of dresses and suits. "You know, I can just pick something up at the mall."

The woman gave me a hard look. I sighed and invited her inside.

"Can't anyone take a joke?"

The woman's mouth twisted as she flounced past me. "You must be Jonah! Wonderful."

I turned with a frown. Sure enough, Apollo was in my living room. Ok. So that was weird.

My patron god raised his eyebrows at the woman and shook his head. "No, not Jonah," he said. "I am Eva's father."

The term sent mixed emotions through me, as it

always did nowadays. Whitner, on the other hand, frowned.

"Her father?" She looked between me and Apollo no less than three times. "But I thought — I saw on the news that you were killed."

"I'm a spirit." Apollo leaned forward until their noses were almost touching. "Boo."

The poor woman screamed, grabbed the two girls she came in with, and ran out the door I was still holding open.

"Was that really necessary?" I ignored the question and narrowed my eyes at him. "I don't think she'll ever come back here again."

"Good," said Apollo with a shrug. "That woman has horrible tastes."

He walked up to the racks left behind. "You've been wearing far too much black in public lately. You need to sparkle."

"Ok." I let my door close and crossed my arms. "Are we talking about clothes? Or is that some strange metaphor to get me talking about my time in the Underworld?"

"Both." Apollo abandoned the racks to take my arm. He led me over to the couch and sat me down. "Eva, tell me what happened to you."

"Eva has been tainted, milord."

I bit back a hiss when Cyrus limped down the stairs. He glared at me as Apollo turned.

"What?"

"Vampire," Cyrus snapped. He held up his hand to show the two puncture wounds in his palm. "The evidence is here, but I witnessed her eyes change."

Apollo's head snapped back around. He reached out to me and clasped my cheek.

"I'm fine."

My father didn't respond as his golden aura erupted. When it faded, he narrowed his eyes at me.

"I do not sense the demon's blood in you, yet something is different. What?"

"Nothing." I pulled away from him. "I am finally standing up for myself against Cyrus and he claims I'm a vampire? That's ridiculous."

"What happened to you, daughter mine?"

"This happened to me." I jerked the collar of my shirt down to expose the bruise Cyrus had left on my chest. "Him accusing me of sleeping with Jonah happened to me. I fought back this time. That's what happened."

"Milord, she is out of her mind. I waited for her to wake up. When she did, she attacked me."

Apollo took me by the elbow to lead me over to the couch. He sat me down then lowered beside me.

"Show me your teeth."

"Seriously?"

"Yes."

I crossed my arms over my chest then smiled at him. Apollo tugged my lip back to examine me. When he was satisfied, he dropped his hand.

"I see no evidence of vampirism. But you must tell us what happened in the Underworld, Eva."

"Where would you like for me to start?" I snapped. "The Incubus? The room of mirrors where souls screamed at me for hours? Or the beatings from Ares? You're going to have to be more specific."

"Ares?" Apollo jerked around towards Cyrus. "You met with Ares in Van Nuys."

"Milord, I told you she has lost her mind."

"Oh, shut up!" I snapped. "Me kicking your ass isn't losing my mind-"

"She has been influenced at the very least." Cyrus

stepped forward. "In order to free her of the influences-"

"I need to know what happened with Ares, Cyrus. I am much more concerned about that than anything influencing Eva at the moment."

Cyrus frowned. He blinked twice then shook his head. "I remember going to Van Nuys. That is it."

"Did something happen to Jonah in Van Nuys?

"No, milord."

"What the hell was Jonah doing in Van Nuys?"

"We must leave you, dear girl. I believe it is time I get your Keeper's version of events that led to your rescue."

Cyrus's jaw tightened then relaxed. "As you wish."

"But-"

"Come with me." Apollo stood. "It is imperative that you remember."

My father and Cyrus vanished which left me still seething on the couch. Seething and confused.

Cyrus and Jonah had met with Ares? What the hell was that about? I had to talk to Jonah. I had to find out what happened.

I ran upstairs to the guest rooms, but they were empty. No one was there—not Jonah, not Reena, not Terrence. I made it back to my office to grab my cell phone off the desk. I started typing before the message screen could fully load.

Jonah, where are you? We got a trip to make.

I tapped my phone against my thigh as I waited for him to respond. I didn't have to wait for long.

Reena and Terrence made me go back to Rome last night. Where are we going?

I don't know why it was so important, but I knew I had to get there as soon as possible.

Van Nuys.

TWELVE

JONAH ROWE

"JONAH, PUT THE PHONE DOWN!"

Reena snatched Jonah's cell phone out of his hands and stuffed it into her pocket. Jonah, already highly incensed, was ready to chuck bricks by this point.

"What the hell, Reena!" he snapped. "That was Eva! That might have been important!"

"Really." Reena looked unmoved and unconvinced. "What did she say?"

"She asked where I was and then texted 'Van Nuys.'"

Reena and Terrence looked at each other. Jonah got even more irritated by that. There wasn't anything he hated more in the world than being in the dark.

"What's up? What do you guys know?" His brother and sister maintained eye contact for several more seconds before Reena shook her head at Terrence.

"Not important at the moment, Jonah," she told him. "Let it go."

Jonah flung his hands up in the air. "I am tired of all of this mystery shit! First, you drag me out of bed, and we use the Astralimes back to Rome, and now

Van Nuys means something cryptic. Why are we here? What are you guys doing?"

"See for yourself, Jonah."

The tunnel ended, and they were in the Glade. The empty space was filled with wooden boxes that were strategically placed here and there. Jonah had to let his eyes adjust a bit; it was three hours later in the day in North Carolina than it had been in California. But they adjusted soon enough, and Jonah looked at his friends in confusion.

"An obstacle course?"

"No." Reena shook her head. "It's more like a shooting range, just with no guns."

"What? You—"

"You have your batons, don't you?" Terrence entered the conversation. "That neat little trick you have where you throw the batons and use the winds to get them back? That's what you'll be doing."

"When the hell did you do this?"

"Malcolm did it for us," answered Reena. "His work ethic is unparalleled when he's bored."

"But what is the point of it?" snapped Jonah. "I'm a soldier now! This paltry… range of yours is an insult to my skills!"

"Well then," Reena stepped back, "whip out your batons and get it done, soldier man. Terrence?"

Jonah saw Terrence pick up some type of mechanism off the ground. Reena pulled a similar one from the pocket of her sweats. She flicked a switch, and a cutout shape of a Spirit Reaper sprung up from behind a wooden box. Jonah flung an orange and reddish-gleaming baton at it and snapped it in two.

Back, he willed the baton. The winds picked up and slapped it back into his palm. The color may have been off, but the ethereality remained the same.

Two more Spirit Reaper cutouts sprang up elsewhere, and Jonah trashed them. Two more. Done. Another. Destroyed.

Jonah felt more and more agitated. At the same time, it didn't hurt to brush up on his skills, even with feeble materials such as these. He had to stay sharp, lest overly soft beds in California made him lose his edge.

Terrence and Reena flipped their switches simultaneously, and a trio of Shade cutouts shot up. Jonah mowed them down with both batons.

"I hope there is a point to this, Terrence, Reena," he warned them, "because I'm gonna be real pissed if there isn't."

Neither of them responded. They just continued handling their switches.

More Spirit Reapers. Dropped. A couple of vampires. Thrashed. A pair of Haunts. Demolished.

Poker-faced, Reena pushed a button, and one final cutout sprung up. Jonah threw both batons with a roar of frustration and bashed a cutout of Eva.

Wait. Eva?

Horrified, Jonah raced to the remains of the cutout, dropped to his knees, and feverishly grabbed through the broken pieces. Even in the gathering night, there was no mistaking the golden eyes. It was indeed Eva.

"Congratulations, Jonah." Reena let her apparatus drop to the ground. "You just beheaded the woman you ran all the way out to California to save."

"Oh my God."

Jonah felt dizzy. His brain couldn't get enough air.

It was a cutout, he kept trying to reassure himself. *It wasn't really Eva you hit. She's safe in L.A. right now.*

But those words didn't mean a damn thing. Yeah,

it was a cutout, but what if it had been Eva's actual head he'd smashed? He'd thrown the batons without thinking. He was frustrated and irritated that Terrence and Reena saw fit to waste his time with the stupid range, and he'd flung the batons. They'd looked just like red-orange lightning —

He scrambled over to the batons. He had been so shocked by what he'd done that he hadn't even bothered to will them back. He grabbed one, but it was still the same color. Now, though, it had a whole new meaning. No longer was it a temporary inconvenience. It was now an abomination. He felt like a stranger in his own body. Yeah, he remembered his name, background, viewpoints — all of it. But he still felt like a stranger.

Reena placed a hand on his shoulder. Terrence clamped the other. Jonah didn't protest either action.

"Something's wrong with me." It cut like a knife to confess that. It felt like he'd just admitted to alcoholism. "I'm out of balance."

"We know, Jonah," said Reena. Her voice was far from soothing, but it no longer had the edge in it that was present earlier. "There was no doubt about it once your essence damn near knocked me out."

"But you didn't believe it, man," Terrence said. "You can be stubborn as all hell at times, dude, and that's when you are yourself. But the way you are right now...it was going to take something drastic to get through to you."

"It was a last resort, Jonah," Reena confessed. "We figured it had something to be something extreme, especially since we've seen the change in your aura color."

Jonah didn't know what to think or how to feel. He was far from fixed. He could still feel the anger and negativity inside him, waiting to strike like a foreign agent. But something had given inside him. Something was different. Like the realization had broken through a wall in his brain. Unfortunately, it didn't feel like enough. Not by a million miles.

"I need some help," Jonah muttered.

"We knew that, too," said Terrence. "And we—well, mostly Reena—found somebody we think can do it."

"Yeah? Who?"

"Another goddess. A minor goddess. Nemesis."

"Nemesis?" He slowly rose to his feet. "If I remember correctly, that's the goddess of vengeance. Do you think it's a good idea for me to be around the vengeance goddess in my current state of mind?"

"Vengeance is indeed in her forte, but to just leave it at that is a broad stroke," Reena explained. "According to my research, Nemesis is also about neutralizing things that are staggeringly out of proportion. Vengeance is only a part of her function. She's also proficient at putting checks on things that have tipped the scales too far one way or the other."

"Balance." Jonah understood. "My anger and other negative aspects of my consciousness have gone too far to one side, and you think that Nemesis can help bring me down out of the rafters."

Reena nodded. "Exactly."

Jonah dropped the piece of Eva's cutout that he still clutched in his hands. He picked up his batons, minimized them, and shoved them into his pocket. He didn't want to see that reddish-orange gleam any more than he had to.

"I'm game," he announced. "What do I have to lose? Where can we find Nemesis?"

"That's where I was of use." It was Terrence's turn

to chime in. "I couldn't believe it when I figured it out, but she is an indie alt-rocker who goes by the name of—"

"Nemesys Blayze." Jonah remembered the name from the tickets he'd seen earlier. "The goddess of vengeance is an indie alt-rocker?"

"Don't hate, man," said Terrence defensively. "Her music is on the level. She is one of my favorites. I blast her music sometimes when I've had a hard day at the high school. I just never knew that she was a damn goddess."

"You had the tickets before you brought me here," said Jonah slowly. "How did you know I'd go for it?"

"You're not a different man, Jonah," said Reena. "You are just in a different emotional state. Terrence and I wagered that there would still be enough of you in there to see reason, particularly after you pulverized Eva."

Jonah winced. "I'm lucky to have you guys for friends. So, where is Nemesis? Or Blayze, or whatever?"

Reena and Terrence looked at each other in that odd way again. "That's the weird thing, Jonah," said Terrence. "She is performing tonight at a club...in Van Nuys."

Jonah blinked. "What? That place that Eva texted me?"

"The very same," nodded Reena. "That's why we were so puzzled when you said Eva texted 'Van Nuys' to you. Where did she get it?"

"Don't know." Jonah shrugged. "What do you think it means?"

"We'll find out soon enough." Reena whipped out her phone, hit a speed dial, and placed it to her ear. "Eva? It's Reena. Can't talk long. We—as in Jonah,

Terrence, and I—are about to use the Astralimes back to California. You need to meet us in Van Nuys. We're going to see Nemesis; she's an alt-rocker who calls herself Nemesys Blayze. All of you meet us at this address…"

THIRTEEN

EVA MCRAYNE

I SHOWED up in Van Nuys alone, quite proud of the fact that I had only four near-misses on the road. And as it would turn out, the drive was good for me. It gave me forty-five precious minutes to think. Don't get me wrong. The memories that ran through my head sucked. But along with the horrors came bits of information that I had pushed aside in my self-pity.

Vital pieces of the puzzle I was trying so hard to put together. Like when Ares said he had a strong connection to Jonah. Or how Hades swore Jonah would be leading his armies before the next—what did he call it? A Panselene?

Thankfully, we live in a digital age. I had just crossed the town limits of Van Nuys when I spoke into my phone to get the answer I was looking for.

The mechanical female voice responded, "Panselene. The term was used by ancient Greeks to denote the full moon. Symbolized by Selene, the goddess of the moon, it was often—"

"Stop," I told the device. Of course, it would be an ancient Greek word. If I'd been focused on what I should have been, I would have asked Cyrus before he disappeared with Apollo. "When is the next full moon?"

"Saturday, January 23rd."

I picked up the phone and flipped it to the GPS screen before slamming on the brakes as the light in front of me turned red. I'll admit it. Driving is not my strong suit. I groaned when I caught sight of the date in the top corner of my phone. Today was January 21st, and night had already fallen. That gave me only two days to figure out just what the hell was wrong with Jonah, and how we could stop it.

I ended up driving across town to get to the address Reena had given me over the phone. When I pulled into the parking lot, I wanted to laugh. The building was nothing but brick covered in flashing lights. It looked like Christmas on bath salts. And from what I could see of the patrons milling around the parking lot, they matched the building to perfection. Ripped shirts and shaved heads were all the rage. I put the Range Rover in park and glanced down at my blouse and jeans.

"No, I'm not overdressed," I muttered to myself. "Not at all."

I rolled my eyes and stepped out. I was so focused on finding Reena and the guys that I didn't hesitate to turn around when someone called my name. The girl who ran up to me wasn't Reena. She had piercings in places on her face that I didn't think were possible. She squealed and clapped her hands together in front of her face.

"Oh, my god! Eva McRayne! Is that you? I, like, watch *Grave Messages* all the time!" She pulled down her shirt to show me the tattoo on her shoulder. It was the symbol of the Sibyl, which Connor had thought would be a great addition to the merchandise. "Sign my tattoo!"

"I really can't." I had no issue whatsoever shooting her down.

I held my hands up as more people joined her. Each one clamored to talk to me. Some reached over to try to touch me. I swallowed down the claustrophobic feeling that threatened to overwhelm me. I bumped into a lanky man behind me who snaked his arm around my shoulder and pulled me close enough that I could smell the beer on his breath as he yelled over the noise of the crowd.

"Eva, baby!" he slurred. "Where have you been all my life? Eh, it doesn't matter. We gonna have fun tonight."

I was just about to slam my boot down on the drunk guy's foot when I heard a very familiar voice yell over the crowd.

"Let her go!" Jonah stormed through the crowd. "You have two seconds."

The man unwound his arm and took a step back, hands raised. "Dude, I didn't know she was here with—"

Jonah clocked the stranger right across the jaw as the crowd started to move back. He glared at the drunk before rolling his eyes at me.

"I sent Terrence and Reena inside then waited out here because I knew you'd cause a small riot," he said. "I can't take you anywhere, Superstar."

"My hero!" I threw my arms around his neck with a grin as I teased him. "You save all the girls from small riots this way?"

The second I touched Jonah, something snapped in my brain. Desire, love—the constant need to be connected to him—they all hit me at once.

I released him and tried to calm my pounding heart while I called out over the noise.

"Missed you, too, Blueberry."

Jonah turned back into a hard-ass the minute I let him go. "Get inside. We can hide you better in there."

I let Jonah take my hand to lead the way. The farther we went into the building, the darker it became. And louder. I covered a single ear with my left hand at the racket coming from the stage. Jonah all but ordered me to take a seat when we reached the booth where Reena and Terrence were already seated.

"Sit down. We've got to talk."

Ok. Scratch that. He did order me. I frowned as I did what I was told.

"How did you know about the concert in Van Nuys?" Jonah leaned his arms against the grubby table. "Reena and Terr—"

He was cut off when a man twice his size approached the table. If I thought I stuck out, this man was a diamond in the proverbial rough. He wore a dark suit, sunglasses, and I didn't miss the black earpiece he wore.

"McRayne?" he barked. "Come with me."

"Dude, we're just sitting here." Jonah started to stand until I put my hand on his arm. "Why don't you go hassle somebody else?"

"Ms. Blayze wants to see you." The man kept his eyes on me. "Your friends can come along."

"Ok," I yelled to his back. "Where are we going?"

The man didn't answer, but the truth was, I didn't expect one. He took us to a small room off to the side and knocked. Even over the noise, I heard the woman's voice call out to him.

"Bring them in, Alastair."

We crowded into a rather tight dressing room. The woman who had spoken was seated in front of a mirror with a strange-looking guitar in her lap. I narrowed my eyes in an attempt to focus them when she sat the instrument aside to stand.

"You are stealing my audience, Sibyl." The woman looked me up and down. "What are you doing here?"

I couldn't think of an answer. I was too busy studying her. Racking my brain in an attempt to identify the woman in front of me. She was tiny, with a slight frame that caused her black and white outfit to hang quite liberally off of her. And it matched her eyes to perfection. One black. One white. I watched while her pink and blue Mohawk bounced with her movements as she closed in the distance between us to point her finger at my nose.

"I want an answer, woman. Now."

"Ms. Blayze," Terrence stepped forward, "we came to you for help. We know who you are. Nemesis. The goddess of balance. Jonah needs your help."

"I'll think about it," interrupted Nemesis. "But only if you stay back here. I heard about what happened outside. And Alastair says the crowd is clamoring for you. This is my show, McRayne. I won't have you ruin it."

"Fine." I mirrored her stance. "We'll stay back here. I won't make a single peep, and your man can tell them I left. Fair?"

Nemesis inclined her head. "That'll work."

She picked up her guitar and disappeared into the shadows. I saw Terrence, who looked so crestfallen, it made my heart hurt.

"You were aware that she was an alt-rocker?" I raised an eyebrow at the three people around me. "I don't think I've ever read about her."

"She's a minor goddess, but she may very well be the only hope Jonah's got," said Terrence as he looked over his shoulder at the door. "And yeah. She is one of my favorite artists. Nemesis is a damn good rocker. I love her stuff."

"Then go." I patted Terrence on the arm. "You

guys go and enjoy the show. I'll stay back here until she is ready to talk to us."

"Really?" Terrence lit up like a kid at Christmas. "But what if—"

"I'll stay with her." Jonah shook his head. "No sense in you wasting money on tickets if you can't get anything out of them."

"Well, if you're sure!" Terrence snagged Reena's arm, and they were gone.

I waited until the door shut before I rubbed my hand over my face. Even I had to say, this meeting was a strange one. Apollo had told Cyrus that Jonah was out of balance. And yet, here we were. In a hole in the wall club talking to the goddess of balance herself. As doubtful as I was, it almost made sense.

But she was a damn wild rocker. My life got stranger with each day that passed.

I heard Jonah clear his throat, so I threw my head back against the chair to look up at him.

"You've been thinking about what I told you."

"I've been thinking about a lot of things, Jonah," I frowned as I caused the chair to swivel. "What exactly are you referring to?"

"Me becoming your co-host on *Grave* and your new Keeper." He reached out to put both hands on either chair arm to stop me. "You know I can do it. You know I'm the best choice."

I studied his face in the dim light. I wanted to kiss him so badly, it hurt. But that was a line I couldn't cross. I didn't dare.

Nobody wants you.

I turned my head away as a sharp pain hit my heart. Jonah didn't want me. He may have played the part of my friend. But anything more was completely off the table.

"I'm waiting."

"First off, you're right. I have been thinking about it."

His eyes gleamed. "And?"

"And I think you coming onto the show is a great idea."

I can't explain what happened next. One minute, I was looking at Jonah. The man my heart had ached for. The next? The room around me disappeared as the feeling of utter panic threatened to take my breath away. Suddenly, Jonah wasn't Jonah anymore. His face changed. His voice deepened. And his eyes glowed a bright orange laced with red that I was all too familiar with.

"I promised I'd make you kneel, bitch." Ares tightened his grip on the chair arms as he leaned forward. "And now's as good a time as any."

"Get away from me!" I screamed my words this time before I grabbed at the arms holding me in place and slammed my forehead into his nose. Ares stumbled back, cupping his hands over his face before he dropped them with a bloody grin.

"You want to play, bitch?" His voice was a frightening calm. "Let's go."

Ares lunged forward. His arm caught me across the throat as he threw me into the small table set up against the wall. I rolled onto my side, holding onto the edge, and connected my kick square in the center of his chest. Ares roared as he fell back. He collapsed to his knees just before a set of batons appeared in his hand. But I was ready. I willed my sword into existence and relished in the feel of the cold hilt against my palm.

I didn't waste my breath speaking. I launched myself forward as the psychotic god rose. He blocked my attacks with ease. He even managed to hit me across the jaw with one end of his baton. Ares dropped one baton as I came in for a stab and grabbed my wrist with his free hand.

"I will take what I want!" he growled.

He dropped me when I kicked him in the knee. His head snapped back when I hit his throat with the base of my sword. The god of war collapsed onto his back in the tiny space when I dropped down and swept his feet out from under him. I straddled him, barely breathing as I pressed the length of my blade against his throat.

"You are not the first god I've humbled, Ares." I pressed against the metal harder. "And you won't be the last."

FOURTEEN

JONAH ROWE

THE WORLD WENT HORRIBLY wrong when Eva head-butted Jonah in the face. He staggered back, stunned that she would do such a thing. He felt the blood trickling down, and it hurt like two kinds of hell.

"Eva, what — ?"

But Eva changed. She wasn't there. Her frame lengthened, her skin became more translucent, and her hair shortened to her skull and became jet-black. Eva wasn't even a woman anymore.

It was Hades.

"You will lead my armies, boy," the god of the Underworld rasped. "Resisting me will come to naught."

The anger that Jonah fought so hard to quell ever since he'd bashed Eva's cutout overtook him so intensely that his skin warmed. "You want to play, bitch? Let's go."

Jonah charged forward. He planned to constrict Hades' throat then throw him off balance. He couldn't think about Eva or anything else. He succeeded in clutching Hades' throat and threw him into a poor excuse of a coffee table. Jonah had to press his advantage, but Hades caught him with a hard kick to his chest. Damn, that hurt. Jonah screamed in agony from it and collapsed to his knees.

He ripped his batons from his pockets, but Hades was ready for that. A sword appeared in his hand that was as black as night. Jonah made up in his mind that there was no way in hell that he was going to get hit by that thing.

Hades swung. Jonah willed the anger to work for him and used that temporary clarity to block it with his batons. Hades attempted to sever muscles in Jonah's left collarbone, which would incapacitate that entire arm. Jonah blocked the slash with his right baton and used the base of the other one to bash Hades in the jaw. He dropped a baton as Hades attempted a full-blown stab. He used the free hand to clutch Hades' sword arm at the wrist.

"Fuck your army!" Jonah snarled. "I walk my own path!"

Hades didn't even respond. He kicked Jonah in the knee. The supreme overlord of the Underworld just did a goddamned cheap shot.

Jonah swore from the stabbing pain, and Hades clocked him in the throat with the base of the night sword. He followed that with a leg sweep. The resulting fall did a number on Jonah's lower back.

Before he could even move, Hades pinned him down. He put that night sword at his throat. When Hades focused his eyes on Jonah, he could barely see any trace of physical life in them at all. And this guy was an Olympian? He wasn't anything like his soap-opera perfect family members.

"You are not the first upstart I've sent to Tartarus, Rowe," growled Hades. "And you won't be the last."

Jonah's throat was still injured from the blow to it, but he found a small piece of his voice. He lifted his hand somewhat.

"Back," he croaked.

The batons flew to his palm, but at the last second, he snatched his hand away. The batons, flying too quickly to stop, slammed full force into Hades' skull. The momentum knocked him clear off of Jonah's chest.

Jonah scrambled to his feet and kicked that night-black sword underneath the wreckage of the coffee table. He grabbed Hades by the throat, which the god attempted to counter by lifting his legs so as to turn it into a chokehold. But Jonah was undeterred. After dozens of training sessions with Reena, a master of chokeholds, he knew what to do.

He hooked Hades' arm, lifted him in mid-choke, and slammed him viciously back onto the floor. It was akin to a wrestling powerbomb.

Hades bellowed in pain. Jonah spat at him.

"Send me to Tartarus, will you?" Jonah bashed Hades in the groin. "Put me in charge of your damn armies?" He kicked Hades in the side. "I hate to break it to you, but I don't do anything I don't want to do. And also—" he paused to slam his foot into Hades' midsection once more, "—you need to keep a better eye on your little wifey. She visited me in the middle of the night to tell me how epic she thought I was. Damn, if she could see me kicking your ass right now!"

Jonah willed his batons to his hands. The one on the left jostled pieces of a broken mirror as it flew back to him. He glanced at it without thinking.

He had to do a double-take.

The broken piece of the mirror didn't reflect Hades writhing in agony on the ground.

It showed Eva writhing in agony on the ground.

Jonah turned to his opponent. There was no sign

of Hades. Eva was on the floor, bleeding and suffering from the effects of Jonah's attack.

He'd been fighting Eva all this time? But she'd turned into Hades! What the hell?

Jonah's confusion and hesitation cost him. He was so dumbstruck that he didn't notice Eva grab a piece of broken wood. He sure as hell noticed when she staggered yo her feet and glared at him. Her golden eyes were those of a snake. And did she have fangs?

"Eva, stop!"

Jonah grunted as she slammed into him. She raised the broken wood over her head then brought it down with a speed that Jonah was barely able to match. He caught her wrist and she made a hissing noise that reminded Jonah of a copperhead. He shoved her off of him and got to his feet as fear propelled him upward.

Eva scrambled back to Jonah faster than usual, but he focused and reluctantly tapped her forehead. Eva yelped as current knocked her back into a wall, crushing several framed photos.

"Eva, something is wrong with you!" Jonah threw at her. "You need to stop!"

She pushed herself up with her arms, but stayed on the floor. Jonah could hear her breathing heavy, but he kept his distance. Her teeth reminded him of the vampires he had fought, but her eyes had been those of a snake.

"Eva?"

"Lilith," She gasped as she fell back against the wall. She kept her eyes closed as she tucked her arm against her stomach. "It's Lilith. She..she comes out. I can't stop her. I can't."

Jonah frowned. The vampire woman? Where was Felix when you needed him?

Cautiously, he approached Eva and placed a hand on her head.

"Primal state comes out when you're afraid or threatened," Jonah murmured. "It must trigger the...the Lilith thing. Let me see if I can balance it. Put it back in the box."

"You are not strong enough, Blue Aura."

Nemesis strolled back in with Reena, Terrence, and Jonathan behind her. She clicked her tongue at the sight of Eva's eyes. Terrence jumped forward.

"Jonah! Move!" She's a vampire!"

"No," Nemesis raised her hand. "She isn't. There is an imbalance in you, Sybbie. But not a taint. Where did you encounter the Queen of the Damned exactly?"

"Underworld."

"Makes sense. And how did she transfer her power to you if not through bite?"

"Absorbed...her. Mind. Made me do it."

"She kissed you, huh?" Nemesis grinned knowingly. "Probably thought it would be fun to sic you out in the open world. If you kept giving in to anger and volatile emotions, eventually the thirst would've taken over and you'd have bitten someone."

"Wait, what?"

Eva rolled her head to the side and looked at the goddess with those wicked eyes. For her part, Nemesis just scoffed.

"Where do you think Kiss of Death comes from, Goldie?"

"But I don't want blood." Eva frowned. "I don't."

"Have you gotten so angry that you've bitten someone?"

"Yes. Cyrus. He started in on me this morning. I bit his hand when he punched me. I didn't try to suck his blood or anything though."

"That's not how it works, babe." Nemesis shook her head. "The rules have evolved somewhat over time, but with Lilith, the original rules apply. You bite someone, then that person must feed off of your blood. If the rumors I've been hearing are true, Alexius is more interested in shedding your blood than drinking it. But had Cyrus kept pushing your buttons, you'd have been a full night stalker. Courtesy of the original vampire."

"Still don't see how that's possible. I have actual sunlight in my veins."

"So? Do you truly think those rules apply to Lilith?"

"Look, as fun as this little conversation is, how does this help Eva?" Jonah collapsed on his ass beside her as his adrenaline wore off. Even knowing what he knew now, he didn't think Eva would bite him.

Take his head off under the influence of a vampire queen? Yes. But bite him? No.

"She'll always have a little Lilith in her. No balance can completely get rid of her influence." Nemesis tapped her chin. "But if you agree to help me, then we can strike up a deal."

"You gonna fix me, too?" Jonah shook out his shoulders. "Or is that not part of the deal?"

"Is something wrong with you?"

"Yeah," Jonah cut his eyes over at Eva. "How I been actin', it ain't me."

"Thank Heaven." A familiar voice entered the scene. "Progress."

Jonathan stepped forward. He regarded Jonah and Eva with concern and pride. "You have finally admitted the truth of your situations to yourselves. It's a huge first step to the restoration of balance."

"But not enough to actually make it happen, Jonathan," Jonah grumbled.

Jonathan didn't even respond to that as the door opened. Terrence and Reena were the first to enter, and the shock on their faces was something else.

"What the hell happened in here?" Terrence demanded. "Jonathan—?"

"It's a long story, Terrence." Jonathan fingered his infinity medallion. "But believe me when I say that this needed to occur."

"Indeed it did, Protector Guide." Nemesis walked in, unfazed by the wreckage of her dressing room. "Anywhere I lay down my guitar and gear also do double duty as my Rehab Room. When two forces are so vastly incommensurate, they must tear each other down to reclaim equilibrium."

"You got the tear down part right." Reena went to Jonah. "Let me take a look at you."

"I'm fine, Reena."

"No, you aren't, Jonah, now let me—"

"I'm good, Reena, just let me stand—"

"Damn it, sit down." Reena pushed Jonah back. "Don't fuck with me."

She ripped her T-shirt, revealing her tank top beneath. Tearing it into strips, she began to bind Jonah's more obvious wounds. Nemesis looked over Reena with interest.

"Mmm," she commented. "Forthright. Steadfast. And sexy as all hell. Tell me, Reena, does your instrument play to my tune?"

"It does," Reena replied, "but I'm taken."

"Relationships can be fluid, baby," Nemesis coaxed. "You and your partner could negotiate... arrangements outside boundaries."

Reena shook her head. "No disrespect, but that's not a path we choose to walk. We are exclusive and purely monogamous."

"That's a damn shame." Nemesis shook her head. "We could have had a lot of fun."

"I imagine we could've." Reena actually grinned. "But you can't miss what you've never had."

"There is more truth in that statement than most mortals would care to admit."

Nemesis gave Reena one last greedy look and then struck a single chord on her odd-looking guitar. It reverberated so intensely that everyone covered their ears and closed their eyes. When they opened them, though, the dressing room was restored to its former state. It hadn't been great to begin with, but there was no wreckage now.

"How did you do that?" Terrence asked.

"Not important." Nemesis wiped the sweat from her brow and focused on Eva and Jonah. "You came to me for help? That can be arranged. For a price. "

Eva frowned. "What price?"

"Be patient and listen, dear Representative." Nemesis gave Eva her full attention. "I have enjoyed my time in the indies, but it is not in my nature to remain in one lane. To do so would be out of balance. So, my price is simple. It's my understanding that Theia Productions has branched out to include music under their umbrella. I want into the fold. I want to be their first recording artist. I want a contract, but I want to maintain creative control. My indie albums will be re-released in the iTunes store, but also in boxed sets for those that are old-fashioned and nostalgic. Alistair remains with me, and I approve every session musician that gets hired. That's my price."

Eva stared at her. Jonah couldn't blame her. To call Nemesis lofty was an understatement.

Nemesis regarded Eva's incredulous face with those heterochromatic eyes. "Don't look at me like it's insurmountable, McRayne," she warned. "You've done a million things since becoming the Sibyl. If you want my help, then fulfilling my request had better be a million and one. So, what's it gonna be?"

There was silence. Even as sore as Jonah was, he thought that that price was a little steep. At least this freak woman didn't ask for anyone's spirit.

All eyes were on Eva. She did another tedious body readjustment as she looked Nemesis in the eye.

"Done."

Nemesis widened her eyes, unmoved. "Go on. You must do it properly."

Eva sighed. "I, Eva McRayne, Representative of Olympus, swear on the River Styx that I will fulfill your request."

"Wonderful!" Nemesis tossed her guitar at the wall, where it stuck as if magnetized. "Now, let's converse. We have much to cover."

FIFTEEN

EVA MCRAYNE

I SPENT the next two hours going over details with Nemesis about her demands. I didn't know anything at all about the music side of Theia Productions, but what choice did I have? I couldn't spend the rest of my immortality waiting to become a vampire. And Jonah...

I winced. I was still in shock over the fight that had us ripping each other apart. If he hadn't been able to stop it, I could have bashed his head in. He'd have probably caved in my skull, too.

But it wasn't the fight that had sting so much as his words. He hadn't been acting like himself. The look he gave me made it clear that he meant that in regards to the things we had done as well. That had hurt. Alot.

"Sibyl, earth to Sibyl." Nemesis snapped her fingers in front of my face. "So, we agreed then? You get me that contract, and I will aid in restoring balance to you and yours."

"I will get you squared away," I nodded with another wince. Jonah had done a number on me when he slammed me against the floor. "But you have to do your part, too. More than just the balance thing. I need you out in Los Angeles. Can you make an awards ceremony on Saturday?"

"Hell yeah, I can!" The goddess grinned so big, I thought her face was going to split in two. "What's it for?"

"The Covington episode of *Grave Messages* is nominated for an Emmy, and it's almost a shoo-in." I pointed at her. "It's a black-tie affair, so keep the slashes and chains to a minimum. All the big wigs from Theia will be there, so I can introduce you to who you need to talk to."

"Yeah?" Nemesis was still smiling, but her face grew dark. "I won't help you until I've signed the paperwork. I want to make sure you will keep your word."

"I swore on the Styx!" I protested. "Is my reputation so shoddy that you don't believe I'll see it through?"

"I just want to be careful," shrugged Nemesis. "You're being influenced right now."

She leaned back when the door burst open.

"About time you two showed up!" she exclaimed. "I was starting to think you'd never get here."

Cyrus ignored the goddess as he stood next to Apollo. Just as he practically ignored me. Whatever. I turned my focus onto Jonah when he re-entered the room with a bag of ice held up to his nose.

Jonah gave me as much of an ass-kicking as I gave him. As such, he looked worse for wear, too. I couldn't stop the guilt that bubbled up in the base of my stomach. I had hurt him. I never thought that had been possible.

But then again, the two of us were so angry. So out of ourselves that I would have been more surprised if something like this didn't happen.

"Hey, Superstar?"

His voice was still sketchy thanks to my blow to his throat. And he had more cuts and bruises than I did. I nodded then reached for his hand. I squeezed it to let him know that I was sorry. That I felt horrible about what happened.

"Nemesis, my dear." Apollo threw a spellbinding grin in our direction. "How is the darker side of life treating you these days?"

The goddess squealed and threw her arms around my father. I rolled my eyes as I remembered Apollo's reputation with the women of Olympus. Even with one who had hit on Reena the moment they met. For her part, Nemesis giggled as she remained on Apollo's neck.

"Very well, actually," she told him. "Your girl here has just agreed to get me a recording deal!!"

"In exchange for your assistance, I'm sure." Apollo looked me over and then turned his attention back to Nemesis as the others filed into the office we had confiscated in the club. He brushed his hand against her jaw to tilt her chin up to face him. "Darling goddess, are you certain you won't go ahead and set Jonah and Eva back to rights again? I would be in debt to you."

"No." Nemesis' face turned dark as she wrenched away from Apollo. "I know how well your word is, Apollo. Don't think for a second I've forgotten about how you left my bed to be with those woodland nymphs."

"Ew." I wrinkled my nose. "Ok, ok. Here's the deal. I'm going to help Nemesis. She is going to help us. That part is settled."

I focused on Cyrus as I folded my arms on the table. "What happened that I don't know about?"

Cyrus turned to Jonah, still glaring despite his next words.

"It seems I owe you an apology, Rowe. If I had known what Ares was going to do, then we would have taken more precautions when we went to him."

"Wait, what?" I stood up with a bit of effort. "What do you mean you went to Ares?"

The following story was one that hit me square in the chest. Cyrus, Jonah, Reena, and Terrence had come to Van Nuys to get the location of the Underworld from Ares. In the process, Jonah had been "blessed" by the god of war. That explained his transformation into Blue Aura Barbarian.

But I paid little attention to Jonah. There was one thing I had to ask Cyrus. A thought that came to me so quick, I had to voice it. I had to hear his answer.

"Did you know that Ares was the one who grabbed me?" I spoke my words slowly because I was afraid of the answer. "Did you set me up—"

"Of course not!" Cyrus didn't yell at me, but there was a sharp tone in his voice that made me step back. "We went there to try to help you!"

"What did I tell you about that tone, pumpkin?" Jonah glared at Cyrus. "You better get yourself in line. Now."

I heard Jonathan clear his throat. I heard the others start talking, but I wasn't paying them any attention when I shook my head. For some reason, Cyrus's reaction didn't make me feel better. I felt worse because I didn't believe him. I turned to face the others.

"I think it's time we start talking about a game plan. Ares and Hades aren't aware of our new alliance with Nemesis, and we need to keep it that way. So, my suggestion? We need to regroup. Hades swore he would have Jonah by the next full moon, which is Saturday. We need to figure out how we are going to keep that from happening."

"Let's not forget his goal for you, Eva," Jonah said. "They didn't just take you hostage for their health."

Jonah's words gave me pause. I hadn't given much thought to Hades' and Ares' motives once I was rescued. Now I didn't know what to think.

"Let's not forget my deal, either." Nemesis skipped over to me to tap me on the nose, which broke me out of my thoughts. "I want it done, Sibyl!"

"I haven't forgotten, Nemesis." I extended my hand to her. "Cell phone."

"What for?" She pulled a thin device from her non-existent skirt. "You gonna go ahead and call them?"

"No." I took the phone and started typing. "I'm giving you my address. Be there no later than three o'clock on Saturday. We have to get you ready to go."

———

"How on earth can you consider yourself a grown-up if you don't know how to tie a damn bow tie?"

I leaned against the door of Jonah's guest room as I watched him fiddle with the black silk for no less than five minutes. Even if I wasn't enamored with him, I would have admired the picture he made in his Armani suit. The cut of the jacket accentuated his build. The black? Emphasized the lean muscle underneath. Jonah looked good as hell

Work. I had to focus on work. Besides, I had already suffered three hours of hair and makeup. Nemesis was bouncing between the walls with her excitement. And the others were gathering downstairs to wait on the limousine. Which meant I had come up here to see what the hell was taking him so long.

Jonah grunted as he tried again, and I took pity on him.

I crossed the room with as much grace as I could muster in my heels. Due to the combination of medical ministrations and my healing powers, the both of us were well on our way to being one hundred percent again, but maneuvering in this outfit was still a lesson in patience and skill. Apollo had decided nothing Wardrobe had brought over would do, so he brought me a floor-length, slinky gown of gold. It was beautiful, but damn if it didn't get in the way. I batted Jonah's hands away to take over.

I couldn't stop myself. I had to touch him somehow. This was as good an excuse as any.

"Watch it, Superstar." He lifted his chin as I maneuvered the bow tie. "I've already kicked your ass once."

I scoffed while I cut my eyes up at him. "You wish. You hit like a girl, Blueberry."

"And you bleed like a pig." He gave me a small smile. "Seriously, Evie. I'm sorry about what happened."

"No, you're not. I'm not, either." I pulled against the sides of the bow. "We needed that to happen. Besides, admit it, Blueberry; you're not used to having a woman on top of you."

His face flushed, and I burst into laughter. He narrowed his eyes at me, but I didn't give him a chance to respond.

"I was serious about the show." I dropped my hands when I finished. "If you want in? You got it. I think you'd be fantastic. And, of course, Theia would pay you a pretty penny. Especially if you stay in Research."

Jonah didn't answer as he pulled me into a hug. I shivered against him. Jonah felt too good. Too right.

He had no idea how dangerous he was to me. Maybe he could sense my thoughts. Or maybe, he was caught up in the moment, but he held me tighter. His breath warm against my throat when he buried his nose against my skin.

Finally, when he released me, he held me at arm's length.

"You really think we can do this?" he asked. "It ain't gonna be pretty, Superstar."

I took a deep breath and nodded. "What choice do we have? Hades and Ares might show up, but we can deal with them. Thanks to Reena and Terrence, we have a shot to get back to normal."

"Normal?" Jonah raised an eyebrow. "What is this normal you speak of, Superstar?"

"You know what I meant." I heard Cyrus calling for us at the bottom of the stairs. "Come on, Blueberry. It's time to show the world what you got."

SIXTEEN

JONAH ROWE

JONAH WASN'T FOND of limousines. He associated them with funerals and bullshit proms.

And now they were on their way to a red carpet?

He could almost see his good friend, Nelson Black, who always told him that his writing would make him wealthy and noteworthy one day. He'd probably say something like, "Tuxes? Limos? Red carpets? That's exactly where you're meant to be, J. You deserve it!"

"Did I really have to trim my beard?" he asked no one in particular. "Growing it out was kinda fun. I finally had my artistic, writer's look."

"Yes." Both Reena and Eva answered the question. Terrence snorted.

Jonah raised an eyebrow. "Would you two be so kind as to tell me why?"

"It made you look extra disheveled once it reached a certain length, Jonah," said Reena. "You men might think that women find wild beards sexy. I have no opinion on the matter myself, but an unruly, scruffy beard on you just doesn't work. The way it looks now, trimmed and manicured? Suits you perfectly. I won't dispute that some men can pull it off. But for you, it's got to be impeccable and stylish. It's just a better look for your features."

Eva closed her eyes. Jonah had a fleeting thought about how she was one of the few women that could make the dark eye shadow look work for her. Most women who did it just looked like raccoons. And the dress that Apollo provided…goddamn. It fit Eva like a glove, accentuated her every curve, and placed her full athletic figure on display. Eva was one of those women who could make a smock and muumuu look appealing. But in this golden dress that was fresh from Olympus, she looked like sex personified.

Jonah was so enthralled with how Eva looked that he almost didn't pay attention to her words.

"Jonah, that wild, Appalachian mountain-man beard didn't just change your face, it changed *you*," Eva said. "In the 'blessing' from Ares. So how you were acting, the things you said and did—you had that…Unabomber beard. I gotta say, it led me to associate you with your dark side. When you trimmed it down, made it tasteful and classy, it was like that other guy was gone. I don't miss him."

Jonah said nothing. It had been fun not shaving, but maybe he had gone a little overboard with its length. He also remembered his dream where he'd encountered his alter ego. That guy didn't have the beard, either. Maybe he was another person when it grew wild like that. Like Eva, he didn't miss that guy, either.

"Things such as excessive facial hair hardly give you an edge, Rowe." Nemesis, who was quite a sight in her black and silvery dress, chimed in. "It's better to just be your authentic self. Playing characters put you out of balance because you tend to forget who you truly are in the process. The reality far outstrips looks and prestige in the eyes of a woman."

Jonah thought about it. It made sense.

Terrence sat forward, inquisitive eyes on the goddess. "Not meaning to disrespect you, Nemesis, because I'm a huge fan and all that, but what exactly is your deal, if you catch my drift?"

Nemesis cast those mismatched eyes on Terrence. "No matter how many eras change, the obsessions with labels and designations remain the same." She sighed. "Look at this right here, darlin'; I'm on the hook to help Sibyl and your Blue Boy here reclaim their balance, but my official label is the goddess of vengeance. It doesn't matter what people call me. It's all semantics. Let's just say that my tastes, much like my purposes, are fluid."

"So, you're saying that dudes still have a chance with you, then?"

"No, darling. Nemesis grinned. "I've already got my man. Alistair. Women are open season; to explore that end of the spectrum is just healthy for balance. But regarding men, it's just Alistair. End of that story."

Terrence sat back, clearly in a struggle to wrap his head around that rationale. But they had other things to worry about than the predilections of Nemesis.

Jonah pulled out his phone and looked up depictions of Ares. He was so pissed off at that god that he didn't know what to do. He didn't know what would happen the next time he saw him, but he was certain there would be violence.

The images popped up, and he scowled at them.

"Such bullshit," he muttered, "because this—" he showed the images to the other passengers in the limo, "—is all I'd ever seen. I had this image in my mind of what Ares looked like. I was more off-base than these stupid sculptures and busts."

"'Off-base' is about the most accurate term there is, Jonah," Nemesis said. "I can assure you that there is not a single depiction of the gods that is accurate on all of Earthplane. In the time of Ancient Greece, there was much miscegenation. Hell, there wasn't even much distinction in terms of ethnicity; the concept of race is a very recent thing in the grand scheme of time. And the gods were no different in that regard. All shapes, sizes, body types, and hues of skin. It was immaterial for millennia. Cyrus will corroborate this; if you went to Mount Olympus, it would look something like your United Nations. Any and every bit of diversity you could imagine. I can tell you for a fact that Ares has always resembled what people nowadays refer to as 'black.' Eris, his sister, has always resembled a person that mortals would refer to as Spanish-born. And those are just two examples of diversity in the divine realm. It was only after certain close-minded people got in charge of everything and wanted to re-write history. That's when all the depictions became European-based and aesthetically one-dimensional. Olympians are just as varied as the multiple colors of Eleventh Percenter auras. It would be unbalanced if everyone were one thing, after all."

"Nemesis speaks the truth," Cyrus agreed. "Olympus is quite the melting pot."

There was a brief silence after that. Jonah disregarded Cyrus's words and grinned at Nemesis.

"That's cool, Nem," he said. "Really refreshing. Now, if only half of Olympus weren't crazy."

Nemesis shrugged and laughed. "Well, we can't all have everything we want."

"But back to Ares, Terrence," Jonah returned his

attention to his brother, "his presence was hardcore, too. Everything about him screamed, 'Run.' But I didn't. I couldn't. The need to help Eva outweighed any reservations I might have had."

Eva looked truly touched at that last part, but she sobered quickly. "Hades had a similar aura, Jonah," she informed him. "You expect him to be fire and brimstone? He's cold. Calculating. He lures you in and then tears you down. He and Ares, I must admit, are quite a duo."

"There is something I haven't told you guys," said Jonah to the group at large. ""Something Hades said in the Underworld. It led me to believe that there is something…beyond Ares and Hades that we don't see."

Eva looked troubled. "I don't know what that might be," she said. "The only one bigger and badder than Ares and Hades is Zeus, and he adores me."

"Eva, the Greek Pantheon is quite large, so I've read," reminded Reena. "They wouldn't have to be Alpha Olympian to be a threat."

"Reena is right, dear Sibyl." Nemesis cut hungry eyes at Reena once more. "And she cuts a damn good profile in a dress, I might add."

Jonah looked over his sister. He had to admit that she was kind of gorgeous. She wore a black dress with conservative splits on both sides. Eva had loaned her a gold bracelet that looped up to mid-forearm, and the look was topped off with flawless makeup and a pristine hairstyle that accentuated every scarlet high-light that Reena had in her black hair. But the funny thing about it was the fact that Reena hated every bit of it.

"Commit this look to memory, Nemesis," Reena grumbled, "because it's never going to happen again."

Nemesis grinned, as did Jonah.

"I'm willing to bet that Kendall has never seen you in a dress," he told her. "She'd probably tear you apart if she saw you like this."

Reena swallowed and took a breath. "Don't put thoughts like that in my head right now, Jonah," she chided. "I've got to stay focused!"

Everyone laughed. Nemesis looked as if she had her own thoughts about Reena but managed to tear her eyes away and focus on Eva again.

"There are many in Olympus who would see you fall," she said, "but your list of supporters ain't shabby, either. You have the might of the Council backing you, after all. That includes Apollo, who is invaluable, and Hermes, who has labeled you his favorite on many occasions. Persephone's on board, too. And of course, the cherry atop the entire sundae is Zeus himself."

Jonah shuddered when he heard Persephone's name but frowned at Nemesis. "You didn't mention yourself on that list."

"That's very true," said Nemesis, who looked neither awkward nor abashed. "My alliance with you all is probationary; the Sibyl has to make good first. When that happens, she will have an ally for life. And given that she is immortal, that stretch is very, very far."

Jonah didn't much care for that conditional shit, but a random thought drew his mind from it. "How exactly do you plan to help me get back to full equilibrium?"

"That will occur after—and only after—my deal gets rolling," Nemesis reiterated, "but beyond that, I can't really tell you, J. Moments such as these must be captured, not predetermined."

Jonah's irritation was about to boil, but Terrence distracted him.

"Jonah, Ares is here! About fifty feet from Joey!"

"What! Where — ?"

The limo came to a halt. Nemesis squealed.

"We're here, loves!" she exclaimed. "One way or another, it's showtime!"

SEVENTEEN

EVA MCRAYNE

I WOULD LOVE to say that I had time to take a look at the man Terrence thought was Ares, but I couldn't see anything past the people swarming to get the first pictures of the car.

"Ok," I coached one last time. "Remember what I told you. Smile. Tell the press short, quick answers. Stand as still as possible for the pictures. And then we'll get inside."

Jonah grumbled something under his breath that I didn't catch when one of the security personnel opened the door he was closest to. I watched as he got out, then the others. Jonah leaned back in to take my hand and help me out. I grinned the moment I stood. The red carpet was a circus. They always were. But somehow, I knew how to control them.

No matter what dark forces lingered in the background.

"Eva!"

"Sibyl!"

The crowds started to scream when they caught sight of me, so I waved and looped my arm with Nemesis. She looked thrilled when the press swarmed us. The first to stop our stroll was Wendy Carrington, the fashion reporter for a show I never watched.

"Eva, darling!" She beckoned her cameraman to focus on us. Jonah and the gang circled me. "Your party looks amazing tonight! Who on earth are you wearing?"

"Wendy, don't be silly." I grinned, then waved once more to the fans being held back by waist-high metal barriers. "You know I don't pay any attention to labels. It's a dress. It looks fantastic. But you, dear woman, are a sight!"

I gestured to her cameraman, who turned his lens onto her. "Isn't she beautiful?"

The woman blushed, and I chalked up the first good review of our outfits. See, the magic of the red carpet wasn't to absorb the flattery. It was to turn the compliments back onto the people who are so willing to give them. They believed that I was special. Maybe I was. But I would never let them think for a minute I considered myself better than they were.

The reporter giggled as she thrust the microphone back at me. "Tell me who you are here with then. What a handsome crew!"

I introduced everyone in short order with brief explanations as to who they were and their role in the episode. But when I got to Nemesis, I tightened my grip on her arm.

"And this is the fabulous Nemesys Blayze," I announced. "Remember her name, Wendy. She is going to be Theia Productions' very first signed artist under the new imprint, Theia Music Group."

The goddess cut her eyes over at me before turning her smile back to the reporter. Wendy took the time to ask everyone at least one question, and I was grateful that Jonah didn't show the irritation I knew he felt in his answers.

I had to tear my eyes off of him. I had to. I was going to give the press a hell of a lot more to talk about than our outfits if they caught me gawking at him.

Focus, Evie. Focus.

We moved down the line, but our interactions with the reporters were the same. It wasn't until we reached the end that we had to pose for pictures in front of a massive Emmys poster. I was placed in the middle of the flashing lights, and I could hear Reena telling Jonah to be quiet as he complained about how blatantly phony all these people were.

All the while, I was wary and watchful. Just past the group of photographers to my left stood two gods I had never wanted to see again.

Ares looked as though he owned the place, dressed in a black suit with diamond cufflinks. Hades was next to him, studying us with a fascination I found quite unnecessary. I tugged at Jonah's arm, and he leaned down so that I could whisper in his ear.

"Trouble." I grinned. "Looks like Hades is going to make good on that promise."

"You sure we have to wait, Evie?" Jonah leaned in as if to kiss my cheek but yelled in my ear over the noise instead. The photographers lined up before us went crazy. "I mean, they are right there."

"Yes." I laughed at the demands to get pictures of me with each member of my party. "I can't fight in a damned dress, Jonah. Much less this one."

I leaned into Jonah's side as he slung his arm around me. Ok. So maybe that wasn't the best idea. I could feel his heart beating beneath my palm. His cologne made me weak in the knees. I started to lean up. Whisper in his ear to take me back to Santa Fe where we could leave all this behind us.

Gods, what was wrong with me? Jonah wasn't

well. He wasn't himself. I had to remember that each time I thought about what had transpired between us over the past few days.

The flashes went crazy. Same with Terrence and Reena. Cyrus and Nemesis. The crowds. The photographers. The reporters. Everyone loved us.

And even though I hated the promotional photographs taken, I had come to terms with their necessity. Tomorrow morning these pictures were going to be all over the internet. In celebrity magazines. I had to do what I could to increase Apollo's popularity. And if that meant I had to look like an idiot, then so be it.

Finally, I waved goodbye to the photographers and led us inside the massive theatre. Connor met me at the door and clasped my hand.

"Good show, Eva." He nodded to the others. "You said you have a recording artist for Cara to meet?"

"Yeah." I nodded before snagging a flute of champagne off a passing tray. "Where is she?"

"Who is Cara, exactly?" Nemesis frowned. "I hope you are talking about—"

"The executive over Theia Music Group," I answered her before turning to the others. "Go. Mingle. Keep an eye on our two party-crashers, will you? I have a deal to seal."

Nemesis giggled. Reena rolled her eyes. And Terrence pulled Jonah away by the arm as he spotted a celebrity in attendance he must have followed. Connor caught my arm as we tried to go past him. He studied me with a critical eye before he spoke.

"No mayhem. No danger. No destruction. Not tonight. Understand?"

"Who? Little ol' me?" I patted his hand. "Can't make any promises, Connor. You know that!"

He started muttering about the cost of doing business, so I ignored him while I searched out the one person we needed. I headed towards Cara Harris despite the well wishers threatening to box me in. I stopped just short of a chubby woman who seemed to be losing a battle with the champagne. Her cheeks were red, her dress was rumpled, and from the look in her eyes, I would have said she started her celebration well before the theatre was opened for the party.

Good. I could use that.

"Cara!" I squealed and grabbed her hand with my free one. "I have been dying to congratulate you myself on your promotion."

"Eva?" She looked confused for a moment, and I couldn't blame her. I'd never set eyes on the woman until Connor pointed her out to me. "Well, I—thank you."

"Listen, this is not a night to talk business, but I have a friend of mine I would love for you to meet." I gestured for a passing waiter who blushed when I smiled at him. I took another flute of the bubbly and pressed it into Cara's hand. "Cara Harris, meet Nemesys Blayze. Now, I know I don't understand a thing about music, and you're a genius at it! But Miss Blayze is the queen of the indies right now. She is the hottest free agent to hit the market in decades."

Nemesis must have heard the sugary sweet tone in my voice and realized I was lying through my teeth. But she didn't show it. Instead, I pushed her forward. "Cara, Nemesys."

"How lovely it is to meet you!" Cara swallowed her drink in a single gulp as she offered a limp hand to my new pal. "Any friend of Eva's is a friend of mine."

"Listen, Cara. You know I have Theia's best interest at heart. And you know I'm in desperate need of a new theme song. I want to request Nemesys to do it, as well as get her signed in Theia Music Group as your first recording artist. Here and now."

"She is really that good?" Cara's eyes widened. "You want her to do the theme music and sign a deal with us?"

"Yes." I nodded as I ignored Nemesis's radiant smile. "Now, if you don't want to sign her, I understand. But by god, I have enough funding to produce it myself. The royalties would far exceed any expense—"

"Eva, darling, that won't be necessary." Cara pulled out her phone and handed it to the woman next to her. "Get the lawyers on the line. I want a contract drawn up tonight for—what was your name again?"

"Nemesys Blayze!" squealed the goddess as she threw her arms around my neck. "Eva, you are the best!"

"I know, I know," I sighed as I worked myself free from her grasp then whispered to her. "Work out the details of the contract now, while she's drunk. Tell her that list of things you wanted. You'll get that and more."

Cara was still yelling at her assistant when Joey bounded over to me. I laughed with real happiness for the first time since this whole damn thing started.

"Grizzly! I've missed you!"

"Evie, oh my god, are you ok?" Joey pulled away to look me over before he crushed me against him again. "I am so sorry I wasn't there when you came home, baby girl. I didn't want to leave, but I had that contract—"

"It was the right move for you to go." I hugged him back. "Everything has gone to hell, Joey. I'm glad you weren't there to get caught in the middle of everything."

"Define hell for me."

"Cyrus is ignoring me. Jonah and I nearly had sex with each other. Then, we nearly ripped each other apart, and not in a good way. We have our chance tonight to set it all back to rights."

"Is there gonna be a fight?" He glanced around then showed me the tiny body camera attached to his lapel. "Cause I can get it on film."

"Why are you acting like a drug dealer from a bad eighties movie?"

"All part of my charm, Evie. You know you love it."

Joey wiggled his eyebrows at me then linked his arm with mine. He led me from one group to another as I charmed the hell out of every producer and celebrity in sight. I knew the power of networking quite well, and I was determined to keep my strings tied to the right people. But I was doing so much more than that. I was keeping an eye on the rest of our party and for our enemies.

"Ok. It's time to get in the theatre, you two." Connor tapped me on the shoulder. "They are about to start."

I gathered up the rest of my people, and we found our seats. Jonah sat down next to me on one side. Joey on the other. I didn't have to see Cyrus to know he was glaring at us. It wasn't my fault he had been glued to Nemesis all night. Hell, the only time he'd acknowledged me with full sentences was when he'd told me about going to Ares. Maybe his pride was hurt because I asked him if he betrayed me.

I needed to talk to him. Because right now? We were going nowhere fast. And to be honest, I didn't want us to go forward. Not together.

The Emmys took forever to get through, thanks to the pauses for the commercial breaks. But we had won three gold statues thanks to the Covington episode. One for Best Documentary, one for Best Presenter, and one for Single-Camera Best Picture Editing. Joey was thrilled, and I was thrilled for him.

When it was time to do the press conferences after the show, the stagehand who had led us backstage touched my arm.

"I need you on the podium, please, Miss McRayne."

"Fine." I gave him an exaggerated groan. "I wish Joey would just do it. He won an award, too."

The man ignored me as he parted the crowd to lead me to the podium that had been set up. I accepted his hand and whistled to get the crowd's attention. When the applause of the press died down, I began to speak.

"The Covington House episode of *Grave Messages* was so staggeringly successful that we won not one, not two, but three Emmys!" I ceased for the following applause. "We've got action. We've got history. But most importantly? We have the Eleventh Percenters making their grand debut!"

I threw my arm out in the direction where Jonah, Reena, and Terrence had gathered next to Joey as another round of applause began. I caught Jonah's eye and winked at him. Then ignored the butterflies erupting in my stomach when he grinned back at me.

When it died down, I glanced out the window against the far wall to see that the moonlight glowed brighter against the pavement with each second that passed. Nearly Panselene time. I had to hurry this up and get our people away from the innocent bystanders crowded around the podium.

"With *Grave Messages*, we strive to give you a show you will never forget."

"Truer words have never been spoken, Sibyl."

229

Hades strolled through the crowd, clapping when the room went silent. I tightened my fists to the point that my knuckles cracked.

"Why, don't look so surprised!" Hades said with a grin. "Surely you haven't forgotten the reason why I am here this evening."

"Hades, everybody," I said through clenched teeth. He was too soon, and I was still in this damn dress. "Give him a round of applause. Come on, don't be shy; let's show him a true California welcome!"

The crowd swarmed around the god of the Underworld, who backed away as he yelled something I couldn't understand. I turned on my heel in an attempt to get to the women's restroom off the right to get some pants on when I heard a massive crack fill the space around me.

I heard screams replace the cheering as a large wooden lion's head broke off the wall. I didn't know whether to run or jump as the massive thing came crashing down right above my head.

EIGHTEEN

JONAH ROWE

THE WHOLE SCENE turned into chaos very quickly, but Jonah never took his eyes off of Eva. Not that he had been able to keep his eyes off of her all night. The way she wore that dress and commanded the entire room of Hollywood elitists had made his mind shift into another realm of thought entirely. But he wasn't thinking about how damn good she looked now. He didn't think about anything except getting her out of harm's way. Jonah broke into a run, then shoved her against the wall before that lion caved in her head.

"Jonah!" She clutched at his jacket before she buried her head into his shoulder to shield her eyes from the dust and bits of wood that flew up from the lion's head crashing through the podium. When the air cleared enough, she yelled. "Are you alright?"

"Dandy," Jonah yelled back. "We gotta get down!"

Eva growled as she took in the rest of the chaos surrounding them. The press was in a struggle between catching the fights on film and running for their lives. "I need two minutes, Blueberry. I can't fight in this damned dress."

"You have no choice, bitch."

Fiery anger engulfed Jonah's insides at the voice that could be heard over the noise. He turned his back on Eva. Ares stood there, the purest malice in his eyes. A two-handed broadsword was in his hands, which he had pointed down. He was completely indifferent to the people who fled all around them.

"If you'd succumbed to the Incubus, this wouldn't be happening," he said as he spat bitterly on the floor. "Instead, you rile the Succubus, who is on edge even at the best of times. And you, Blue Aura—you can't appreciate a good thing to save your life."

"Succubus? What the hell is he talking about?"

"Griselda, his secretary," Jonah answered her without taking his eyes off of the god. "The Incubus you killed must have been her mate."

"Very good, Blue Aura." Ares gave them both a cold grin. "Now, move aside. I am under orders not to harm you."

Jonah had no interest in conversation. It was another opportunity for Ares to get in his head again. "Just bring it, man."

Ares tightened his grip on his broadsword. "Indeed, I shall, boy."

He stepped back, lifted one hand from the hilt, and did that horizontal hand-slashing thing again. Once more, it left a temporary burning flame in its wake. Seconds later, several members of the press and the celebrities who had been trapped with them ceased their escape attempts and turned to Jonah, Eva, and their friends with blind abhorrence in their eyes that had not been there seconds before. Jonah and Eva looked at each other in alarm.

"What the hell, man?" Jonah demanded. "You're gonna possess innocent people to believe they're soldiers? You'll get them killed!"

Ares scoffed. "This is Los Angeles, Jonah. No one

is innocent. As you know yourself from my blessing, once it's in you, you have an inordinate capacity for violence, a high pain threshold, and insatiable blood-lust. If you could see their thoughts at this moment, you would feel anything but pity for them."

"How blind you are, half-brother dear."

Nemesis stood near the ruined podium and cracked her knuckles. Ares glared at her.

"You have no business here, you barely-divine whore," he growled. "You'd best clear out before I cleave your head in two."

Nemesis stuck out her hands, and her strangely shaped guitar appeared in them. "See, it's words like that that get your ass flipped, kicked, and split."

She struck a sharp chord. Everyone's weapons appeared in the hands. Jonah, Terrence, and Cyrus remained in their tuxes, but Eva's and Reena's evening gowns morphed into tank tops and black camo pants. Funnily enough, both of them still had the makeup. Reena still managed to look badass while Eva looked like a version of Battlefield Barbie.

"I could kiss you, Nem!" she cried. "This is more like it!"

"Who are you telling?" Reena breathed. "You know how much I hate the drafts that dresses cause?"

But Jonah paid them no attention. Once again, his batons were blue. The color may as well have been blinding. All was balanced and copacetic. He was himself again.

"Nemesis?"

The goddess scoffed. "What were you expecting? Something dramatic? No. The Sibyl held up her end, and now I've done so as well. Now, kick ass!"

The fight broke out in earnest. Jonah only had eyes for Ares, but a couple of possessed photographers cornered him. He cold-cocked one in the face and then shoved him into the other guy. A middle-aged, round-bellied man charged him and barreled him off of his feet. Luckily for Jonah, he hadn't lost grip on his batons and clocked the guy across the back of his skull.

"Sorry, man," he grunted as he turned over to get up.

"Jonah!"

Jonah glanced over just in the nick of time. A woman who looked faker than a blow-up doll saw him on his hands and knees and attempted to curb stomp his head. He barely got out of the way; he could feel the gust of wind she made as her high-heeled foot slammed down. She scratched him across the face, which pissed him off. She then threw a punch, which he blocked with a baton. When she wailed in agony and rage, Jonah gave her a hard shove, and she crumpled to the floor after hitting her head against a camera.

He saw Terrence catch a woman dressed to the nines with a double-leg takedown after she attempted to stab him with broken glass. He stood with an apologetic look on his face and looked over at who Jonah had just defeated.

"Is that—is that Starla St. Jove?"

"Yeah," Jonah sighed. "The non-acting dumbass who got hacked up in *Homecoming III* and gutted with her tiara in *Spring Formal VI*. Besides those movies and a couple of Old Navy commercials, I haven't seen her in much else."

"Until tonight." Terrence shook his head. "I always read that L.A. drove people crazy, but I never imagined it'd be like this!"

A cameraman came out of nowhere and barreled into them. Jonah hit the ground and groaned. That hurt like hell.

Then he looked up.

The cameraman was Joey. Terrence, who hadn't seen his face before he went down, rose with hellfire in his eyes and stormed forward to brain Joey in the head.

"Terrence, wait!" Jonah raised his hands. "It's Joey!"

Terrence froze. Jonah dropped one baton and removed his tuxedo coat. Joey looked ravenous; he looked like he wanted to feast on their corpses. Jonah reminded himself that Joey, along with the rest of these people, was possessed. They were innocent of all wrongdoing.

Admittedly, it was a tough sell because Joey rang his bell quite hard.

Jonah maintained eye contact with Joey for a few more seconds and then glanced at Terrence. "*Now!*"

Terrence got it. He ran full blast into Joey's back, which propelled him forward. Jonah used his tux coat to shroud Joey's head and then crowned him with a forearm. He was out cold.

"Jonah!" Eva yelled. "Blue and Gold!"

Jonah ran toward Eva without hesitation. She was having trouble with a possessed celebrity's bodyguard. He threw a quick nod to Eva, and she kicked the man in the chest, which sent him staggering back. Jonah dipped low, grabbed the man at his knees, and lifted him off of the ground. Then Eva turned her sword flat-side, took a running start, and swatted the guy across the chest with it. The man nearly did a full circle in the air before crashing on the ground. Jonah helped Eva to her feet.

"Did you think we'd actually get to do that double-team move when we practiced it?"

Eva looked more than a little pleased. "I always

hoped so," she confessed, "but that's a tactic I can only do with someone I trust."

Jonah smirked. He was touched that she said that, but he'd never tell her.

He looked around. Reena and Nemesis stood nearby, several bow-tied bandits at their feet. Cyrus, despite his lack of a sword, held his own quite well against Griselda the Succubus, but then Eva helped him finally put the animal down. With the sword through her heart, the bestial bitch went out the same way as her mate.

A muscle worked in Ares' temple as he stood by. Hades, on the other hand, was nowhere to be seen.

"Even after all that shit, we're still standing." Jonah had to say it. He simply couldn't resist. "Got anything else, Army Man?"

Ares growled. "If you think I need backup to destroy the likes of you, then you are sadly mistaken —"

"My dear son. Please shut your mouth."

Jonah blinked. Eva nearly dropped her sword. It'd been a while since Jonah had heard that voice, but there was no mistaking it.

Hera.

She stood on the remains of the podium next to her brother, Hades. That must have been where he disappeared off to. He went to retrieve his equally evil sister.

Many things about her were the same. The black hair was perfect and strategically positioned around a golden crown. The face was still ravishingly beautiful, but it appealed to no one because the bitch ruined the ride by being one step above clinically insane. But there was one change. She wasn't clad in the chiton dress and jewels that Jonah had seen before. This time she donned some sort of dense animal hide of some kind. There was protective padding at her forearms, thighs, and shins. She looked as wicked and ready for battle as the knife in her right hand.

"Well, ain't this a bitch," murmured Nemesis.

No one responded to that. Jonah was too dumbstruck at the sight of the goddess, but nowhere near as much as Eva and Ares.

"Mother?" Incredulity did a weird thing to his severe, hard face. "What are you doing here?"

Hera ignored him. To Jonah, it looked like once she'd told Ares to shut up, she'd forgotten he was even there.

Eva gaped at the goddess. "But—you shouldn't be here. You took an oath on the Styx!"

Hera smiled. "Why do you think you have not seen me until now, dear Sibyl? Why do you think that Hades has been the one tormenting you? I have done nothing but speak a few words here and there. Superfluous, yet still effective. Just ask Cyrus."

Jonah frowned. He didn't miss just how confident this woman was. How exactly had she danced around the issue?

"First of all, Juno Helakos made an oath on the Styx, not I," said Hera. "And that oath stipulated that I would not harm the Sibyl in Rome. Well, we're in Los Angeles. The City of Angels. Empty words, but there you are. And my oath did not stretch to these immaterial Eleventh Percenters. I am not even harming you, Sibyl. I'm simply supervising your abduction to Tartarus, where my dear eldest brother will be the one that hurts you."

Now Ares looked unnerved. Very slowly, he backed away from his mother and uncle. "Mother, those loopholes will mean nothing to Father. You know that there are grave consequences for dancing around consecrated oaths! Do you not remember what Father's wrath is like?"

Again, Hera ignored her son. Jonah stepped up.

"So, you've screwed with people again," he said. "You used us—even Ares and Hades—"

"She did not use me in any way, Blue Aura." Hades narrowed his eyes at Jonah. "I would have to confess that I believe you are a larger affront to me than this Sibyl. What with all your 'life never ends' propaganda and talk of your Planes and the Other Side. It's blasphemy to me. You will lead my armies, and I won't even have to hear your arguments when you do so."

"The hell does that mean?"

Hades appraised him. "Your body does not need to be physically alive to be my general."

Jonah looked at Eva and the others. It sounded like Hades and Ares had truly thought this through. He didn't know what to do, but he certainly wouldn't go quietly.

"As for my disappointment of a son," Hera finally acknowledged Ares, "I needed someone stupid enough to unleash savagery without clear cause and reason. And he couldn't even do that properly. My powers are blunted, but I still have plenty—"

She flung a hand, and Ares slammed against a far wall so hard, he cracked it and slid down.

Jonah was stunned. Hera played her own kid. He remembered the story of her pitching her other son off of Mount Olympus, but this was just sick.

She closed her eyes, and shades formed here, there, all over the place. Jonah didn't like this at all. Even with a goddess on their side, they were badly outnumbered.

"Your destructive influence ends now, Eva McRayne." Hera snapped her fingers, and the Shades snapped to attention. "Take the Sibyl for me, the Blue Aura for my brother, and slaughter the rest. And as for the bottom-level goddess, well…Hades will think of something."

Nemesis didn't say a word. Jonah suspected that she didn't want to betray fear. He couldn't look at Eva anymore. Or Terrence. Or even, Reena. How could he? What emotion could he convey in his face that might reassure them? Five, maybe six shades lumbered forward.

And their heads exploded. They literally exploded.

Their bodies fell to the ground and then dissipated into shadow and dark mist.

Jonah looked at Eva, stunned. She shrugged. Terrence and Reena had nothing.

Nemesis spread her hands and said, "Nope."

He saw that even Hera and Hades looked baffled.

But one person didn't.

Ares had done it. He'd dropped the broadsword when his mother repelled him, but both of his hands glowed with reddish-orange flames. He had done it from a kneeling position, but now he rose, fury in every inch of his being.

"Mother, you've taken advantage of my powers and my purpose for the final time," he growled. "I see now that I was but a mere pawn. There are repercussions for such treachery, as well as flouting oaths. Your first consequence, Mother and Uncle, is that I atone for my sins by becoming the Sibyl's newest Olympian ally."

"Excuse me?" Eva whirled around.

"Huh?" Jonah demanded while Reena shook her head and Terrence gaped.

"Oh!" Nemesis looked aroused. "The plot thickens."

Ares ignored them all. He walked forward and stood in front of Eva and Jonah. "I swear on the River Styx that I am now an ally to the Sibyl and will never renege. She and I will never be friends, but such things are immaterial. Mother, Uncle, if you desire your plans to come to fruition, you will have to deal with all of us."

Jonah didn't know what to think about this new development. Hera and Hades, on the other hand, quivered with rage.

"You heard him," whispered Hera. "Deal with them all. Don't let any of them escape!"

NINETEEN

EVA MCRAYNE

I NEEDED somebody to hit pause for me. A rewind button. Something to help me work my mind around the puzzle flying together faster than I could comprehend the picture. Hera was behind all of this? Ares was now my ally?

I ran my sword through the Shade that blocked my view of the stage until I could see the single figure who had been hell-bent on destroying me from the word go.

"You broke your oath, Hera," I said to her. "That means I get to break mine."

I moved past Ares. I watched her as she smirked at her brother. Hades tapped his fingers in front of his face before gesturing towards us.

"I tire of this," He murmured. "Grab the Sibyl and the Blue Aura so we can be done with this fiasco."

Fiasco was right. Shades began pouring out of the walls until the room was shrouded in shadows. I kept my back against Jonah's as we were swarmed by darkness. Even Ares, the big bastard of war, seemed to be having a hard time pushing them back. I blocked a set of arms grabbing for me and turned to see Jonah blast three of our opponents into oblivion. Terrence and Reena held their ground, but we were all struggling to keep ourselves together.

We needed a miracle. A Hail Mary. Anything to gain the upper hand in the madness created by a vengeful god.

I kept my eyes on Hera, dressed in the ridiculous Amazon costume. Well, except for her crown. I frowned as I slashed away another Shade. In the mirror, the goddess wore her crown. When she was shaped as a Native American, she was wearing her crown. Why?

I almost laughed aloud at my thoughts as I came up with an answer. Surely not. Surely it wouldn't be that easy to see her fall.

But this would have to be a team effort. And just like the Covington House, Jonah and I would have to mix our worlds. My whole plan hinged on timing. Just as Hera had quarterbacked this whole plot, I had to quarterback her downfall.

Here went nothing.

"Hey, Asswipe!" I yelled at Ares over the melee. "You can create explosions, right? Like a cannon?"

"Asswipe?" He grunted as he pushed a Shade away from him. "Millennia of civilization and the best word out of your language you can call me is 'Asswipe?'"

"I'm kinda busy at the moment." I dared to glance over at him. "Can you?"

"I am sure I could. But the resulting explosion—"

"Don't worry your simple little head with that," I told him as I turned to Jonah. "Blueberry, what will I owe you for the most powerful wind ethereality you can muster?"

Jonah instantly understood. "To see the bitch fall, it's on the house."

"Excellent." Two bolts in place. Now for the last. "Reena, you up for a run?"

"Why?" asked Reena.

"I need you to grab Hera's crown before the smoke clears. We're gonna need it."

"Her what?" Reena demanded. "Are you insane?"

"Just do it. I'll explain later."

Reena sighed, gave me a sharp nod, and popped her neck muscles. All systems were a go.

We pushed and stabbed and bashed our way to a table, where me, Terrence, Nemesis, and Cyrus dove behind. Jonah's hands began to glow blue, and the winds picked up. Time to see if my quarterbacking skills were up to par.

"Ares, *now*!"

The resulting blast of orange light shook the entire room. Jonah raised cerulean blue-glowing hands, and with a grunt of concentration, used the winds to deflect the flames and the majority of the force from us. I had never seen Jonah exude that much power, but Reena didn't stay to marvel. She sped out from our hiding place, and I heard Hera scream. Seconds later, Reena knelt next to me with Hera's garish headpiece in her hands.

"You owe me big time, Evie," Reena grumbled as she passed me the headpiece. "She could have barbecued me."

"She still might."

I heard the goddess shrieking. I rose to my feet to see the theatre lobby cleared of Shades and two very stunned deities standing on my stage.

"Looking for this?" I stepped around the table as the others gathered behind me. "You seem a little— different without it."

Hera's eyes had dimmed. Her grace and beauty? All gone. Replaced with the appearance of an old hag only seen in fairy tales. She screamed and put her hands over her face.

"Brother," she rasped, "stop her!"

Hades reached out to do gods knew what, but Ares was faster. He threw a spear that caught flames in mid-flight through the dissipating smoke and skewered the god of the Underworld right through the stomach. Hades stared at the weapon before turning his cold eyes up to us.

"We will meet again, Nephew," he promised. "I will not forget this treachery."

He disappeared, and the smoking spear clattered to the ground where he once stood. Hera screamed again as she rushed me. She was fast, but her blunted powers put her at a disadvantage. I grabbed the crown by its base and smashed it against the side of her face. The great goddess of the heavens crumpled in a heap at my feet.

"I am done with you. I am done with your lies. Your treachery. Do you want to keep playing games with us, Hera? That's fine. But we will win every time."

She tried to rise. She tried to reach for her crown. In the end, she was too weak.

"Eva. Explain this to me." Jonah spoke up from behind me. "What on earth did you do to Hera?"

"Her crown is the true source of her power." I bounced the heavy thing in my hands. "Given to her by Zeus on their wedding day. It holds every power the Great One ever bestowed upon her. Lightning. Atmosphere. Beauty. She has never done anything to preserve herself, she just relied on her crown. Consequently, without it? She looks like this."

"You wretched—" Hera clawed at my foot, so I pulled it away. "Return what is mine!"

"No. I'm not finished yet." I turned to my companions. "Ever notice how she is always wearing her crown? It was so much more than a symbol to her. Yes, she is an Olympian. Yes, she has the blood of the Titans running through her veins. But Hera was only meant to be an ornament. Not a powerhouse."

I turned my attention back to her. "That's the true secret of the gods, isn't it? You all share the same blood, yes. But what truly makes you special is what you are gifted with. Apollo was given the Sun. Hermes was given his sandals and wings. Zeus? His lightning bolts. But you needed this trinket to matter. Without it, though?" I dropped the crown just out of her reach. "You're a fucking joke."

Ares gave us all a hard look and went away without another word. Whatever.

I turned and walked out to the lobby, where Joey knelt in the corner with a knot on his head and a blood trickle down his mouth. He stood, so I wrapped my arms around his neck.

"Glad to have you back, Zombie Joe." I grinned when I realized the rest of my crew were following behind me. "You didn't break my Emmy, did you?"

"Jonah," Joey ignored me as he looked around me. "You ok, man? Wasn't my plan to get all possessed up and go UFC on people."

Jonah must have waved his apology away because he said nothing. I tapped his body camera to get Joey's attention back on me.

"Yeah." He winced and favored the knot on his head. "Me and about twenty-five other photographers."

I turned back to see Hera had disappeared. She wasn't coming out of that mansion in Beverly Hills for a long while. I knew my head was going to be on a chopping block, but right then?

I couldn't have cared less. I stepped out to another

sea of flashing bulbs, cheers, and press shouting their questions. They got the show of a lifetime, alright.

Now, it was time to play the star.

TWENTY

JONAH ROWE

JONAH DIDN'T THINK that it would ever end. Eva played her part so well, and Nemesis ate it up, too, but Jonah could see through all of these phony people.

By the time their collective returned to Eva's condo, Eva had been offered four-holiday specials and three other black-tie events for *Grave Messages*, Nemesis had gotten five offers to jump ship despite having just signed her deal with Theia Music Group, Reena had been told she'd be the next Michelle Rodriguez, and Cyrus, Terrence, and Jonah had been offered bodyguard gigs from some pop princess outfit from the early 2000s about to embark on a reunion tour. The lead singer even promised them that they'd make somewhere in the zone of $3500 a week during the duration. Starla St. Jove cried that a lawsuit would come Theia's way by morning, but Eva's boss, Connor something-or-other, wrote her a check right there. She took one look at it and was instantly everyone's best friend.

They all plopped down on Eva's furniture, with wine flowing all around. Jonah passed and got some

Tampico. Reena, who took water, asked Eva point-blank, "Evie, how do you do this?"

Eva tilted her head back and rested her glass on the knee of her camo pants. "Doing it's the easy part. It's making it look easy where the challenge comes in."

They all laughed. God, it was a good feeling after all that had happened. Nemesis finished her glass and sat forward. "So, Ares is now an ally? I so didn't see that coming."

"To hell with him," Eva snorted. "I don't trust him. I'll never stop hating him, whatever his choices."

"I'm right there with you," Jonah agreed. "I don't trust him as far as I can throw him, and he's a big bastard."

"His oath on the Styx binds him to his choices," Cyrus said. "I assure you that while it may have seemed surprising, in many ways, it was not. Hera has betrayed a great many individuals in the name of her goals. She has never understood that one cannot simply treat others like trinkets to be worn and stored at leisure."

Jonah still wasn't convinced. Apparently, Eva wasn't either.

"I don't know how much stake I place on Ares' cute little oath," she told Cyrus. "You saw how his mommy flouted her own."

"True," Nemesis chimed in, "but didn't you see? Breakin' her oath has already brought grievous consequences to Hera, Eva! Her treachery has now led her husband and both of her sons to support you and distance themselves from her. She and Hades are now pariahs in Olympus, a place where she still cannot return, and you also discovered her power source. She has had to return to her lonely mansion in Beverly Hills lookin' like a withered, dry piece of shit. If those things aren't comeuppance for breaking her oath, I don't know what is."

Eva looked pensive but didn't say anything. Terrence sat forward.

"What's your power source, Nem?"

Nemesis's heterochromatic eyes sharpened. "I like you, Sweetpea, but not that much."

They shared another laugh, and then Jonah had a distinct feeling that sobered him somewhat.

"Excuse me," he said to the room at large. "I'll be right back."

He went up to the guest room. Jonathan kept his promise. Yay.

Jonah gathered up the package that his mentor left on the bed and headed back downstairs, where everyone looked at him in puzzlement. He ignored the confused looks and went to Cyrus.

"Look, dude," he began after swallowing some pride, "when our minds were being screwed with, things happened and things were said that can't be taken back. I own that. We ain't best friends, but hey, this isn't high school. I'm not apologizing, because I wasn't in control of my actions. That being said, accept this peace offering."

He extended the package. Cyrus, curiosity piqued, took it from him, and unwrapped it. It was a single-edged sword. The base was bound in leather and grooved to perfection. The blade itself was dark, but the outer edges were lined in gold. Cyrus held it aloft and eyed it with surprise and approval. Terrence took it in with inquisitive eyes.

"Jonah, you gave him a machete?"

"Not a machete, Terrence," Cyrus said, whose eyes never left the sword. "It is a makhaira. A Greek cavalry sword with an expanded convex portion to the cutting section."

"What he said," Jonah nodded. "That very action concentrated the weight, and by extension the momentum, to the bottom part of the blade. It allows more cutting force, see."

Everyone stared at Jonah. He shrugged.

"Ares' possession gave me an understanding of all weaponry," he explained. "Of course, just about all of it faded once I got re-balanced, but I remembered the blade name, did some research, and told Jonathan that I wanted to make up for what I did to Cyrus's sword. He said to leave it to him and ask no questions. He got the sword made; I have no idea who did it or where it happened. The point is that Cyrus has a new sword. It's mainly ethereal steel because we don't deal with gold, but Jonathan lined it with gold traces, which I suppose are for nostalgic purposes. But, Cyrus, you have my hope that this sword will be as good for you as the last one."

Jonah wasn't about to lay it on thick. He wasn't fond of Cyrus and he wasn't ashamed to admit it. But the fact remained that when he was possessed, he destroyed the guy's sword. He was ready to get that off of his conscience. Nothing sucked worse than owing a debt to someone you didn't care for.

Cyrus mimed some battle movements and already looked accustomed to the new weapon. He looked at Jonah with an inscrutable expression. "This is an incredible piece of work, Rowe. Many thanks to Jonathan, and also to you."

He willed the sword to vanish and extended his hand. After a second or two, Jonah took it. That was that.

Eva looked out of the window. "Sun's coming up," she announced. "You all know what that means."

"Yep," said Terrence, "bed."

No one knew how long they slept. It didn't even matter. Nemesis left to get some final details of her deal ironed out and told Reena that if she ever desired "a good time," just give her a call.

Jonah was surprised when Reena politely said she'd keep it in mind, but she later told him that that was a lie because she wasn't willing to screw up what she had for any fling, regardless of how hot she was. When Jonah laughingly observed the fact that Reena noticed that Nemesis was hot, she'd unabashedly shrugged.

"I'm taken, not blind," she said.

Eva packed the next day with a lot of stuff. It was fun seeing all the sights, trying L.A. cuisine, and taking advantage of Eva's clever techniques of dodging fans and paparazzi.

The high lasted for the majority of the day, but by 2 A.M., Jonah was seated on rocks near Eva's condo, looking at the L.A. skyline trying to wind down. It was quite a sight, he couldn't lie, but the sprawling vastness of it matched his thoughts.

"Can't sleep either, huh?"

Eva was behind him, wine glass in tow. Jonah decided not to give her grief for it, but Eva caught his glance.

"Don't worry," she promised. "It's the last one for a while. Reena is very persuasive about healthy living."

"You ought to live with her," Jonah murmured.

Several seconds of silence. Then—

"I can't believe the things I did and said," he burst out. "I can't believe that I had that in me."

"You didn't, Jonah," Eva insisted. "You were possessed. You were sick. And now, you're better."

"That is a tiny comfort," Jonah grumbled. "The possession is gone, but I still remember everything. No memory gaps now. That is just bullshit."

Eva lowered herself next to him. "Yeah, well, I was nearly at the end of my rope in the Underworld."

"I've been to the very end of my rope twice in my life," he told her. "Once was when Nana passed into Spirit. The second one was—recently."

"I'm well aware," said Eva. "Do you want to talk about it more? I know enough about what Vera did, but if you need to talk it out, I'm listening."

"Nah," Jonah shook his head. "I'm good."

Eva actually smiled, but it faded quickly. "Terrence and Reena also told me that you guys have a lot on your plate back in Rome."

"That's one way to put it," Jonah said. "It's an understatement, but whatever. There is a lot of stuff to keep us busy. This little excursion, as crazy as it was, was a welcome distraction. But I have something to confess." He sighed. "Remember back when Rome and the parallel lines and all that screwed with your Sibyl powers, and you thought about stashing yourself there to be normal again? I think that I was trying to do something similar back when I wanted to bully myself onto your show in my unbalanced state."

Eva nodded. "I came to that same conclusion."

Jonah gave Eva a sideways glance. She shrugged.

"Okay, Reena came to the conclusion," she confessed. "After she explained what was going on in Rome, I agreed with her. But I'll tell you the same thing you told me back when I wanted to run. You can't abandon the folks who need you. It seems like they need you more than just about anything else."

"I know," said Jonah, "and it fuckin' blows. What if I fail?"

"What if you don't?"

"What if I do?" Jonah asked stubbornly.

"What if you don't?" Eva repeated, just as stubbornly.

Jonah stared at her. Eva stared right back.

"You aren't going to let me have my pity party, are you?"

"After all the shit I've gone through concerning depression, not a chance in hell," Eva replied. "And you are not welcome on my show as an escape or a refuge, Jonah. A guest and valued partner with a unique skill set? Yes. But not as a way to shirk the responsibilities that you have now."

Jonah shook his head with narrow eyes at Eva. Then he flung his arm around her shoulder.

"Love you, Superstar."

"Love ya back, Blueberry," Eva cleared her throat. "And don't worry. I'm sure that there will be plenty of opportunities for you to be on *Grave Messages* in the future. But only after you do what you have to do in Rome. It's only the same thing that you would've told me."

"You know," said Jonah with a snicker, "Nana would've liked you."

"That's the sweetest thing you've ever said to me."

"So when are you going to tell me about the night before all this started?" Jonah pointed to the wine glass. "The one that ended with the razor?"

"You talked to Joey, then." Eva twirled the glass by the stem. "I won't get away with 'I don't want to talk about it', right?"

"Right."

Eva kept her gaze out on the skyline. Jonah nudged her with his arm and she jumped a little.

""It's just disturbing. I don't want to put that on you."

"Spill it, Superstar."

Jonah could tell she didn't want to talk. Eva watched the city lights spread out beneath them. When it became obvious that Jonah wasn't going to fill the silence, she gave in.

"When I got home from Santa Fe, Cyrus was here. He was waiting on me, I suppose. Beat the absolute hell out of me for going off with you." Eva rubbed her forehead with one hand. "It triggered memories of my mom. Suicide seemed to be the only way to make it stop."

Jonah's fists instantly tightened as hot rage filled his body. "Why didn't you tell me, Eva? You should have called me"

"Because I wasn't in my right mind," Eva glanced over at him. "I'm still not. I wanted to protect you from that."

Jonah stared at her. It took a minute before he trusted himself to speak. "Eva, I'd have killed that motherfucker."

"I know that," She crossed her arms over her knees. "That's another reason why I didn't tell you. You wouldn't be tainting your good soul on that bastard. Not for me."

"But-"

"But nothing. It happened. It's over. Now, I am trying to square myself with it."

"After he got called out, it shouldn't have happened at all." Jonah seethed as she turned to meet his gaze. "And he dared to put hands on you again? Tell me he'll get punished in Tartarus. Tell me they'll hurt him. Tell me he'll get the same as he gave you."

"Apollo doesn't know." She cleared her throat. "I haven't told anyone the truth except you and Joey."

"Joey knew about Cyrus beating you?"

"Yeah. He knows."

"Why didn't he tell Apollo?"

"It's not right that Joey be put in that position. Just as it wouldn't have been right for me to run to you with this shit. I'm not willing to disturb your peace of mind like that. The only reason I'm doing it now is because you want me to talk about it."

Jonah felt the need to punch something. Anything. He tried to loosen his fists, but his fingers wouldn't budge.

"Eva, if he touches you again, it won't be about souls being tainted. It will be about a bastard getting his. I can't *believe* I got his sword replaced. I should've shoved it through his face."

"You replaced his sword because you're a good person, Jonah."

"That night in the garage, when he busted your nose. Jesus. He did it right in front of me."

"It doesn't matter, Jonah."

Jonah growled deep in his throat. He should have taken him down then. He had his chance. He'd had plenty of chances.

"Eva, I would have taken him down for you had I known."

"Jonah, you were possessed then. You would have taken down anyone."

"This is different."

She leaned over and brushed a kiss across his cheek. Jonah closed his eyes at the gesture.

"Thank you for caring."

There was something else. Something he needed to say. The timing was horrible after what she had just told him, but it had to be done.

Here goes nothing.

"Evie, about the other night. I want to apologize."

"About what?" She pulled back to pull her knees up to her chest as she studied him. After a moment, she rested her head against them. "Jonah, there's absolutely nothing to apologize for."

"I shouldn't have done what I did. In the garage." Jonah picked up a rock, rubbed it between his fingers, then tossed it over the edge of the cliff. "I was possessed. I wasn't in my right mind. You know me better than that, Superstar. You are a woman of substance who deserves to be treated with deference and honor, not thrown about like a piece of meat. If I hurt you, I'm sorry."

She didn't respond right away. Instead, she sat up then looped her arm through his before putting her head back on his shoulder.

Jonah rested his head against hers then buried his nose in her hair. He still had that undeniable need for her. It took everything he had not to take the moment and make it more. As he had wanted to do in Santa Fe. As he had almost done that night in her garage. He remembered every detail. Every scent. The feel of her skin. Her willingness to let him do...anything. As wonderful an experience being with Eva was sure to be, he never would have wanted an encounter with her while under possession. He had more respect for Eva than that. She was more than just a quick lay. He'd only known Eva for just over six months, but they were close. Too close for him to act out and ruin the friendship they were still trying to build.

TWENTY-ONE

EVA MCRAYNE

I SHOULD HAVE SEEN this coming. Jonah didn't want me. I should have known that. The possession had been twisting his words. His thoughts. His desires. Jonah Rowe under Ares' possession had wanted me. The version of the man I had fallen head over heels for did not.

I stared out over the cliff as I felt a familiar numbness overwhelm me. I was trying to decide if I should jump. I had plenty of reasons. I had a whole lifetime worth of reasons.

I stayed rooted in place. I longed for the darkness, but I was terrified of it. Joey had told me to take it one minute at a time. So I was. One minute, I would step to the edge. The next minute, I would step back and think of Jonah.

I'd told him never to apologize for actions beyond his control. Then, I apologized for not getting him the help he so obviously needed.

"Jonah, I owe you a huge apology as well." I stared at the empty wine glass in my hands and wished I hadn't thrown the alcohol over the cliff. "I should have known better. I should have gotten you help. I'm so sorry that I encouraged you. I never want to put you in a compromising situation. I promise it won't happen again."

"What are *you* apologizing for?" Jonah had said. "Eva, I remember everything. I can tell you beyond a shadow of a doubt that apart from being so damn direct, I regret nothing. You're gorgeous, beauty personified. I just don't appreciate myself approaching you like that while under Ares' influence is all."

"I'm apologizing because I knew something was wrong." I looked straight out at the city lights. "I knew something was wrong, but I let myself get caught up in those moments. I should have been more forthcoming about getting you help, Jonah, and I didn't. I hope you can forgive me for that."

"Eva." Jonah clamped my shoulder. I closed my eyes. "Do not apologize. You are guilty of nothing. Nothing. You've experienced a lot of wrong in your life; maybe that leads you to be apologetic. But please, please don't be sorry. I'm not going away."

"Please don't," I managed to whisper. "I couldn't stand it if I pushed you away. I couldn't."

"Eva, come here." Jonah wrapped me up in a hug that surprised me. "I don't know all of your past or the people who've made you believe you're a problem. But that's not us. That's not Jonathan. That's not me. We ain't abandoning you. Ever. Stop thinking we will."

It took a moment, but I held him back. It took me even longer to respond.

"Thank you for that," I murmured against his shoulder. "I know that's not you or Jonathan or any of the Elevenths. I just...need to put Evangelina away."

"No, you don't," Jonah tightened his grip before he released me. It took everything I had to release him, too. "Evangelina is part of who you are. You can't bury her any more than I can bury my anger. All you need to do right now is acknowledge that you're a work in progress, and don't have to get it all done tonight."

"I understand."

"But?"

"No buts. I understand what you're saying."

"Will you try it?"

"Acknowledging the worst parts of myself? Yes. But I have to do that on my terms. I know that, too."

"Yeah, me too," Jonah pulled his knees up and looped his arms around them. "Ares' rage overtook me so easily because I have unacknowledged shit of my own, so me, too. But the best part is what I just said. We don't have to get it done tonight.

"You have so much good in you, Jonah. I wasn't kidding when I said your grandmother would be so proud of you."

"How do you know?"

"Because I know you. Because I see you and your actions. You are a true hero, Jonah. In every sense of the word."

We sat in silence for a while, lost in our own thoughts, I suppose. Finally, Jonah stood and squeezed my shoulder.

"I'm heading back to Rome early tomorrow so I better get some sleep."

"Big plans?"

"Yeah," He smiled a little as he pulled out his phone. "I've been texting this girl back home. Met her in one of my classes at LSTU. I'm taking her out later tonight for dinner and a movie."

It felt like I stared at Jonah forever, but I knew it was just a few seconds. On the outside, I was perfect. I smiled up at him as if my heart hadn't broken in two at his words.

He didn't want me. Jonah had never wanted me. I was an idiot for thinking otherwise.

"Yeah? Congratulations. What's her name?"

Jonah gave me a curious look, but I wasn't about to let on where my head was.

"Lola Barnhardt," He answered. "She was in my classes. We'll just see how it goes, you know?"

See how it goes, huh? Right. I knew exactly where it was going to go.

"It sounds lovely," I stood and dusted my ass off. "How long have you known her?"

"For a little while," He pulled up a picture on his phone and passed it over. "We've been chatting since graduation. She was dating a business major. Got bored with him though."

I took the phone to study the woman in the photograph. Long dark hair, almond shaped green eyes. Curves that didn't seem to appreciate the low cut blouse she was wearing.

"She's gorgeous, Jonah." I passed the phone back. "I'm sure things will go very well for you."

"We'll see," Jonah said. "But I'm having fun just chilling out with you right now. Mind free and no influence from gods or vampires. Ain't life great?"

Jonah laughed, and I smiled a little. I didn't have it in me to laugh with him.

"Yeah," I looked down at my boots then back to him. "Living our best lives."

"Listen-"

"But," I spoke over him. "You go on to bed. It's been a long day of me dragging you all over Los Angeles. And you said it yourself. You wanted to rest up for tomorrow."

"You coming inside?"

"No. Not for awhile." I crossed my arms over my chest. "I need to be alone with my thoughts for a bit."

"No better place for peace and serenity than right here," He kept smiling at me. "Night, Superstar. Love ya."

"Good night."

I watched him until he went back to the condo. When Jonah disappeared inside, I stepped closer to the edge as I tried to wrap my mind around his date.

The woman he was after was gorgeous. The exact opposite of me. I would have laughed if it didn't hurt so fucking bad. No, it didn't hurt. It resignated. The smile on Jonah's face when he showed me her picture burned. The excitement in his voice when he told me about their date struck a chord in me I didn't know I had.

So here I was. Standing on the precipice. Waiting for my heart to finish icing over. Despite that, I wondered what was wrong with me. What was so wrong with me that everyone I loved ran to someone else?

"Eva"

I stiffened as Cyrus approached me from behind. I tightened my arms but I didn't turn around to face him.

"Come to gloat?"

"About Rowe?" The keeper chuckled as he stood beside me. "No, though I do believe I will say I told you so."

"Oh, fuck off."

"I have heard rumors that Apollo is looking to replace me. I need you to tell him you will refuse a new keeper. I need for you to renounce this nonsense and allow us to resume our relationship."

"Relationship," I laughed, but there was no mirth in the sound. "What relationship, Cyrus? What were we? We weren't friends, that's for sure. You killed any notion of that. We weren't lovers. You killed that, too, every chance you got. So what exactly are we going to restore? The perpetual embarrassment? Smacking me around? What?"

"Eva, it is imperative you speak on my behalf. I will lose a millenia worth of work-"

I stared at Cyrus in the darkness. I wanted to see the keeper I'd met five years before. I wanted to see the man who had been infinitely patient with me in the very beginning.

I couldn't see him. I couldn't see anything except the irritation on his face every time he had to speak with me. I remembered every bruise and broken bone I had received from him. I heard his hateful words repeated time and time again. I wasn't good enough. No one could ever love me. I would always be alone.

"You're right, Cyrus."

I saw his shoulders drop with relief before I spoke again.

"You're right. I'm not good enough, no matter what I do. And you're right about another thing. No one will ever love me so I should expect to spend my life alone." I met his gaze. "Alone. As in, without you. Without anyone."

"Eva-"

"No. There is nothing to reconnect. There never was." I found a strength I didn't realize I had. "I will talk to Apollo in the morning. I will make sure you are reassigned within the Order of the Keepers. But as far as remaining my keeper? Those days are over."

"Do you mean to say that you're requesting dissolving our bond?"

"I'm not requesting anything. I am taking active steps to make sure it happens." I tugged my hair away from my face as the winds picked up. "This is goodbye, Cyrus."

A vice grip clamped the back of my neck, but instead of the fear I was used to, I relished in the flash of pain that traveled down my spine.

"You will do as you are told or so help me, you will meet your end tonight."

"Promise?"

I brought the heel of my boot against Cyrus' shin and he grunted as he released me. I willed my sword in my hand then turned to face him.

"I have absolutely nothing to lose, Cyrus. You really want to do this?"

Cyrus was a good foot taller than me. The years he had spent as a soldier had hardened his body into granite. His immortality ensured he would stay that way. So when he slammed into me, I went down hard. I cracked my head against the rocks before I brought the hilt of my sword against the side of his head.

"Five years together and this is the most action I have ever gotten out of you," I looped my leg around his and jerked so that I rolled the two of us. "I gotta say, I'm disappointed. Your performance is lacking."

Cyrus snarled and punched me across the jaw twice. I was knocked off of him, but I laughed as I layed in the dirt.

"Jonah is right. You really are a bitch."

I rolled away from his boot before he could stomp my head in. I was almost back to the very edge of the cliff when I heard a familiar voice yell out my name from the backyard.

"Eva!"

"Jonah, stay back-"

I grunted when Cyrus jerked me up by the throat. He tightened his grip so hard, I started seeing dots black out the city lights below me.

Fear - actual fear - rushed through me as I realized the position I was in. Cyrus was still my keeper. If he slipped, that was it for me.

I want you to know that when it's over for you? It's over.

Joey's words flooded my mind followed by something Jonathan had told me when all of this began.

Jonah needs you to be waiting when the battles are over. He needs you physically alive.

I dug my nails into Cyrus' wrist to hold on. He was breathing heavy from our fight. His hatred for me as evident now as it had ever been. I couldn't die this way. Not now. Not yet.

"One more inch forward, you blue bastard, and I drop her. One more inch."

TWENTY-TWO

JONAH ROWE

JONAH WAS FILLED with fear when he saw Cyrus with Eva by the throat. But more prevalent than that was rage. The rage that eclipsed all fear, and all the doubt that came with it. It was Felix, after all, who taught him the Golden Rule.

"Despair illuminates nothing. Anger illuminates a map."

Jonah relished the anger caused by the sight of this motherfucker threatening Eva, yet again. He'd never learn.

Jonah would have to teach him.

"No witty comebacks, boy?" Cyrus snapped. "No icy wit? No verbiage about my manhood?"

Jonah raised his left hand, but kept the right one out of sight. He said one word.

"Here."

In response, the winds picked up in a vacuum to Jonah's palm. Both Cyrus and Eva were yanked from the cliff's edge in the suction of Jonah's vacuum caused by the winds. When Cyrus reached Jonah, there was a sickening squelching sound. Cyrus gasped in surprise and pain, but Jonah just watched him, hatred in his eyes.

"Feel that?" He whispered. "That is a gift for Eva.

I was going to give it to her because I forgot about it earlier. But for now, I see the best place for it is in your guts."

Cyrus doubled over from the blade in his stomach. If there was such a thing as justice, then he wouldn't survive that wound.

Jonah knew better than to believe in justice.

He knelt down next to Eva, who was leaning up on her side. He couldn't see shit in the dark, but he knew she was gasping for air. She was alive.

Jonah pulled out his cellphone and hit the contact he had for Apollo. Two seconds into that phone call, two men appeared out of the shadows.

"You are in need of assistance, Blue Aura?"

"Thanks, Apollo." Jonah disconnected the call. "Cyrus Alexius is to be taken to Tartarus on Apollo's orders."

"The charge?"

"Attempted murder of the Representative."

The second man knelt next to Cyrus. Jonah watched as they disappeared and the first man approached them. He knelt next to Eva and put his hand on her shoulder.

"Eva, I am Ulysses. Are you alright?"

"Fine," She gasped. "Fine. Just...fucking hate...heights."

"Allow us to take you inside." The keeper stood and lifted Eva to her feet. Jonah rose with them. "Jonah, are you well?"

"Not a scratch on me."

Eva looked up at him and he could have sworn she was searching for any sign of injuries on him. Jonah resisted the urge to shove the keeper out of the way so that he could step in. Sweep her off her feet as he had done when he was possessed.

Possessed. He told himself. *I was possessed. It didn't mean anything.*

Jonah followed the two of them to the kitchen. "You said your name was Ulysses?"

"I did. A pleasure, Jonah."

"Yeah, listen, can the other guy bring Eva's dagger back? I wanted to give it to her tonight. Good thing it slipped my mind."

"My dagger?" She was over by the sink, washing the blood from her face. "I don't have a dagger."

"Not yet. I left it in Cyrus."

Eva didn't respond right away. Instead, she turned the water off and folded the towel over her hands.

"Thank you, Jonah.

"For what?"

"For stepping in. You saved my ass and I appreciate that."

Jonah shrugged. "I told you I got your back, Superstar."

Jonah looked over the Keeper who stayed behind. Like Cyrus, the guy was hard, poised, and looked ready for any attack, like a snake coiled and ready. But unlike Cyrus, this guy had an indefinable air of warmth about him. No predatory or untoward vibes came off of him. His aura wasn't threatening and...he had a manbun. Hard to be evil if you sported a manbun in Jonah's mind.

"Good thing you guys were close by," He said. "Any lingering and I'm sure Cyrus would have tried something else, even with his guts hanging out."

Ulysses growled in his throat, but Jonah knew it was in reference to Cyrus. "Olmos and I have been watching you guys since the Emmys," he said. "A lot of disturbing things have come to light about Cyrus, but we couldn't hit him head on. Run the risk of him escaping to his true masters."

"Pardon?"

"Cyrus is a Titan spy and assassin," Ulysses revealed. "He's been as such since Dionysia, the Second Sibyl and his lover, was due to expire after giving the mirror to the third Sibyl. He struck a deal with them to keep her alive. They attempted to make her a sort of anti-Sibyl. She became a monster and had to be put down."

Jonah and Eva stared at him. What the actual hell?

Ulysses raised his hands. "This came to light recently. Alexius has had the greatest cover known to exist. After thousands of years, his mask started slipping with you, Eva. You were his downfall. Well, you and this boy's dagger."

Eva stared at the Keeper as she fell back against the sink. Jonah cursed under his breath at the revelation. He was surprised, sure. But he wasn't shocked.

Nothing about the Olympians really shocked him anymore.

"Where is he now?" Jonah demanded. "Apollo said Tartarus-"

"The traitor is indeed at Tartarus. He should be receiving his trial before the Furies as we speak."

The Furies, huh?

"As for Eva's dagger, I will go retrieve it. I assume you will be staying the night, Blue Aura?"

"Um, yeah. Me and my two friends are crashing here tonight. We're leaving out by noon."

"Very well," Ulysses studied Eva again. "Are you sure I can't do anything else, Representative?"

"No. I'm sure."

"Why in the morning? Can't you just bring it straight back?"

"I could," Ulysses nodded. "But one would think the weapon should be cleaned and polished first. Until the morning."

Eva watched Ulysses vanish before she headed to the fridge. All the while, Jonah watched her. When she reached the counter to pass him his bottled water, he caught her hand.

"Let me look at you, Superstar. You got in one hell of a fight."

"I'm o.k. Really. It's not the first time I've taken a hit. It won't be the last."

"You up to telling me what happened?"

"No."

"Come on, Evie. Don't do that. Don't start putting up walls that I'm gonna have to knock through to get answers from you."

"What walls?"

Jonah waited. She pulled her hand free to sit on the edge of a barstool. She stared out the kitchen window before she gave him the answers he was looking for.

"Cyrus needed me to tell Apollo not to replace him. Apparently, the Council is on the hunt for another damn babysister for me. I told him I didn't want him as a keeper. I told him I didn't want any keeper. I was better off alone." She took a swig of her water. "Good call on my part."

"Because Cyrus is a traitor?"

"Because I have a horrible taste in men." She shrugged. "I didn't see Cyrus as a traitor. I was too blinded, I guess."

"Eva, don't do that." Jonah hoped the tone he had wasn't authoritative or iron. He wasn't trying to be Cyrus. "That's a very slippery slope. Don't judge all men by the worst of us. Don't make every man in existence pay for Cyrus' mistakes."

"I'm not judging men at all. I'm judging myself. Obviously, I need to work on myself more. What's the saying about loving yourself before anyone else can truly love you?"

"You don't love yourself?"

"I think we both know the answer to that question."

Jonah nodded slowly. "I guess we can work on self-love together. I'm lacking in that department too."

"I know."

Jonah raised his eyebrows at her. She shrugged.

"I do. I see it every time you look in the mirror. I can practically hear what you're remembering. All the assholes who told you that you'd never amount to anything. I know, Jonah, because I hear the same thing." She turned around and rested her elbows on the counter between them. "I also know that telling you how great you are doesn't do shit because you've convinced yourself that the lies are the truth."

"When you hear the same shit for years, it sticks more than anything," Jonah opened his water. "But I'm a work in progress. I'm not where I was."

"I agree with that. I think you've gotten a lot more confident since I met you."

Jonah sipped his water before he eyed her.

"How'd this conversation get turned around to talking about me?"

"Because there's no point in talking about me." Eva twisted the bottle in her hands. "Where do you want me to start? Looks? I think you're handsome and any girl would be lucky to have you by their side. This Lola woman better be on her Ps and Qs or someone else is going to come along to snatch you away. Brains? You're brilliant. Fighting ability? I know no one better."

Jonah shook his head. "And now, Eva, follow your own train of thinking."

Eva closed her eyes. "Jonah-"

"Shut up," Jonah said. There was no force or malice in his tone. Just necessity. "Eva, you're gorgeous. Unequivocally one of the most beautiful women I've ever seen. You haven't had the best luck in relationships, I'll grant you that. But that says more about the guys than it does about you. Eva, that gold dress made *me* weak in the knees, and I respect you too much to view you as just a hot piece of ass. Any man you know should worship the ground you *consider* walking on. For God's sakes , Eva, remember that guy whose house you purged of the poltergeists and he decided he loved you? He proposed to you four times, said he'd finally divorce his incarcerated wife, and even volunteered to renounce his Presbyterian faith and start worshipping Apollo. Superstar, men don't volunteer to switch *gods* for just anyone."

"Don't do that, Jonah. It's cruel."

Jonah froze with his water bottle to his lips. "Don't do what? Tell you the truth?"

"Give me hope." She stood. "I'm gorgeous because the magazines say I am. The gold dress made you weak in the knees because you were possessed, Jonah. And the man you talked about? He was committed to an asylum four weeks after we filmed the episode. A diagnosed schizophrenic."

"Eva-"

"You don't know what it's like, Jonah. You don't." Eva sounded tired. Resigned. "I'm so glad that you don't understand what it's like for me. All I have ever known is pain and violence. So please, don't give me hope that things could change. It'll break my heart when it doesn't."

Jonah placed a hand on Eva's arm. It took a minute, but she turned to face him. He clasped her chin between two fingers and forced her to meet his eyes.

"Eva, risks can suck," He admitted. "And sometimes, our hearts get broken. Sometimes, we miss the mark. But it's only through heat and pressure that we reach the diamonds."

"I don't think there are diamonds for people like me. Only bits of gravel."

Jonah lifted up Eva's wrist and studied the pale white lines there. It wasn't right that she had been pushed to that point twice in her life. It wasn't right; the words she said now.

He thought back to his first impression of Eva. The spoiled, vapid celebrity. The A Lister who crushed those beneath her without a single glance. Now, he knew better.

"Every scar is a mark of survival, Eva. It's a mark that you made it through the heat and the pressure. Someday, someone will come along to appreciate the diamond that pressure created."

"No, they won't." Eva slipped her arm out of his grasp. "I'm done, Jonah. I'm just done. If the Fates have made it so that I'm to be alone, then I've learned that lesson. I can't do this to myself anymore. I won't."

Jonah wasn't going to prod Eva any further. She was set in her thoughts at the moment. So he said just one thing. And one thing only.

"If you want to make God laugh, show Him your plans."

"I don't believe in God, so if he laughs, I'm stabbing him in the throat."

Jonah couldn't help but chuckle at that. "You heading up, Superstar?"

"Yeah. I have something I want to look into."

"What's that?"

"The oath of Hestia." She went towards the stairs but stopped when she had her hand on the banister. "Good night again, Blueberry. Thank you for listening."

Jonah wondered what the oath of Hestia was, but knew the conversation with Eva was over for the night. So he simply nodded.

"You're welcome, Superstar."

She slipped inside her room and Jonah waited until he heard the door latch. He was halfway down the hall when he realized that before tonight, Eva would have hugged him goodbye.

Tomorrow, He told himself. *She'll be back to rights tomorrow. Tonight was just a shock. Sleep will help. Always does.*

When Jonah reached the guest room, there was a note on his pillow with a black rose on top of it. Frowning, he opened the note and read.

Dearest Jonah,

I want you to know that I watched you and the others take down your enemies at the gala affair. The Sybil may have fashioned herself the centerpiece, but in my eyes, the stage belonged irrevocably to you. You are a most remarkable specimen of man; a man lost in a world of lost men. Your performance the other night when dealing with my aunt and husband only reiterated my belief that your considerable talents are being wasted on mediocre matters. Your "purpose?" It's too small a thing.

At the same time, I am not my husband. Coercions... betrayals...I've no need of these things. When the time is right, you will come to me of your own volition. At that time, I will personally mentor, guide you, mold you, and craft you into what a champion should be.

Worry not of when. I'm a goddess. If there is one thing I understand above all else, it is patience.

That said, I'll be waiting.

Your number one fan,

P.

Jonah swallowed. Persephone.

He ripped up the note. He had no time for that shit.

But then again, she said she had all the time in the world. What did she mean when she said he'd come of his own volition?

Painstakingly, he pushed it to the back of his mind. It was a matter for a later date. Hopefully, a much later date.

END OF BOOK 2

Dear reader,

We hope you enjoyed reading *Gods & Thieves*. Please take a moment to leave a review, even if it's a short one. Your opinion is important to us.

Discover more books by Cynthia D. Witherspoon at https://www.nextchapter.pub/authors/cynthia-d-witherspoon

Want to know when one of our books is free or discounted? Join the newsletter at http://eepurl.com/bqqB3H

Best regards,

Cynthia D. Witherspoon and the Next Chapter Team

ABOUT THE AUTHORS

T.H. Morris has been writing in some way, shape, or form ever since he was strong enough to hold a pen or pencil, and was born and raised in Colerain, North Carolina. He has been living in Greensboro, North Carolina, for the past twelve years. He is an avid reader, primarily in the genres of science fiction and fantasy because he enjoys immersing himself in the worlds that have been created. He began writing The 11th Percent in 2011. He resides in Colorado with his wife, Candace.

Cynthia D. Witherspoon is an award-winning writer of Southern Gothic, Paranormal Romance, and Urban Fantasy. She currently resides in South Carolina, but spent three years in Fayetteville, Arkansas. Always an avid reader, she began writing short stories in college. She graduated with a Bachelor's Degree in History from Converse College, and earned a Masters in Forensic Science at Oklahoma State University Center for Health Sciences.

Gods & Thieves
ISBN: 978-4-86745-340-7
Mass Market Paperback Edition

Published by
Next Chapter
1-60-20 Minami-Otsuka
170-0005 Toshima-Ku, Tokyo
+818035793528

29th April 2021